THE

BARN STORMERS

*Being the Tragical Side
of a Comedy*

MRS. HARCOURT WILLIAMSON
Author of "A Provincial Lady."

New York
Frederick A. Stokes Company
PUBLISHERS

By FREDERICK A. STOKES COMPANY

CONTENTS.

iv   Contents.

Contents.

Contents.

The Barn Stormers.

*

CHAPTER I.

"All out of work, and cold for action."

WANTED—For extensive repertoire, juvenile leading lady. Must be tall, handsome, young, have fine
figure, and fashionable wardrobe on and off the stage.
Send photo, and write immediately, stating experience, age, weight, and lowest salary, to Scott Ambler
Comedy Company, Bagra, Ohio, week of 21st–28th.

Monica Nairne laid down the paper, which was suggestively entitled *The New York Clipper*, and walked
deliberately toward the mirror attached to an article
of furniture she had lately learned to designate as her
bureau.

The cat, which had been coiled in her lap, jumped
down with a mewing protest, but Monica turned to
reprove it as she moved across the room. " I can't
afford to support *you* any longer, you know," she de-
clared; "and when we can't afford to support a mere
under-bred cat one's adopted from ship-board it's a
sign that one has fallen upon evil times."

She stared into the mirror, her elbows resting on
the cushion of her handkerchief case, her face between

her hands. "You're far from bad-looking," she said, addressing the reflection that returned her eminently critical gaze, for Monica had lived alone for the space of two months and had contracted the first habit of the hermit—talking to herself; "*I* should distinctly call you pretty, if not handsome. I wonder if you would be Mr. Scott Ambler's 'style'? You are honestly 'juvenile,' too. Only I have a vague idea that that expression has some esoteric meaning in stage parlance, which I don't exactly comprehend. Goodness alone knows what you *weigh*, though, my dear! And what business that is of Mr. Scott Ambler's I should be glad to have explained!"

She went back to the *Clipper* again, and there seemed to be a subtle attraction about the smell of fresh printer's ink, as she carefully conned the important paragraph once more. Looking up from it into space, she tried to project upon the virgin camera of her mind a prophetic photograph of Mr. Scott Ambler and his Comedy Company. But the magician, Experience, was absent, and the instrument refused to work.

On the first page of the paper was a coarsely reproduced portrait of an exuberant young woman, in a low gown and a Gainsborough hat. Monica imagined herself thus apparelled, and there was a certain shuddering fascination in the idea.

She had never yet possessed a really low-necked dress. In the French convent, where she had spent half her life, she had even been obliged to take her daily bath in a robe ample as charity, lest her guardian angel, a spirit of the masculine gender, supposed never to leave his post, should be offended by her nakedness. But she was going to be an actress now, and could only hope that her tutelary genius might be ready to accommodate himself to circumstances.

"Not that I *would* wear a hat with it," she reassured herself, with pride of nationality. "I would show them that, though it may be all well enough before audiences in the States, it would never be considered good form at home. I daresay they would soon begin copying the English ways."

"They" meant the members of the Scott Ambler Comedy Company, for already Monica had more than half resolved to answer the advertisement.

On the table were writing paper and pens. There was a short article, partially completed, on "Poverty as a Crime," which Monica had begun the previous evening. She had herself been driven to the sin of tight-lacing, because she had outgrown all her old frocks, and could not afford to buy any new ones; and she had even visions of cheating a street car conductor with a false coin which, through another's dishonesty, had come into her possession. But here was hope; and she need not, perhaps, resort as yet to the desperate expedient of turning her own misfortunes into "copy." She was glad of this, for her efforts in journalism had so far been unsuccessful, though she had still abundant faith in herself as an actress.

After wrestling for a time with an illusive pocket, she eventually excavated her purse, and placed it as a warning between the *Clipper* and yesterday's abortive bid for literary fortune.

The morocco sides of the receptacle in question came together like a pair of sucked-in cheeks. Elephants, not to say mastodons, might have trod upon the thing for years, ruefully thought Monica ; and yet she had considered herself so wealthy only eight weeks ago, when she had landed from Southampton, with an independent fortune consisting of thirty pounds.

But then she had taken up her quarters at a really good New York boarding-house, recommended by a travelled friend, and the leanness of her purse was, if she had only known it, decidedly a foregone conclusion.

She had believed in her own gifts as extraordinary, had been convinced that an English girl of good breeding and good appearance had but to pick and choose among theatrical managers in the States. She had also fancied herself practical in deciding that the proper beginning was to secure a desirable address, and then nonchalantly wait for something to turn up.

" But things *don't* turn up," she had had to conclude in sadness, " except the points of one's patent leather boots, worn out in trying for engagements. And nothing ever does seem to come off in my life—except buttons."

Yet, after many days, behold something *had* " turned up "—this rakish *Clipper*, left in a street car by her nearest neighbour. It merely remained to be seen whether it also would " come off," and that could only be ascertained by writing, and waiting in forced patience for an answer.

She wrote accordingly, and soliloquised, tearing up two or three sheets of paper in the laudable effort to do herself full justice, without unduly exaggerating, in description.

" Age, twenty-one, and waist measure to match (at least I think I can still manage it !). Height, five feet four; hair, dark brown, naturally wavy, warranted no curl papers; eyes, bluish grey, black lashes, considered effective; mouth said to be mobile; features expressive; nose better suited to comedy than tragedy; good contralto voice, much praised by teacher of elocution in England. H'm! I trust these are the sort of points one is supposed to mention. It seems like describing a 'lost, strayed, or stolen.' I can't think of anything more. Oh, yes—complexion! Lights up well on the stage, with a little rouge. That's business-like! And teeth—a most important item. Exceptionally fine, though perhaps safer not to mention that I haven't yet cut the four wisdom ones in the corners. Experience! Ah, *there's* the rub! Let me see."

At this critical juncture there was considerable biting of the more business-like end of the pen.

"Have played successfully in England, 'Pauline' in 'The Lady of Lyons,' and 'Polly Eccles' in 'Caste' (that'll show them how versatile I am); beside a great many other parts of equal importance. If I go on to say it was only as an amateur, they won't have me. I've learned enough in my two months' dreary round of New York managers and dramatic agents to be sure of that. How can I *ever* gain any experience if nobody will give me a chance? How am I to go on living if I can't get work? And I don't want the other thing yet. Not that I'd so much mind *dying*, but there'd be the awful waste of time in *stay-ing* dead. 'Poverty as a Crime' again! that's one more example. Here I am now, in self-defence, pledged to a course of deceit."

The salary to be decided upon was another stum-

bling-block, and, at last, leaving a space for the inser-
tion, and a blank to be filled in with the item of her
weight, she obeyed the summons of the luncheon bell.

Though Mrs. Potter's boarding-house was in Madison Avenue, a fashionable street, and an exorbitant
price was charged for the tiny fifth-storey back bedroom occupied by the English girl, rigid economy was
practised in the matter of luncheons. The dashing
young gentlemen from Wall Street were mercifully
absent at that hour, and as Mrs. Potter did not consider the appetites of her own sex worth consulting,
the menu, like history, had a way of repeating itself.

"The same yesterday, and to-day, and for ever,"
Monica had felt inclined to quote from Hebrews,
chapter xiii., and 8th verse, when she had been
treated to tinned corn beef and pickles six days out
of the seven. But, after all, she was young, and to
her mind, as yet, dinner was a mere incident of dining. She recked little what she ate, and to-day less
than ever.

"How much should you think that I weighed?"
she inquired abruptly, when the tinned beef had grace-
fully given way to apple sauce and cookies.

Mrs. Potter looked as though she were not quite
sure whether or no an invidious though veiled allu-
sion to her catering was intended. Otherwise she
did not appear to be surprised. Evidently the question of a human being's weight formed an ordinary
topic of conjecture in America.

"Would you like me," she asked, agreeably, "to
guess much or little?"

"That's the trouble. I'm not quite sure which is
required," answered Monica; "and a great deal may

depend upon a stone or two." She looked cautiously around. The last boarder was about leaving the table. People did not wait for ceremony at Mrs. Potter's, and luncheon was a movable feast. "You see," Monica went on confidentially, "I am thinking of taking an engagement; and they—er—want to know how much I weigh."

"*Oh!* One hundred and fifteen pounds," retorted Mrs. Potter, without hesitation, surveying Monica's proportions as though she had been a joint of meat. "A very proper weight for a young lady."

The English girl gasped. The computation sounded enormous until she had hastily reckoned it into stones.

"It's a travelling company," she continued, having already, earlier in her acquaintance with Mrs. Potter, briefly touched upon her aspirations. "I don't know at all what salary I ought to say. If I go I'm to have good parts."

"You'll want to stop at the best hotels, of course, then," advised the landlady; "and you'll have to buy plenty of handsome dresses. I should set my figure high. Yes, the weight low and the figure high! Say —well, say fifty dollars a week."

"Ten pounds," Monica calculated, doing a sum upon her fingers. The very thought of so munificent a sum, pouring in weekly, made her feel already every inch an actress.

Light of foot and of heart, she ran upstairs, carrying some food for Dinah, the ship's cat, for which she paid Mrs. Potter at the rate of a "dime" a week.

"I can afford to support you after all," she murmured, "if only Mr. Scott Ambler admires my photograph. Now, to fill up those blanks! Fifty dollars

salary—one hundred and fifteen pounds in weight.
What a pity it can't be somehow reversed!"

When Monica had posted the letter, big with her
future fate, she allowed herself to stroll past the
Broadway shops, even more brilliant than those of
Bond Street. She had kept away from them before,
being naturally an extravagant and impulsive little
person, and not wishing to lead herself into temptation. But now she deliberately paused before that in
which the most fascinating fripperies were displayed.

Bewildering visions showed her to herself, clothed
in the latest substitute for samite, mystic, wonderful,
and, above all, delightfully expensive. At last, in all
probability, she was to have her chance. All her
chances thus far had run away from her to other
people, less deserving; but something told her it
would be different after to-day.

Out of fifty dollars a week she could save at least
twenty-five. There would be twenty pounds laid
away in a month. Why, she would make her fortune
at that rate. What would the hard-visaged, harder-
hearted woman, whose terrible words had sent her
out of England, think if she could only be informed
of the pariah's brilliant prospects?

She would probably grow even more wizened and
yellow, and increase her daily doses of tea, from the
rate of 1,460 cups per year to twice that number.
Monica was pleased with this fancy. Even her mer-
curial spirits had been shadowed of late with the
greyness and uncertainty of her own future. But now
she was happy. And, woman-like, she showed it by
recklessly entering the shop, and revelling in the purchase of things she did not need.

There were ups and downs of feeling during the two blank days that followed. Towards the end despair had the whip hand of hope. After all, it had only been chance which had brought her the advertisement, though now she had come to look upon an engagement with the Scott Ambler Comedy Company as her one means of salvation.

On the third morning a letter arrived. She had tried to teach herself not to expect it before, but, as a matter of fact, she had nearly given it up. She had been too late, or the London photograph had not come up to Mr. Ambler's requirements for a "juvenile lead!"

But here was the letter at last, in a wonderful envelope, which she hardly knew whether to admire or to laugh at, with its bold advertisement of the company's tour and repertoire in lurid red and blue.

Her heart thumped like a hammer against her side as she opened it. Mr. Ambler's handwriting was hardly scholarly ; but that was a detail.

"Pleased with photograph—nationality no objection—experience stated sounds promising—" (Monica's eyes began to sparkle.) "But—" (oh, there was a *but !*) "the salary named—far too large. Business does not run to more than eight dollars a week for juvenile lead—management also paying expenses, that is, board, travelling, etc. If terms are accepted, please wire, when railway fare will be telegraphed by management, to 42nd Street Depot—to be called for at ticket office—shall expect to hear at once."

The letter dropped from Monica's hand, alighting upon Dinah's back. Where were all the glorious visions now ? The sparkle had gone from her eyes, and her hopes, as from last's night champagne.

Still—what was she to do? There was the future to be faced—no hope from New York managers or theatrical agents, who had seen other prettier faces than hers; and the article on "Poverty as a Crime" (finished and despatched when doubt of Mr. Ambler's answer began to gnaw) had been already returned, rejected.

Eight dollars over and above her board! It was a pittance. She could not possibly accept it. She would even be ashamed to tell Mrs. Potter that it had been offered. What a drop from the magnificent fifty of her dreams!

Stay! There were a few lines on the second page, which, until the sheet fell from Dinah's indignant back, Monica had not observed. Even men did not disdain postscripts, it would seem.

"P. S.—If I do not hear from you by four o'clock on Tuesday afternoon, shall conclude you do not wish to close with offer, and shall accept services of another lady who has already applied for the position."

Good gracious! And this was Wednesday morning! The shock of those potent words, the "other lady," was too much for Monica's mental balance. Poignant jealousy set in. Rather than that greedy wretch should have the engagement, Monica would take it herself, even if there had been no salary attached at all.

She dressed hastily, and pale with the excitement of her decision, flew out into the street, and sent her acceptance along the wires to Mr. Scott Ambler, Colosseum Theatre, Bagra, Ohio.

CHAPTER II.

" It shall be so my care
To have you royally appointed as if
The scene you play were mine."

IF a London detective were but informed that his quarry had escaped his clutches *via* Waterloo, or Euston, or Paddington Station, he would, at all events, know whether the scent was to be followed into the south, the north, or toward the setting sun. But this advantage would be lost at the 42nd Street Station in New York.

As all roads are advertisingly supposed to lead to Earl's Court, so, contrariwise, all roads branch forth from 42nd Street. The big station is a labyrinth of railway trucks, a confusion of incoming and outgoing locomotives, a babel of strange and hideous noises.

To Monica Nairne, who had never yet taken a journey since landing from Southampton in New York, the place was appalling. She did not know what to do with her luggage. Nobody seemed inclined to enlighten her. She ran down the wrong platform, and had to rush frantically back again. She was obliged to unearth her ticket from a sequestered corner of her travelling bag, to be punched by a supercilious potentate, just as the train she wanted began gliding slowly out of the station.

With Dinah mewing advice from under one arm,

and her bag swinging from the other, she ran along
the platform. Somebody "boosted" her up—for
regulations are not quite so strict in New York as in
London, and charming young ladies are allowed to
risk their lives, and their cats', if they please.

Holding on by the iron railing, she scrambled up
the steps, precipitated herself through a door and a
vestibule, to sink down, panting, in a blue, brocaded
chair. She was in a compartment resembling a comfortable little library or drawing-room, and when she
had collected her scattered wits, she gazed at her surroundings in surprise.

"It can't be a train," she thought, dazedly. But
already the station was left behind, and through the
curtained, plate-glass windows, the high bricked walls
of a cutting were to be seen. "It's more like 'Alice's
Adventures in Wonderland' than anything else,"
Monica continued to reflect—for she had been taught
to read on Lewis Carroll. "I've popped into the
Rabbit Hole, and I'm falling now, though it doesn't
feel like it. There are the shelves and the maps, only
I don't see any jars of marmalade, and I've brought
my Dinah with me."

Beside the blue chairs there was a sofa with frilled
silk cushions, a big, manly-looking writing desk, a
table upholding the latest thing in typewriters, and
Turkish rugs on a floor of polished wood. Paintings
of American scenery were set into panels between the
wide windows ; over the table hung a map, and the
remaining wall space was filled in with bookshelves,
protected by glass doors. One door at the end of the
car led into the vestibule through which she had made
her late desperate plunge, and another at the opposite

end of the snug little apartment was hidden by an
embroidered portière.

"I suppose the way into the Queen's beautiful gar-
den lies behind that curtain, if only I dared look,"
soliloquised Monica. "The one thing missing is the
glass table with the golden key."

She allowed her eyes to rest upon the books at-
tractively arranged along the four rows of shelves,
and she wondered if they were placed there for the
benefit of passengers.

"Perhaps there's a slot, and I should be expected
to drop a penny in it," she thought. "What a relief
it would be if they were only labelled, like the things
in Alice's Wonderland, '*Take me*'! But I believe at
all events, I'll risk it."

She placed Dinah on a rug so deep that the cat began to pick its way industriously out with curving
claws. Then dedicating a grateful sigh to the generous railway company who threw in unlimited litera-
ture with the price of the ticket, she silently drew out
a volume. It was a novel which she had wished for
some time to read.

As she was conscientiously reclosing the glass doors
(Monica had been taught, since childhood, never to
leave anything open, not even her mouth), the portière
was pushed suddenly aside from the farther doorway.

"The White Rabbit!" flashed, lightning-like, into
Monica's Wonderland-haunted mind. But it was not
the White Rabbit. It was merely a man, neither
very young nor very good-looking, but with a typical
American face, keen-eyed, sharp-featured, clean-
shaven, and in his arms he held Dinah the cat. For
an instant, surprise slightly arched his heavily marked

brows. His glance quickly took in Monica, her travelling bag and her chosen novel. Then his eyes twinkled, and he smiled—a queer little three-cornered smile, that lifted up one corner of his mouth.

"I beg your pardon," he said. "Is this your cat?"

"Oh, yes, thank you," returned Monica, receiving the animal with gratitude. "She must have run out through that door when I wasn't looking; but I assure you it sha'n't happen again. I hope cats aren't forbidden?"

"Only to restaurant keepers; they make them into rabbit-pies."

"I mean in railway carriages," supplemented Monica, with dignity.

"They're not in this one, anyhow."

"Oh! Are you the—the conductor—if that is the right word?"

The sharp-featured man looked out upon the moving landscape, and smiled.

"No, I'm not the conductor, I'm a—well, I guess I'm a sort of passenger. I hope you won't mind my coming in here, will you?"

"Not at all," she replied, still with purposeful primness.

He had rather a nice voice for an American, Monica thought; but she resented the whimsical element in his smile, and wished him to know it. Then, suddenly, she remembered that she was adventuring in the land of the free, in manners as well as in soul, and that, besides, she was now on her way toward becoming a full-fledged actress. She had cast off all the old traditions in which her past had been steeped, and begun life in a new world—alone.

It therefore behoved her to live up to her adopted *rôle.*

" Everybody has an equal right here," she added, conciliatingly.

" Well, hardly *everybody*, perhaps," corrected the stranger; "but I guess no one is going to question either yours or mine."

Monica murmured something polite and indefinite, settling herself among the cushions in the corner of the sofa with her book. The man also sat down at the desk, making a great show of rummaging among pens and papers, but not writing at all. Presently he spoke again.

There was something attractive as well as shrewd in the expression of his face, and Monica was not blind to it. If she had been in England she would have kept her eyes upon her book; but it wasn't England.

" Excuse me," he said, "wouldn't you like to look over some London papers and magazines? There are plenty of them somewhere about."

Monica could not help smiling. " You guessed I was English, then ? "

" That wasn't very hard to find out. I know England fairly well myself." He got up, and dragging some papers from a rack beside the desk, selected a few, and laid them on the end of the sofa.

Scarcely had he re-seated himself, when once more the portière rings jingled along their rod of brass, and a singular-looking young man came in. He had the face of a boy, and the expression of an octogenarian. His eyes widened at sight of the grey frock on the blue sofa, and stopped abruptly on the threshold.

"You won't want me now, sir, I presume?" he nasally enquired.

"Not now," said the other; "by and by, perhaps. Take the typewriter to your own place, and then we sha'n't disturb the—er—the passengers."

The youth, hiding an incipient grin with the palm of his long hand, seized the typewriter and vanished.

"I should not have been at all disturbed," pronounced Monica. "And I seem to be the only passenger in this compartment—beside yourself. It is odd, too, because I had heard that travelling was so crowded in the States."

"That's so—in some 'compartments.' But there are different kinds, you know. This kind is—er—sort of reserved."

"Oh, I hope I haven't got in first-class by mistake!" Monica exclaimed. "Mrs. Potter, that is my landlady, told me there were no such things as first and second and third class in America."

"She was quite right, and so are you," soothed the fellow-passenger. "You just stay where you are, and make yourself comfortable."

Monica had half started up, but sat down again, breathing more freely.

"This is the first time I've been in an American railway train," she vouchsafed, growing more and more friendly and at her ease. "It seems wonderfully nice. We've nothing half so smart at home."

"Just you wait till lunch time," said her companion, "and you'll see something smarter yet. They —they do you very well on board of this car."

"Oh, but," objected Monica, modestly, "I've got my own lunch in my bag, and Dinah's too. Mrs.

Potter put it up, so I know without looking what it will be. Corned beef, and, perhaps, if she felt very good-natured, a currant jelly sandwich made of bread."

"Still, it's a pity to let the stuff in the dining-room go begging, isn't it?" suggested the man. "It's—we get it for nothing, you know."

"What a remarkable country!" laughed Monica. "In that case I'll save Mrs. Potter's contribution for another occasion."

"I would. You're sure you haven't got any friends on board some other car you'd like to treat? You might as well have them in, you know."

"I haven't a friend in all America," she answered, confidentially.

"The—dickens you haven't! What—over here alone? Not a relation in the country?"

"Well, you see," blushing slightly, "I'm not a typical English girl—not the kind you read about in books written by Americans. I had very good reasons for coming. And—I only said I hadn't any *friends*. I have—at least I think I have—a relation; but I haven't found her yet. Perhaps I sha'n't find her at all; but I mean to try."

"That sounds romantic," he commented.

"It might be, in a story-book. But things seem different in real life—especially in one's own life when one's got used to it. I don't even know the name of this relation of mine now, though I have her photograph, taken a good many years ago. When I was in New York, I showed it to people I got acquainted with, hoping they might recognise it—for one never can tell, and the world is such a little place."

"I should think it would appear to be a pretty big

one to a young lady without any blood relations to her name."

"Oh, don't say *blood* relations, please!" smiled Monica. "That always seemed such a horrible, sanguinary expression to me, and ever since I was a child I have associated it with the only person I really hate. *She* is a '*blood* relation,' if you like! But I will show you the photograph, if you don't mind. I should think that you had travelled over the country a great deal—haven't you?"

"I rather guess I have. Do show it. I'll be very pleased."

"I always carry it with me," explained Monica.

Opening her little Gladstone, she fumbled about for a moment among brushes and combs and flasks of eau-de-cologne, bringing out at last a framed photograph, representing a pretty woman dressed in the fashion of fourteen or fifteen years before.

"Of course it would be too good to be true that you should know her?" she said, almost breathlessly, as the sharp-featured man examined the portrait.

He shook his head. "No, I can't say I do. And yet, by Jove, there's something that looks kind of familiar about it, too! I've always prided myself on my memory for faces. But—I'm not sure of this one. I shall begin looking round, now I've seen it, though; and who knows but I'll light on it some day? I suppose I mustn't ask what relation she is to you?"

"No, I think you mustn't ask *that*." And Monica was demure again.

"You'll have to let me know your name and address if I'm to help you find your missing relative. Isn't that so?"

"My name is Monica Nairne, but the address won't be so easy. I am just going,"—and she tried to keep the ring of self-importance from her voice—"to join a travelling theatrical company."

"Oh, indeed?" The sharp-featured man looked thoughtful. "Had any experience—on the other side the herring-pond?"

"No! That was what all the agents asked me!" Monica laughed. "They always glowered, and said, 'What have you done?' which I feared at first referred to my criminal record."

"Do you know anything about the manager?"

"N—ot exactly. I answered an advertisement."

"H'm! Don't think me impertinent. We Americans are such nuts on asking questions; but we don't mean any harm. Would you mind telling me where you are to join?"

Monica told him.

"You expect you'll like it?"

She informed him she was looking forward to her new life with glowing anticipations.

The cat, which was a friendly animal, with curiously little reserve for its kind, had made an exploring expedition to that region of the stranger's body, which, had he been a woman, would have been known as his lap.

"It's just possible," he said, stroking the creature's head with a meditative air, "that you will be disappointed in things. I don't want to discourage you—but life's full of disappointments, and they may not even let you travel with your cat. I know something of theatrical folks' superstitions, and most of them think that a cat 'hoodoos' the company."

Monica was grieved at this.   Dinah and she had
shared so many joys and sorrows.

"I wish I'd left her at Mrs. Potter's, then," she
sighed.

"*I'll* keep her for you if you like—and I'll promise
to keep her well.   You shall have her back again
whenever you choose to send.   I'm superstitious, too,
but I believe she'll bring me luck.   Won't you, old
puss in boots?"

"If Dinah is puss in boots, shall I call her new
master the Marquis of Carabas?" began Monica, and
then gave a slight start as a picturesque gentleman of
colour appeared in the doorway, like a very black
"Jack-in-the-box," to announce that "luncheon is
sarved, sah."

"May the Marquis of Carabas have the pleasure of
taking you into the dining-room?"

The sharp-featured man arose, and Monica observed for the first time that he was very tall.   It was
a relief to her sense of the proprieties that he was also
old, thirty-eight or forty at the least.

"I thought you were joking before," she hesitated.
"Surely luncheon isn't meant for everybody—for
nothing?"

"It's meant for us."

"There's a mystery somewhere, I know," said
Monica, firmly.   "I shall not go in until you explain."

He shrugged his shoulders in a thoroughly American way.   In fact, everything that this man said or
did seemed to be an unconscious tribute to his pa-
triotism.

"Now, then, Miss Nairne, if you're going to take
that sort of stand with me, all my pleasant little

game's spoiled.   But promise first you'll go and have
lunch with me just the same, and I'll tell you the
secret."

Monica thought for a moment, and then could not
resist the bribe. She promised, with the facial expression of one who, with little faith, taps a doubtful
egg.

"Well, this car happens to be my private one. I
sort of jaunt round the country in it, combining business with pleasure; and I never saw so much chance
of catching on to more than my share of the latter as
I did when I popped in here and found you. Now,
don't look shocked. It's a straight deal, and I'm
going to hold you to your promise."

CHAPTER III.

THE Marquis of Carabas' private car was "switched off" the train after dinner that night, and Monica was escorted by a mild-mannered, white-eyed darkey into a sleeping-car, crowded with passengers. Her railway fare, telegraphed by Mr. Scott Ambler, had not comprehended the price of a berth; but so strongly did the Marquis of Carabas advise her to purchase one, describing the horrors of a long night spent in an ordinary "day coach," that Monica yielded, and counted out three of her few remaining dollar bills.

She rather wondered that the marquis had not volunteered to tell her his name. But he had not done so, and she did not wish to ask. He had certainly been kind to her, never presuming on her naïve confidences, and she felt that he was fit to be trusted, even with the guardianship of Dinah. Still, she would have preferred to know his name.

It was surprising, too, after all his friendliness, that he did not escort her into the car wherein her long journey was to be completed.

"Good-bye, and good luck," he said, insisting upon shaking hands. "'Scott Ambler Comedy Company.' I sha'n't forget, and I shall follow your route in the dramatic papers. Some fine morning, when you least expect it, I . . . but sufficient for the day is the evil thereof. Good-bye; I'll take care of the cat."

And then the white-jacketed black man had been sent for to carry Monica's bag, and lead her through car after car, until her destination was attained.

Everything interested her—the people playing cards; the toddling babies, trotting down the long aisles between the sections, making friends with good-natured passengers; the frankly shrill laughter and conversation; the night porters making down the beds; the ladies calmly putting up their front hair in curl-papers within eye-shot of the madding crowd.

Bagra, Ohio, was only to be reached by changing trains, and Monica's friend, the Marquis of Carabas, had given her explicit directions as to what she was to do. She was to breakfast in the public dining-car, then change at Ardabula Junction for the Bagra train.

Until she was called upon to pay for breakfast, she had had no occasion, since purchasing her berth, to open her purse. As she took it from her bag, a certain unfamiliar rotundity of outline struck her. The thing looked gorged, like a boa-constrictor after a meal of half a dozen rabbits.

She undid the fastening dazedly, and peeped in. There were her eight dollar bills, and her small change in silver—all that had lain between her and starvation, failing the Ambler Comedy Company; but an inner compartment concealed some plethoric obstruction, which had not, to her knowledge, previously existed.

So tightly filled it was, that the leaves started apart with the lifting of the clasp, and the blood rushed to Monica's face as she spied a thick roll of crisp new paper money.

She must be dreaming, she told herself, or else she had picked up some one else's purse by mistake. But, no, it was her own—the little pocket-book given her by one whose photograph was slipped beneath her pillow every night—except last night! For the first time, she had forgotten it last night!

It almost seemed that this guilty forgetfulness might account for the inexplicable change in the contents of the purse. Slowly she drew forth the roll of greenbacks, and, flattening the bills out upon the breakfast-table, proceeded in growing bewilderment to count them.

Each one was of the value of ten dollars, a sum which Monica's hardly acquired knowledge of American currency informed her was equal to two pounds. There were fifteen of these little bills, and therefore, in some magical way, she found herself suddenly as rich as she had been on her advent in New York.

With a quickly beating heart, and a face that still burned hotly, she projected her recollection back to yesterday, trying to recall if at any time she and her bag had been separated. She had left it on the floor near the sofa, when she had accompanied the Marquis of Carabas into his gorgeous dining-room for luncheon But then, after that, she had taken out money to procure her berth. Surely she must have noticed if the purse had then been thus unusually bloated.

Again, she had left the bag forgotten and alone at dinner-time. She had recklessly absented herself from it for an hour at least. What had the wretched thing been doing while she had been away?

"That a purse of mine should ever be a thief!" she mentally exclaimed, with severe condemnation; but even as she did so, her real thoughts had travelled to the Marquis of Carabas. How he had managed it she could not tell; but she was sure that somehow the mystery had been of his arranging. It had been rather an expensive trick for him; but perhaps thirty pounds would seem no more in his eyes than to her had been the three dollars spent by his advice upon a berth in the sleeping-car.

This would account for his having kept his name a secret while informed of hers. Of course, if she had been given any idea as to his local habitation and his name, she would instantly have sent his horrid old money back to him. Yes, it *was* horrid, and it had been detestable of him to put it there. Perhaps he was not what he seemed, and had had some dark and sinister design in this deed that he had done. Very likely it was a recognised trick in America, where people were said to be so sharp, and every one of the bills had in all probability a secret, mysterious mark. She would thwart him, however, if he had intended to catch her in any way, for she would never spend a penny of the money. She would rather starve first.

When she had got away from the breakfast-table, and was again in the section of the sleeper which had been sacred to her throughout the night (it had been transformed from a bed to a seat during her absence), Monica buttoned the roll of money inside the bosom of her travelling dress. She did not wish to run the risk of its being lost, though she did not in the least look upon it as her own property; and in some way, she did not yet know how, she wrathfully resolved to return it to its owner.

At last the change of trains was safely accomplished, ·

and after an hour in a day coach (which seemed par-.
ticularly mean and common in her eyes, after the
gorgeous experience of yesterday), an excitable brakes-
man opened the door of the car to shout "Bagra!"

Monica gathered up her few belongings, and, without waiting for the train to stop, stepped out upon
the platform.

CHAPTER IV.

" My little body is aweary of this world ! "

A COLD drizzling rain had begun to fall, making brown mud puddles in the tracts of snow left by the " January thaw." Beyond the platform, into which they were slowing down, stretched a depressing vista of sodden fields. No indications of a town were anywhere visible, though above a distant hill-top rose the wooden frames of two or three cheap, roughly built cabins.

Monica's heart seemed suddenly to collapse. Could this be Bagra? For an instant she hoped that she had not heard aright; but there, staring her in the face, was a board with the name of the place in large, black, uneven letters. There could no longer be any doubt.

She reluctantly alighted upon the station platform, and—several boxes having been pitched with extraordinary ferocity from the baggage-car—the train, with a puffing sigh of relief, steamed away. Monica Nairne was left alone in the world, with a bag, an umbrella, and a mackintosh ; and she felt, for the first time in her somewhat eventful life, like a poor, little, withered leaf, blown helplessly before the blast.

The depôt, as no doubt the inhabitants of the alleged town of Bagra would have styled it, was an unpainted frame building, consisting of a general wait-

ing-room, and a sanctum for the "ticket agent."
Through the open door, Monica could see in the centre of the room a huge iron stove, white hot, and surrounded by a species of trough, filled with sawdust.
This, though she was for the present in happy ignorance of the fact, was generously provided as a receptacle for superfluous tobacco. Outside the one grimy
window ran a long, low bench, on which several hope-
less-looking specimens of manhood aimlessly sprawled
about. They had blank, yellow faces; blank, colourless eyes, like those of a well-boiled fish. They had
straggling beards of nondescript brown; wide, flat
felt hats were stuck anyhow on their towsled heads,
and over their filthy shirts, stained with a fortnight's
traces of tobacco, were buttoned threadbare coats.
Large, mud-caked boots were thrust out before them
as they lolloped over the bench, gazing with dreamy
curiosity at the one arrival by the morning train, and
chewing reflectively, as a cow relishingly, though half
unconsciously, manipulates her cud.

Monica returned the general stare with a vaguely
questioning one. The only thought suggested by the
dim countenances of the loafers was that their re-
semblance to each other was extraordinary. She remembered how, when she had been a child, she had
sometimes folded layers of brown paper together,
and by cutting out one figure, had produced a long
row of crude "paper dolls."

These men might have been made in the same
fashion. Like the earth before creation, they seemed
without form and void.

They had slouched forth from some unspeakable
homes, merely for the excitement of seeing the train

come in. They had done the same thing every day
since they could recollect; and if they died, some
other mushroom presentments, exactly resembling
these, would immediately spring up to take their
places. No one would miss them, or, perhaps, even
know that they had gone.

Three or four preternaturally lean and long-legged
pigs, with their tails all out of curl, grunted and wal-
lowed in the mud on the other side of the double
railway track. They were, perhaps, the more pros-
perous animals of the two; but the combination was
well-nigh more than Monica was able to endure.

Tears filled her eyes as she strained them wistfully
after the fast receding train. She would thankfully
have jumped into the next one, to go anywhere, away
from Bagra and the Ambler Comedy Company, while
all her bright visions of the future receded into a mental background allotted to anachronomic myths.

" Excuse me ; might you be Miss Nairne ? " spoke
a voice in her ear, and she felt herself smartly touched
upon the shoulder.

Monica hastily turned to experience another shock,
and to lose another illusion.

A short, stout man of middle-age, in a moth-eaten
fur overcoat, smiled encouragingly at her with a part-
ing of thin lips over prominent brown teeth. He
had small, shrewd, grey eyes, bold and self-assured
of glance; a nose, whose skyward aspirations his
whole personality took pains to contradict ; sallow,
freckled skin; a square jaw; and a dominating silk
hat, which vainly endeavoured to proclaim him gentleman.

Having "taken in " the candidate from head to

foot with a single sweep of whitish eyelash, he did not wait for her reply.

"Of *course* you're Miss Nairne. That photo of yours didn't tell no lies," he pronounced, affably. "I'm Mr. Ambler. Sorry I was late meetin' you; reckoned to be in time, but I guess the cars got ahead of me this morning."

"It—it didn't matter," faltered Monica, overwhelmed with despondency. Indeed, nothing seemed now to matter very much.

"Say," went on Mr. Ambler briskly, intent on the business of the moment, "have you got your checks handy? Give 'em to me if you have, and I'll see to havin' your baggage sent up to the hotel on a truck. There ain't no conveyances in the whole of this orn'ary town, so we'll have to trapse up on shank's mare. It's only about a mile. Hope you don't object to mud?"

Monica murmured something indefinite and hopeless as she retrieved from the depths of her pocket the two square bits of numbered brass, which represented her boxes. These she put into the bare, stumpy hand of Mr. Ambler, being treated to a flashing glimpse of mourning nails as she did so; and after a few moments' parley with an invisible official, she and her future manager began their pilgrimage.

Monica's brain reeled under Mr. Ambler's loquacity and freedom of all conventionalities of grammar; for he was, so far, well satisfied with his new acquisition, and desired to make himself agreeable in her eyes. Indeed, as her daintiness more and more impressed itself upon his calculating mind, he even regretted that he had not shaved himself that morning.

He questioned her about her journey, and finally inquired if she wasn't "pretty sharp set." "Hungry, you know," he condescendingly explained, when the English violet eyes looked mystified. "We must stir our stumps a bit faster if you want any decent dinner, I'm afraid. The others'll all have had theirs by the time we git up to the hotel."

"Do people dine so early, then, in this part of the country?" questioned Monica in surprise, for consultation of her watch had lately told her that it was not yet one o'clock.

"You can bet your sweet life they do. Why, the hotel folks would like to have you dine at breakfast time so as to get the cookin' and the dishes out o' the way. They're in that much of a hurry in these parts that I tell 'em they'd give you to-morrow's bread yesterday if they could."

They walked on very rapidly in the middle of the road until, at the top of the hill Monica had seen, they found themselves provided with a bricked sidewalk. They were now approaching the environs of the town. On either side of the wide street were low one or two-storey houses, mostly of frame, painted white, with green outside blinds, retired in little front yards fenced off with painted palings.

All seemed quiet and deserted, a fact which Monica attributed to the prevailing dinner hour, when suddenly, round a corner, swung a party of small boys and girls, coming toward them at full trot.

"Hi! hi! Look at the show folks! Look at the show woman!" shrieked a youth at the top of his voice ; and, with magical effect, faces appeared at half the windows. Children rushed from doors and gates,

panting to join the procession. Everywhere the shout
was taken up. "Say, look at the show folks!" and
youthful warriors responded as though to a thrilling
battle-cry.

Monica was bathed in a cold perspiration. Never
had she been subjected to such an ordeal. Fox's
"Book of Martyrs" had been compiled a century or
so too early. If there could only be a later edition,
she felt that she would be entitled to a place next the
gentleman with the bags of gunpowder under his
arms.

"Don't mind a little thing like this," chuckled Mr.
Ambler, amused at her visible distress. "Why, it's a
compliment, and works up business for to-night. It'll
be all over town now that we've got a new lady. You
see, we've been playin' here most a week, and they
know us as well as they do their own gran'-mothers."

The mile which lay between the depôt and the
hotel seemed, in Monica's sensitive imagination, to
expand into twice the distance. But at last the ordeal
was over.

Having passed several shops built of brick and wood,
the windows of which gave equal prominence to dry
goods, millinery, and provisions, Mr. Ambler paused
before a two-storey frame building, whose windows,
innocent of shutters, stared forth like lidless eyes.

"Ryder House" was the concise legend placed
above the front door; and Mr. Ambler's pause told
Monica that they had reached their destination.

Gallantly he stood aside from the portal, motioning
her to pass in. She did so, and was instantly whelmed
in an atmosphere where the fragrance of fried onions
mingled with the pungent steam of boiling soap-suds.

The hall-way was bare, the stairs uncarpeted. Beside a closed door in the interior stood a large article of dark brown earthenware, frankly advertising itself as a spittoon. Monica shuddered as she glanced at it, averting her eyes, and thankfully obeyed Mr. Ambler's invitation to proceed above.

"I'll show you your room," he said, "and you slick yourself up a mite if you like while they're dishin' our dinner. I shall hev the pleasure of takin' mine with you; and when we're through, I'll introduce you to the folks. There's a young lady, our pianist, shares your bedroom with you; but I rather guess she's out just now."

A shudder ran down Monica's spine at this intelligence. So she was not even to have the privilege of being miserable alone!

Mr. Ambler flung open a door, and the newly fledged actress stepped over the threshold. To her unaccustomed eyes, it looked an *outré* and squalid interior.

The room was of a fairly good size, and was lighted by a couple of windows, rakishly protected by scarlet paper muslin shades, one of which was hanging loosely from the stick. The floor was bare round the edges, and apparently clean, while a big square of rag carpet, such as the English girl had never seen, concealed the centre portion. There was one washstand, covered with folded newspaper, and adorned by one cracked earthenware jug, set dangerously askew in a basin of mean proportions. A dwindling cake of yellow kitchen soap lay stranded in a tea saucer, and glass there was none. Monica nervously wondered if the pianist never brushed her teeth.

A base burner stove gave forth a faint, not unpleas-

ant, odour of lately kindled fire, and behind it stood a
rough packing-box, piled with powdery lumps of "soft
coal."

The bureau boasted a greenish mirror, so small and
so high that it would be impossible to keep in touch,
through its medium, with any portions of the anat-
omy below the collar bone. But, fortunately, there
were two beds, covered with light-coloured patch-work
quilts, on one of which reposed, with a pathetically
hopeless drop of its limp folds, the absent pianist's purple print or calico wrapper.

Somehow Monica's heart warmed towards that
wrapper. If anything, it looked sadder than herself.
She envied its lack of responsibility, and wished that
she too might hang head downwards over the foot of
a bed, rather than be under obligation to descend and
dine with her manager.

As she washed her hands and face with hard water,
icy in temperature, she found herself glancing at the
garment from time to time, half unconsciously building up before her mental vision a supposititious personality for its owner.

Her idea had been to delay the evil moment of going downstairs, but scarcely had she began to arrange
her brushes and little dainty belongings (which looked
sadly out of place on the newspaper spread bureau)
when there came a resounding rap at the door.

"Dinner's ready!" shouted Mr. Ambler, and the
girl, leaving her travelling bag spread open, hurriedly
joined him.

Over the mantelpiece in the dining-room was a
chromo representing the "Maiden's Prayer," while
beneath, on a green crochetted mat, stood a lamp with

a white globe, over which sprawled an exaggerated presentment of tomatoes.

These were the only attempts at decoration, and so far from successful were they that Monica rejoiced there were no more.

The table was covered with a red cloth, the principal advantage of which lay in the fact that it was warranted not to show spots under a fortnight's wear. There were small musty serviettes to match, and the one supplied to Monica was so impregnated with the scent of tobacco as to suggest that the last person who had used it had been greatly addicted to the friendly weed.

Mr. Ambler made skillful play with his two-pronged steel fork and battered, horn-handled knife, more particularly with the latter, discussing theatrical gossip with his mouth full, and occasionally, in an absent-minded manner, employing his red serviette as a pocket-handkerchief.

The fried steak, tinned corn, pickles, and apple-pie did not, however, appeal to Monica's appetite or imagination.

She played with a bit of bread, and, leaning back nervously in her chair, listened to Mr. Ambler as he found time between mouthfuls to explain her future duties.

"You'll have plenty of hard work cut out for you," he said; "but I guess you're too sensible to mind that. We have a repertoire of twenty-one plays, stay a week in every town we go to, and put on a different piece every night. Our juvenile, Miss Minks, has left us suddenly to be married, only waiting till we should have a satisfactory answer to our advertisement, be-

fore she cut sticks and went. We had to do a play in
which she'd only a walking part last night, and will
again this evening, as you can't be expected to get up
in anything at quite such a short notice as *that*. But
· by to-morrow you can be ready with something, can't
you ? Say, just a short comedy old woman's part."

Monica opened her pretty eyes in bewilderment.

" Why," she exclaimed, " what an odd thing for a
leading lady to do ! "

" Oh, but, my dear," corrected Mr. Ambler, with
the nonchalantly affectionate air of the elderly, provincial theatrical manager, " you're not engaged as
our *leading* lady, you know. There's a big difference
between leads and *juvenile* leads, ain't there ? "

The hot blood burned in a spot of rose colour on
Monica's usually pale cheeks. This was that " esoteric
meaning," then, over which she had laughingly wondered in reading the advertisement. It came home
to her very disagreeably now, for, inexperienced as
she was, she had felt pluckily ready to bear many
hardships for the doubtful glory of being a " leading
lady," and gaining experience in good parts. The intimation of her mistake came upon her with such a
shock that she could but ask, in a spiritless way,
wherein the difference was supposed to lie.

" Wall, my wife is *leadin'* lady," explained Mr.
Ambler, as though that question was for ever settled.
" She's a *vurry* strong actress, and plays all the emo-
tionals. But there's often a pritty, sympathetic kind
o' part left for you, and when there isn't, why, you'll
get all the more experience takin' 'em as they come,
—old ladies, adventuresses, female detectives and the
like. Of course, our singin' and dancin' soubrette

comes in for the saucy servant girls and pert misses, and
Miss Thomas—that's the pianist—has to be ready for
anything small and easy that can be done after she's
finished playin' the overture. You'll find that there'll
be some daisy parts for you."

Having disposed of this subject, and shown the new
juvenile lady that, affable as he was, he was not to be
trifled with, he pushed back his chair with a scraping
of its legs along the boarding of the bare floor.

"You're through, ain't you?" he politely questioned, having recourse to his tooth-pick, and rolling
his tongue providently round the interior of his
mouth. "Come on, then, I'll take you up to the stage
manager's room, and he'll hand you over your new
parts."

Something in the small, glittering eye of the man
dominated Monica, despite her disgust for his vulgarity. It had been on the tip of her tongue to say that,
having made such an unfortunate mistake in the nature
of her engagement, she would be reluctantly com-
pelled to return at once whence she had come; but
she found herself actually fearing to do so. Notwithstanding the superficial friendliness and irritating
condescension of his manner, her instinct detected the
ruthless animal underneath. He was a man who
would storm and swear at a woman, and stop at no
unscrupulous act which would serve his own crude
interests. Monica did not *know* this. Her independent experience of the world had not been sufficient to
teach her many of the secrets of human nature as
yet. But she felt all that she would have been unable
to catalogue in Mr. Ambler's character, and she mor-
ally weakened before his brutal strength. She had no

one in all the world who would protect or care for her ; she had very little money which she might call her own, and she dared not, in the very first hour of coming to this desolate place, offend the person highest in authority.

Creature of a lower order as he was, already the manager of the Ambler Comedy Company had assumed a certain savage importance in the eyes of its newest member.

CHAPTER V.

"In honest, civil, godly company . . .
We'll drink within."

MR. MONTGOMERY, the stage manager and leading
man (no one knew with what name he had begun life),
came to his bedroom door in person. In the Ambler
Company it was the correct thing to receive visitors
in the sanctity of the chamber, and no one would for
a moment have thought of questioning the propriety
of the custom. Indeed, life would scarcely have been
worth living had all sociability been confined to the
public parlour of the hotel, even in hostelries where
such an institution existed.

Mr. Cassius Montgomery was a tall man, and would
have appeared even taller had he not been in his
"stocking feet," an accident for which he carelessly,
but with some dignity, apologised to Miss Nairne,
though without making any effort to remedy it. His
long neck was also untrammelled by the confinement
of a collar, and he was clad in a flowered dressing-
gown, which fluttered about his knees. He had a
flabby, bilious face, not ill-featured, and his weak eyes
were protected from the garish light of day by a pair
of blue spectacles.

The presence of Mrs. Montgomery, to a certain
degree, saved the situation, so far as Monica's feelings
were concerned, for the English maiden, bred in pro-

vincial refinement, had never before been introduced to a person of the opposite sex in his bedroom.

A plump little form scrambled off an untidy bed, with a generous display of rotund calf and wrinkled stocking, as Monica reluctantly appeared at the door. " Good gracious me ! " piped a childish voice. A pair of fat hands ran themselves renovatingly through a curly shock of bleached golden hair, and the soubrette of the company skipped forward to welcome the new arrival.

Mr. Montgomery introduced her with a sweep of his hand. " My wife, known in private as Mrs. Montgomery, but professionally styled Miss Fanny Free. You'll see her billed as the ' Little Human Flower.' "

The buxom blossom in question grinned. " I'm a Daisy," she said. " That's about as near a flower as I come, I guess. '*Fancy* Free,' they used to call me before I got married ; but now my husband doesn't like it if they do. I guess it too near hits the mark to suit him—ain't that so, Cash ? "

She was really pretty, in a gaudy, artificial way, but the small round face was so good-natured, with its wealth of dimples, that Monica felt oddly drawn to her at once.

"You'll have to take us just as you find us," she went on. " We ain't much on ceremony. Wages don't run to it in this shebang, do they, Mr. Ambler ? Won't you sit down and make yourself at home, Miss Nairne ? I was reading such a *sweet* detective story, curled up on the bed, when I ought to have been studying my new part or dressing. But of two evils, I say, always choose the least ; so I guess, if you don't mind, I'll just do up my hair for the night."

The Human Flower was evidently a favourite with Mr. Ambler, for she patted him gaily on his bald spot, as she flitted past, and invited him to "roll a curl-paper."

This he jovially refused to do, and retired, having been invited by Mr. and Mrs. Montgomery to return in half an hour, bringing Mrs. Ambler—professionally, Miss Marguerite Neland.

"Say, fetch 'em *all* along, won't you? That's a dear man!" the little lady screamed. "We'll get some beer in, and have a regular bang-up time."

"Our room's a sort of meetin' place for the crowd," she informed Monica, when the door had closed. "We like 'em all to feel at home here, and we hope you will, too. You must just drop in whenever you're lonesome. Now, when you and Cash have got through talkin' business, they'll all come in, and you'll get to know everybody at once."

Having thus put the shrinking stranger at her ease, the Human Flower went gaily about her own avocations, breaking from time to time into song or a step of her newest dance, and occasionally engaging her husband's services to put his long forefinger on her forehead to keep a twisting curl-paper in place.

He took her solemnly, and excused her frivolity to Monica with his eyes.

Shuffling to a large trunk in the corner of the room, he exhumed from beneath a motley collection of wigs and shabby stage clothing a pile of MSS., which he gave to Monica, explaining to her, in a painstaking manner, that they were her parts in the various plays of the repertoire.

"I suppose, as your letter said you were an ex-

perienced actress, you're a quick study, and can get
up in a new piece for every night of the week till
you've learned the lot," he said, mournfully. "This is
a pretty hard-working company, Miss Nairne."

"We're regular *barn stormers*, if you know what
that means," chimed in Miss Fanny Free. "And
what's more, we're *pirates*. That's what they call us
because we steal other people's plays, and don't pay
any royalties for 'em. Ha, ha! you seem ready to
cry, my dear—but cheer up! Though we're a queer
lot, we're not so bad as we look, and you'll get some
fun out of us—you see if you don't!"

By the time that Monica had received all her instructions from Mr. Montgomery, and Mrs. Montgomery's yellow head had assumed the aspect of a
"fretful porcupine," the members of the company,
invited to the impromptu reception, came knocking at
the door and trooping in.

First appeared Mr. and Mrs. Ambler; and Monica
had enough human naughtiness in her heart to be
pleased as well as shocked at seeing that her hated
rival, the leading lady, was a *passée* mountain of flesh.

"*Sha'n't* I make her look old?" reflected the juvenile lead, with sinful inward satisfaction.

"We call her the 'Mullingar Heifer,' behind her
back, and goodness knows it's *broad* enough," whispered the Human Flower, in a safe corner. "She's
the only being on earth Mr. Ambler's afraid of, and
my! can't she bullyrag, for all she looks so mild!"

Next in order appeared a shrivelled elderly female,
answering to the name of Mrs. Patton, and afflicted
with a constant sniffle, which came almost as regularly
as the ticking of the clock. "Husband was the old

property man, just ran away from her," exclaimed
Mrs. Montgomery. "If you want some fun get her
to talk about him. She'll do it like a bird."

Even as she spoke, the new property man, Mr.
Todd, a gay, untidy youth, with a *retroussé* nose
(of whom Mr. Montgomery was evidently jealous),
lounged in, and was regarded with acid disapproval
by Mrs. Patton.

There was an old man also, a gnarled personality,
with a thin supply of grey hair, apparently buttoned
to the scalp with a surprising quantity of warts. He
was introduced as Mr. Wilts, with the addition of a
hasty character sketch by Mrs. Montgomery, setting
forth that hundreds of years ago he had acted in
really good companies, and was now only happy when
abusing other people's stage business and grammar.

Surely now, Monica thought, she had met all her
fellow actors, save the retiring pianist. She had
shaken hands with everybody, shudderingly, achingly
conscious the while of her own superiority, and irritably anxious to slily wipe her fingers after the touch
of each clammy, vulgar palm.

But she was mistaken. There were more to come.
Somebody pounded with facetious ferocity on the
door, and two young men, arm in arm, swaggered
jauntily into the midst of the assemblage.

One was handsome, as a healthy animal is handsome, and would have made a fine appearance behind
the bar of some second or third-rate hotel. His black
hair was sleekly oiled into a curl over his flat forehead;
his full red lips smiled under a waxed moustache,
showing strong white teeth; and his blue chin was
deeply cleft in the centre. He wore a tall celluloid

collar, a crimson tie, and though his trousers were too tight and too short, and his shiny boots of common make, he had the air of being irresistible among women.

His companion was a small man, with a slight stoop, and legs so much bowed as to have earned him the sobriquet from reckless little Fanny Free of the "Picture Frame," because, as she announced, "you saw the landscape through a sort of frame, whenever he went out walking." He had a pale, young face, with beautifully chiselled features, a sensitive mouth, and the brown wistful eyes of a misunderstood dog. As for his clothes—the flannel shirt, the worn and patched coat—they would scarcely have been beyond the ambition of a coal-heaver.

These were the "heavy man," Mr. Jim Crawford, and the comedian, Mr. William Nickson.

Monica was introduced to both. They were of a different class and of different types from any she had come into close contact with until this memorable day; but great as was the gulf which she was conscious must divide them from her, a strange, shocked, electric thrill of premonition set them at once apart from all the others in her fastidious mind.

"Now, every one's here, who's going to work the growler for us?" cheerfully enquired the Human Flower; and, somewhat to Monica's mystification, she proceeded to empty the contents of the water jug economically into the one and only basin. The men, laughing, held up their not immaculate hands, but Mrs. Montgomery coquettishly forbade them all to speak at once.

"Miss Thomas ain't here," suggested Mr. Nickson,

letting his wistful gaze travel round the stuffy crowded bedroom.

" No, she ain't, and she ain't likely to be, I guess," volunteered Mrs. Ambler.   " She's got the sulks."

The merriment of the company was in no wise interrupted by this announcement, and shouts of laughter arose as Messrs. Crawford and Todd wrestled for possession of the water jug. Holding it between them, they hurled themselves simultaneously from the room, and could be heard sliding and plunging down the stairs, giving vent, as they progressed, to sundry demoniac yells.

Monica could have hidden her face between her hands in sheer humiliation, and yet the sense of humour within her mingled a wild desire for laughter with her shame.

The two returned presently with the jug, or pitcher, as they termed it, frothing over the top with beer. " Tooth mugs " from several apartments were called into requisition, and a tin of oysters, which Mr. Todd had generously purchased, was handed among the ladies. Superfluous hairpins were snatched from frizzy locks, and prodded into the bivalves, which succulent viands were thus triumphantly conveyed to waiting lips, and promptly swallowed whole.

Under the influence of the sparkling beverage, of which Monica could not be induced to partake, though ardently pressed to do so by Mr. Crawford, the members of the Ambler Comedy Company waxed additionally hilarious—all save poor Mrs. Patton, who was reduced to the opposite extreme of emotion, perchance by the memory of happier days. Taking a seat close to Monica, she began to recite, in a sobbing monotone, the history of her late bereavement.

" My Gawd ! how I loved that man ! " she moaned. "I used to sit up *all night*, sewin' *spangles* on his tights—and *now*, look what he's been and gone and done ! "

Encouraged by the newcomer's silent sympathy, she proceeded, relating details so essentially connubial in their nature that, in self-defence, the blushing Monica arose to go.

Mr. and Mrs. Montgomery had been very kind, she murmured, and—and—it had been a pleasure to meet the members of the company ; but they would understand how much studying she would need to do. Every moment was of value now, and she hoped they would pardon her if she excused herself.

It was the handsome animal, Crawford, who gallantly sprang to open the door for her ; but the effect of his killing glance was slightly modified by the exclamation, uttered as soon as her back was supposed to be safely turned, by Mrs. Ambler :

" Well I *never !* What a stuck-up piece ! "

Carrying her pile of MSS., Monica proceeded slowly to her own bedroom. For the moment she had forgotten that she was not to be the sole occupant, and with a passionate longing to fling herself on the bed and have a good cry, she impetuously threw open the door.

Then, on the threshold, she stopped, arrested by a startling picture within.

CHAPTER VI.

"Gods! should you have ta'en vengeance on my faults!"

A TALL, thin girl, with a quantity of bright-red hair hanging about a face as colourless as the white-washed walls, bent over the bed which Monica had taken for her own, and had evidently been rummaging among the contents of the open travelling bag. At the instant of interruption she had unfastened the purse to take therefrom a roll of money, and now stood committed to her shame, quivering under the lash of sure detection.

Neither spoke. The English girl drew in her breath sharply, and a wave of physical sickness swept over her. It was as though she had unsuspectingly put out her fingers in the darkness, and they had come in contact with the cold back of a toad.

The thief remained motionless, watching her with deep-set dark eyes full of feigned defiance and despair.

It would have been useless for Monica to pretend not to have seen, even had she chosen such a course, for the gaze of the two girls had met with an electric shock of mutual understanding. She came into the room and closed the door behind her.

" I thought it was locked," panted the other.

" The end of the bolt is broken off," Monica said, quietly. " I noticed it when I was in here before."

It struck her with a sense of strangeness that their utterances in a crisis at once so dreadful and so em-

barrassing should have been so common-place and in-
formatory. But she knew not either what to say or
what to do. It was horrible to feel that her room-
mate was a thief, a sly creature who had taken advantage of an unsuspecting stranger's absence to pry
into her property, and filch her pitiful store of
money; and yet Monica was conscious of being sorry
for the wretched, white-faced thing, more sorry than
she had ever been for anybody in her life.

"Well," said the girl, hoarsely, "is that all you've
got to say? I suppose you think I was going to rob
you."

Monica sat down, not through any particular desire
to assume a sitting posture, but because of a sickly
weakness in the region of her knees.

"No," she said, choking a little, after an instant's
pause. "I know that's—impossible. My purse fell
out on the floor, perhaps. You had picked it up, and
—and—it's quite easily explained."

The deep-set brown eyes stared at Monica for a
long moment, and then the purse was tossed so violently upon the bed that a little loose silver sprang
out, and, rolling over the patchwork counterpane, fell
jingling to the floor. But the detected thief did not
stoop to pick it up.

"Do you really think that?" she questioned, an
odd catch in her voice.

"Yes," Monica answered, stoutly, "I *will* think
that."

"Well, then, it ain't true."

The red-haired girl stood erect now, her nostrils
quivering like those of a vicious horse.

"I did mean to steal your money. I counted it.

There was eight dollars and seventy-five cents. I thought if I took four dollars, maybe you wouldn't remember just how much you'd had, and, anyhow, you'd never know I'd done it. You'd think 'twas a servant somewhere, and you couldn't be sure, so you wouldn't have dared to accuse anybody."

Monica, too, was pale, and very quiet; but as she spoke sudden tears stung her eyelids, though they did not fall.

"I don't accuse anybody now," she answered.

"What?" exclaimed the other, sharply. "Ain't you going to tell?"

"No, I'm not."

"Mind, I don't ask you not to."

"That doesn't make any difference," said Monica. "If you begged me to tell I shouldn't do it. Why, you're only a young girl—alone—like myself."

A curious shuddering sigh whistled between the pale thief's uneven, half-closed teeth; and then, with a suddenness which startled Monica, she cast herself upon the bed, plucking with a pair of incongruously beautiful hands at the tawdry coverlet. She did not cry at first, though the other girl, above the beating of her own frightened heart, could hear a gritting together of teeth and panting breaths that finally culminated in a burst of sobbing, swift and fierce as a tornado.

"Alone! That's it—that's it! Oh, God! You don't know—you don't know what it's been!"

Monica went closer to hear the spasmodic utterances, and then, half shrinking from the possible consequences of her own temerity, laid a hand upon the heaving shoulder clad in purple calico.

" I don't know," she said, " but I can guess, perhaps. I've been finding out lately how hard things
can be."

The girl lifted a face so swollen and blotched with
tears as to be actually hideous.

" Would you have stolen?" she thickly gasped.

" I—don't know," stammered Monica. " I had to
pull myself up short, or I'd have cheated a tram-car
conductor the other day." Then she fell into hysterical laughter. " I—I *wanted* to do it."

The red-haired girl sat up, wallowing in tumbled
bed coverings, and with a sharp grip on Monica's arm,
pulled the trim grey figure down beside her abject one.

" You're an angel—just an angel, to tell me that,"
she said ; and Monica understood, even though angels
are not supposed to have dealings, particularly dishon-
est ones, with conductors of street-cars.

Out from a pocket of the purple wrapper (which
now appealed to the new juvenile's pity even more
poignantly than when untenanted) came a square of
whitish cotton that had seen better days. And then
followed that enemy to the romance of tears in all
women, plain or beautiful—except those favoured
ones of story books—the fatal necessity for resorting
to the handkerchief.

" See here," said Miss Thomas, still panting, " I
want to tell you how I came to do it. If you'd been
rough with me, like I deserved, I'd have died sooner
than say a word. But I guess you're different from
anybody I ever came across; and I guess you're
real."

" Very real," agreed Monica, smiling, and not only
continuing to sit beside the youthful thief, but gently

smoothing the poor, pretty hands that reached out to touch her dress.

"I'm going away," began the pianist. "I'm goin' to be discharged. They haven't said anything to me; but I know what they're up to, for somebody told me in confidence, so I shouldn't be surprised. When they go out of this town, Monday morning, they're goin' to leave me here, stranded without a cent; that's what Mr. and Mrs. Ambler—hateful cat! —'s going to do. My friend spoke to Mr. Ambler about it when he heard the rumour, and tried to get him not to; but Ambler just swore, and said 'twasn't any business of his whether I'd got money of my own or not. Anyhow, *he* didn't owe me a dollar, and as I didn't suit him, I should just get fired and do the best I could. You see, if I won't do what he wants me to, he *can* fire me if he likes without givin' any notice. And, besides, what could I do? I haven't the money to go to law, and he knows it. My friend, Mr. Nickson, would lend me some in a minute, if he had it; he's that generous he'd sell the clothes off his back, only they ain't fit to sell. But he's in debt to the management, and won't get a cent till the debt's all wiped out. He's got to stay on, and when he saves up he'll send to me. But I've just nearly gone crazy since I heard the news, thinking how I'd manage. That's why I was goin' to take your money. So now you know."

"You poor girl!" soothed Monica. "What a wicked man Mr. Ambler must be!"

"Sh! don't talk so loud. Mrs. Ambler sometimes listens at the door. She's the nastiest thing! He *is* wicked; but he's awful mad at me."

"Why is he sending you away?" Monica asked, all sorts of plans for the miserable girl's welfare simmering in her brain.

Miss Thomas straightened herself jerkily.

"For one thing, I don't bang the piano loud enough to suit him. I can't! It seems like being cruel to something I love, and hurting it when it can't help itself. Besides, I don't like taking the money in at the door, which he makes me do pretty often. The ten cent boys from the back of the house smack their lips at me, and make hissing noises, and call me 'red head.' I suppose I've been a fool to mind; but I've got a temper as red as my hair, and I spoke out sharp once or twice, and he said I sent away money. Besides, I'm near-sighted, and have to wear glasses on the stage, and Mrs. Ambler's got him to think it looks too queer with some of the costumes. He just says I'm obstinate because I won't take 'em off. That isn't all, either. The worst's coming, and I guess this was the last straw that made up his mind to fire me. They're goin' to put up 'The Octoroon' next week, and Ambler said I had to play 'Weenty Paul.' I *never* took a boy's part, and I can't—I told him I couldn't. Though I'm travellin' around with show folks, I ain't that kind, and I only came to play the piano; I didn't know I should have to act. You've no idea how strict I was brought up till my mother died and my father married again. I'd rather die than have to walk out on the stage and show my legs. It would seem right wicked, that it would, and besides —they—they're so *awful* thin! Nick would see 'em, and—and—but now it's too late; I almost wish I hadn't held out so firm."

"Perhaps it *isn't* too late," said Monica, feeling like a species of secondary Providence, " if you would like to stay."

"Oh, I *would* like it!" the girl cried, wistfully. "I hate the Amblers, and there's others I don't care for much, but—there's Nick. He's been so good to me since I came, and—he'd miss me, I guess. Then, now —there's *you.* If you could only forgive me, and try to look over what I've done, I could worship you. I could lie down in the mud puddles and let you walk over me. But it *is* too late. They've engaged another girl somewhere, Nick found out, and they've sent her money, in advance, for her ticket, and some new clothes. 'Tain't likely they'd waste a penny on me, even if I took everything back and went down on my bended knees."

"No-o," Monica dubiously admitted. "But if somebody repaid them all they'd spent, and asked as a great favour that you should be kept on?"

"Why—but there ain't anybody who'd do it! Nick can't, and the only person in the company who can get any favours out of Mr. Ambler is Mrs. Montgomery—Fanny Free. But she hasn't got a red cent."

"She shall ask him, then, and *I* will pay," Monica solemnly pronounced.

The Marquis of Carabas' thirty pounds seemed to burn against her bosom. Only this morning she had vowed never to touch the money. Now, once a hole was made in it, it was as good as spent. But the pianist should stay.

"There isn't a minute to lose," she said. "I'll go and see if it can be arranged at once."

Monica rose, and the other girl sprang from the bed

as she left it, the mattress rheumatically squeaking with joy at their departure.

She was taller than Monica, and as she put her hands on the pretty, grey-clad shoulders, she appeared, with her reddened face and her dishevelled shock of vivid hair, like a creature of another world.

" *You'll* do all this for me?" she asked, dazedly. " For me, who sneaked into your bag, and would have stolen your money, if you hadn't come and caught me? Say, whether I stay or go, I won't forget this to my dying day; and I tell you, I'd give every drop of blood in my body to do you one mite of good."

Monica was to remember this, strangely enough, upon a later day.

CHAPTER VII.

"Are we all met?
Pat, pat ; and here's a marvellous convenient place
for our rehearsal."

"YOU know, if we keep you on, you've got to play
'Weenty Paul.'"

Thus said Mr. Scott Ambler to the pianist, when
thirty dollars of the Marquis of Carabas' money had
gone into his pocket, and a telegram had been despatched countermanding the engagement of the substitute. By this little transaction, he had been made
the richer for ten dollars, the secret of which financial
deal sat sweetly in his mind, and caused him to feel,
for the moment, at peace with all his world.

It was the morning after Monica's arrival at Bagra,
and was Saturday, the last but one of their stay. The
new juvenile lady had been excused from appearing at
the theatre the night before, though Mrs. Ambler had
suggested that she should "walk on" as "Child's
Head" in "Macbeth," just to get her hand in. She
had spent her time in studying "Mademoiselle Danglars" in "Monte Cristo," and was now about to go to
the theatre with the old members of the company for
rehearsal.

Miss Della Thomas was to show the newcomer the
way, and it was as the two girls were about to leave
the hotel that Mr. Ambler made his attack.

"I sent you word last night I intended to play it all right," she answered sulkily, and then the strangely allied friends were allowed to go their way.

Monica had now no wish to leave the company. She had not ceased to feel the sordid vulgarity of her surroundings and her enforced companionship; but suddenly she had found a new interest in life—even life as it was to be lived among Mr. Ambler's comedians. The personality of the pale, unlettered girl, with fiery hair and burning eyes, had taken a strong hold upon Monica. She felt the magnetic thrill of her adorer's ardent passion of gratitude and admiration. Perhaps she was innocently vain or self-conscious enough to feel an added charm in the odd friendship because of Della's appreciation of the difference between them. It was pleasant to be worshipped; and sunning herself in the warm rays of this humble love, she forgot for the moment that she had cause to be lonely, sad, or desolate.

Defrauded of the leading parts she had hoped for, there was still a certain weird charm of novelty in her situation, and after the first shock of disillusionment had partially passed away, Monica was fortunately endowed with sufficient sense of humour—so rare a gift in a woman—to skim the cream, and shut her eyes upon the dregs, of her environment.

There were parts to learn, and old things to alter, and new things to buy, and—there was a rehearsal, actually at a *theatre*, her very first experience of the sort.

When she had returned to Leeds, " finished " at the convent, and already conscious to the full of histrionic talent, which she was fain to believe genius, she

had acted with an amateur dramatic club, giving per-
formances in private houses. Though the very thought
of " being a professional " actress had tingled through
her veins like sparkling wine, she had never dreamed
of such a lot for herself, until one day, she suddenly
found herself standing among the ruins of the life
which had seemed hers. Then, for reasons which had
in an hour of resentful exaltation appeared wise ones,
she had flown to America, there to find Will-o-the-
Wisp—and a Career—with a capital C.

The career, to be sure, was beginning in a very
different way from what she had expected; still, she
felt brighter and more inclined to see the fun in everything than she would have believed possible the day
before.

The company straggled along the " dirt " side-walk,
made hard with powdered clamshells and ashes, in
couples, at irregular distances. Monica walked briskly,
turning occasionally to gaze with wondering amusement at the eccentric pictorial advertisements with
which ·the Ambler Company was locally billed, and
would have passed a barn-like frame structure had not
Della Thomas pulled her by the dress.

" This is the hall," she announced.

Monica stared mildly. " Hall? What hall ? "

" Where we play at night. Where we're going to rehearse."

Down went the neat provincial theatre, that the
English girl had mentally builded, with a crash !

They went up a flight of filthy stairs, covered with
footprints—not in the " sands," but in the mud of
time—peanut shells, and harmful, unnecessary corpses
of tobacco.

At the top was a dim window, where, during business hours, tickets were sold, and beyond, a double doorway, which led into the auditorium. As there was no stage entrance, the performers must needs pass in at night, shoulder to shoulder with those who had paid to see them act.

Already several members of the company had arrived, and were warming themselves at the red hot soft coal stove, or sprawling on the rough benches and deal chairs provided for the audience. On a dirty little stage, somewhat resembling a box set on its side, and flanked by half-a-dozen unshaded kerosene lamps (which did duty as footlights), prowled Mr. Montgomery, waiting the assembling of his flock.

Monica's heart began thumping rather painfully. She took herself to task for her nervousness. Why should she care what impression her acting at rehearsal might make upon these poor ignorant barn stormers? Nevertheless, she had to admit that she did care very much. Mademoiselle Danglars (who had been allotted but a small part in the version of "Monte Cristo" as played by the Ambler Company), not being supposed to have been born in the first act, naturally had nothing to do in the beginning, save look on while the others rehearsed. But Mr. Montgomery, who seemed to be everywhere at once (a phenomenon easily accounted for by the fact that he "doubled" two parts, beside the leading one), found time to intimate that she might make herself useful in the evening.

"We are accustomed to having Saturday matinees," he hastily explained, "and give away a big dressed doll to that child in the audience who draws the lucky number with her ticket. You've no idea what a crowd the scheme brings in! But Bagra is rather dead and alive for that, so we're doin' no matinee to-day, and shall have the more time to get ready for to-night. This will be our first performance of ' Monte Cristo,' and as most of the people are playin' two or three parts each (you see it's a small company and a big cast), you can help enormously. For instance, you can assist me with my changes, and work the sea at the end of the second act."

"Work the sea?" Monica repeated, helplessly. But already Mr. Montgomery was at the other side of the stage, "doing" De Villefort with his voice and Monte Cristo with his person. No attempt at acting was made by any one, and Mr. and Mrs. Ambler and Mr. Montgomery availed themselves of "star" privileges, to the extent of cutting out all their own long speeches, merely "coming down to cues," which they conde- scended to shout with more or less distinctness.

Mrs. Ambler (or Miss Marguerite Neland, as she preferred to be called) had played " Mercèdes " before during a previous season, evidently fancying herself very much in the part. She and her husband and the stage manager contrived invariably to take the centre of the stage, and to stand as far back, or "up," as possible, which Monica learned for the first time was considered the most desirable position. She watched all that went on with breathless interest, hoping to glean a few points in professional stage business for herself.

She had not realised her own ignorance before. Even these people, so far beneath her in intelligence and education, showed a familiarity with the jargon of the stage manager and prompter, which excited her envy. They went about what they had to do easily, showing a calmness and unconcern which she would gladly have shared with them.

At last the dread moment arrived for Mademoiselle Danglars to go on. By this period in the proceedings Mrs. Ambler was quarrelling with Mr. Ambler, whom she accused of having tried to "queer her business." What this meant Monica did not know, but she sagely concluded it must have been something culpable in the extreme, Mrs. Ambler having called Mr. Ambler a "nasty thing," and Mr. Ambler having responded that she was "another," and might "go there herself" as soon as ever she pleased, and be jiggered to her.

There was much loud talking and stamping of feet on the stage, accompanied by covert snickering in the wings from the Human Flower, and Monica fondly hoped to benefit by the general disturbance. Every one in authority being more or less occupied, there was the less chance that amateurishness on her part would be noticed. She had reckoned without her host—or, rather, without her manager—however. Hardly had Mademoiselle Danglars been good-naturedly led by the fair Flower into her proper entrance, when Mr. Ambler, free for the moment to make some one else miserable, darted to the opposite wing, for the evident purpose of criticising the new member's performance.

Small as the part was, Monica had studied for several hours, practising what she fondly believed to be appropriate gestures, long after Della Thomas had gone to sleep with her face turned toward the wall. She had had reason to flatter herself that she knew every line, though studying had been an effort, as she

had had to accustom herself for the first time to studying a MS. part written down with only the cues of the
preceding speeches. Now, however, no sooner had
she begun to speak, than every word went from her,
beginning to circle elusively round her head, she
fancied, like a flock of frightened birds.

People roared at her confusingly. The cues did
not seem the same when uttered aloud as when she
had read them written down. It was terribly difficult
to "pick them up" without hesitating, and to remember which had been cues for speakers, and which
for entrances, exits, or stage business. Womanfully
she tried to appear the experienced actress, and the
debonair smile which she assumed as a mask seemed
to become so hardened with constant use that she felt
it might have to be knocked off her face with a hammer.

"You come down now, Miss Nairne! Up stage,
quick as you can! Off, left upper entrance!" were
the bewildering cries which rang in her ears.

The poor little amateur star of drawing-rooms had
never been familiarised with the mysteries of "up and
down stage," etc., and now that they were suddenly
sprung upon her without explanation, her distress
waxed so extreme that beads of perspiration made little
rings of her dark hair cling damply to her forehead.

"Say, Miss Nairne, you don't seem to be quite as
quick to follow stage directions as such an experienced
lady as you ought to be—eh?" remarked Mr. Ambler,
appearing like a gnome at her elbow, when she stood
panting and collecting her scattered wits in the wings.

The girl jumped at the sound of the rasping voice
so close to her ear. For an instant she was non-

plussed, and yesterday's shrinking fear of the man overpowered her more strongly than ever. Then, catching a malicious gleam in the ox-eyes of her inquisitor's fat wife, her courage mounted with the occasion.

"*English* stage managers' directions are very different from *American* stage managers'," she retorted, with a telling toss of the head; "and *much* less obscure."

She had scored. Mr. Ambler was temporarily silenced, if not convinced, by her audacious mendacity; and, as he turned away, grunting under his breath, she saw the magnificent Crawford making the motions of dumb applause. She could not hide a nervous blush and hysterical smile, which were naturally misunderstood; and Mr. Crawford shortly after edged his way across the stage in her direction.

"Say," he whispered, "how are you going to get your things to the hall to-night, Miss Nairne? I s'pose you'll have quite a bundle, won't you?"

"I dare say I can pay some boy from the hotel to carry everything I shall need," she answered, trying not to be too stiff or ungracious.

"But *I'm* acquainted with a boy would like to do it for you without any pay, except 'thank you.' A boy about my size. I'll tote you around to the hall, too, if you'll let me, and back again. Nick always goes with Della, you know, and perhaps you wouldn't like to walk three."

"You are very kind," said Monica, with pink cheeks; "but I couldn't think of troubling you. And since I have been in the States, I have been about a great deal alone. I am not at all afraid."

"I guess you don't know what a place like this is on Saturday night, or you wouldn't be so sure," persisted Crawford.

He looked at her, evidently willing to give her the opportunity of changing her mind; but she did not speak again, apparently absorbing herself in the MS. part she held, until Crawford turned on his heel and walked jauntily away.

Monica was very busy throughout the day, altering a frock for Mademoiselle Danglars, a task in which Della Thomas begged to assist, and threw herself, heart and soul.

"I can do things with my fingers," she said, proudly. "Sewing comes next to playing with me. I can hear a sort of tune in my head, and follow it as the needle goes pricking through the cloth. I've got nice hands, haven't I? If it wasn't for them, I might be even a worse girl than I am. Seems as though things must go awful hard with me, like yesterday, before I can bear to use 'em to do anything mean."

Sometimes throughout the day Della would start, and look up wistfully as a step passed along the uncarpeted hall, or a tap come at the door. But when only the fly-away little soubrette appeared for a chat, or Mrs. Ambler to cast a critical and jealous eye over Monica's wardrobe spread out upon the bed, her face would fall into its old heavy, almost sullen lines once more. Monica did not know that Della's days had been made happy by an afternoon call from Nick, who sat tilted up against the wall near the stove, with his unblacked boots on the rung of his chair, and said unutterable things with his eyes which his shy lips could not speak. Monica did not know that Della, instinctively feeling that her new friend would not approve these invasions of the sanctity of their chamber, had awkwardly told Nick that he must not come any more, thereby offending his sensitive *amour propre*, and making herself utterly miserable.

So Monica grew happier every moment, finding great pleasure in talking of the convent, and of England, with the girl who was so humble, so admiringly imitative of her good manners, and so ready to listen to all she had to tell. A girl who loved music as Della did must have much that was worth cultivating in mind and soul, and it was sweet for Monica to feel that she might be finding her mission in judiciously bringing it out.

Della was almost pretty when her heavy face wore certain expressions, Monica told herself to-day. The dark, near-sighted eyes could flash with the fire of sudden passion, or light with a clear lustre of crude intelligence; and the alabaster skin and glowing hair were beautiful. She did not love cold water, or walking for the joy of healthful exercise, and she shared the soubrette's fondness for lying on the bed in un-aired, baking rooms, reading trashy novels. Tales of the English aristocracy, written by American retired shop-girls, were what Della liked best, and she had had her name printed on the programmes as Miss De Audrey Thomas, because there had been a haughty and beautiful Lady de Audrey in the prettiest story she had ever read.

But Monica already saw possibilities of better things. She had great hopes of the girl, and, somehow, severely as she condemned the Marquis of Carabas, she now thought of his twinkling eyes and his

whimsical mouth, and vaguely wished she might tell
him all about Della Thomas, and the varied experiences of the last twenty-eight hours.

Nursing her innocent sense ot self-importance and
her charitable intentions, Monica did not dream that
her refining influence had begun by breaking a humble love idyll in twain.

Della talked rather feverishly at the supper-table,
where the company assembled early to partake of
pork and beans, cranberry sauce and seed cake; but
Nick, who sat opposite, did not raise his dog-like,
hazel eyes. He had no personal enmity towards the
new juvenile lady. He even honestly admired her
beauty and dainty ways, which were of a kind that he
had never seen before, and were meekly accepted by
him as belonging to another sphere than his. But he
did resent what he believed to be Della's desertion of
him for the acquaintance of a day. He tingled all
over at the thought that she was ashamed of him and
his bad boots and his stumpy hands. He was sure
that she had really kept him from her room, whither,
heretofore, he had been free to go every day, because
he was not good enough in her eyes to associate with
the grand young lady from England. She had forgotten that he might have had new clothes if he had
not lent her three weeks' salary to send home to her
cross step-mother. Not that he wanted it from her
again. He would rather die than take it. But she
need not have whistled him down the wind for the
sake of a girl she had only known a few hours. Not
that it mattered. He would soon show her that if she
didn't want him, he could do without her. And so,
that night, when Monica had sent her parcel, tied up

in a sheet, to the theatre, by a beady-eyed negro boy, Della delayed their departure with various excuses, all in vain.

Monica had forgotten the information received that morning regarding the evening custom of Mr. Nickson and Miss Thomas, and now she rather impatiently asked for what they were waiting.

"Nothing," said Della dully; and they started out into the poorly lighted street.

CHAPTER VIII.

" And thy sea marge, sterile and rocky hard,
Where thou thyself dost air."

ALL was excitement at the theatre. Behind a piece
of sheeting at the left of the stage the ladies were
busily beautifying themselves, and dark figures, buxom
and lean, could be seen with alarming distinctness
silhouetted upon the transparent partition. Another
curtain of the same description was designed to veil
the toilet of the gentlemen from public view, but owing to its inadequate length, legs in all stages of
deshabille seemed, like moving fringe, to decorate the
bottom of the drapery.

Mr. Montgomery, dressed according to his own
conception of a cross between a Corsican peasant and
a sailor, strode about the stage, directing the two
local assistants, whose services were thrown in with
the theatre, and who would later figure in red calico
as peasants, and in fearful and wonderful uniforms as
guests at the De Moncerfs' ball.

" Hurry up, and get into your things, Miss Nairne,"
he cried; "and when you're through, stand around
behind the scenes, please, and be ready to help me.
I've got enough on my shoulders to drive a dozen
men crazy " (which was a shot at the management for
keeping down expenses, and was responded to behind
the right-hand partition by a defiant shuffling of Mr.
Ambler's legs).

Monica flew to obey, but the scene in the ladies'
dressing-room caused her to retreat, gasping. Fortunately for all concerned, Della was already out in
front, having removed her hat and jacket and gone to
her beloved piano, which she would have to desert
presently for the exigencies of a "walking part" or
two.

The three women, who already occupied the four-
foot-by-ten space, however, had appropriated it all,
and flowed over with their belongings into the narrow
passage-way between the curtain and the wings. Mrs.
Ambler's plenteous form reposed on poor Monica's
bundle of frocks, as she strapped red ribbons round
her singularly well-developed ankles, and rejoiced in
the thought that her weight might not be conducive
to the preservation of the leading juvenile's finery.

Mrs. Patton, as a Corsican peasant, was a sight to
beggar description; but her cast-off petticoats took up
as much room on floor and wall as did the gay flounces
and cheap laces of that spoiled beauty, Fanny Free.

Even the third among these estimable dames, who
was good-nature personified, had now no time to
think of any woman's rights save her own; and as
Monica would not demand her due share of the room,
she performed her first professional toilet, abject, in
a triangular corner behind the wash-stand.

The first act was over before she had finished and
could report herself for duty to Mr. Montgomery.
Now, to "help him ring his changes," and to learn the
baffling mystery of that unforgotten sentence, "working the sea," Mademoiselle Danglars not being due
till the fourth act.

The stage was hung, rather than set, with a prison

scene, which Mr. Nickson, the artistic member of the Ambler Company, had painted, and of which he was justly proud. Monica, on her way to find the master of proceedings, peeped through an aperture in the canvas, and was thrilled at beholding him as Edmund Dantes in his cell. Such was his costume, or lack of it, that she could not restrain a little gasp. The upper portion of his body alone was clad in a ragged and curiously interesting relic, which might in the days of its glory have been a meal sack. His collar bones were modestly concealed behind a beard, supposed to have attained an abnormal length during residence in prison, while beneath the realistically tattered edges of his sole garment, descending to his hips, spindled two long white stalks, far more resembling spears of celery than the legs of an able-bodied sailor. They were the only legs that Mr. Montgomery possessed, however, and though he scrupled not to reveal their attenuated proportions, he had compromised with his own and the audience's modesty by covering them with cotton tights several sizes too large for him.

This was his conception of Edmund Dantes' prison toilet; and so marked was the effect of its classical simplicity upon Monica, that she remained breathless till the close of the scene.

For the end, a tableau had been arranged, which was intended to be one of the masterpieces of the performance. Scarcely had the curtain gone down, with wild applause and whistling from the little boys at the back of the house, than Mr. Montgomery, like a huge brown and white "daddy-long-legs," scuttled into the wings toward Monica.

"Quick! quick!" he ejaculated, in stifled accents,

"now's your time you're wanted to work the sea!"
It was no moment to ask questions, but only to do or
die.

Every man in the company seemed suddenly to be
busy on the stage helping the local talent to tear
down old scenery and put up new. Sky, and a
painted background of turbulent ocean, took the place
of the prison wall, through which the deceased abbé
had lately made an effective, if laboured, entrance.
Mr. Todd, the property man, slammed down a box
on the centre of the stage, which Edmund Dantes
mounted, swearing and dancing as though it had been
a hot ploughshare, in his frenzy of excitement.

"Where are the rocks?" he groaned. "What the
devil has gone wrong with those rocks?"

Mr. Nickson, panting, dragged on a board, painted
to represent the most rugged and convulsed effort of
nature in the granite line, and balanced it against and
in front of the box on which the escaped prisoner had
taken his stand.

"That won't do," wailed Mr. Montgomery. "Here,
Miss Nairne, squat down behind the rock and hold
fast on to it, while you throw up the salt for the
waves. Now, where the dickens *is* that salt? Will
anybody bring the waves?"

The abbé—his white beard tucked rakishly under
one arm—rushed on, bearing a tin wash-basin, filled
to the brim with glittering white particles of rock-salt.
"The kind," Monica hastily reflected, "that they
freeze ices with."

"Now, curtain's going up!" prompted Mr. Montgomery. "Stoop down your head so they can't see
you from the front. Throw the salt—plenty of it—as

though it was the spray dashing against the rocks ! *So !* "

Monica crouched, feeling as though she were a spirit of ocean. Up went the curtain, and simultaneously up went the salt. What matter if in inadvertence and too great enthusiasm the breaking spray rattled down into the kerosene lamps which formed the foot-lights, and even dashed into Edmund's speaking eye? The effect was fine, being realistic in the extreme, and all would have gone well, to the fall of the curtain, had it not been for one untoward circumstance.

Somehow, Monica, grubbing on her knees, and spasmodically grasping a point of rock with one hand, while she manipulated the majesty of ocean with the other, was unfortunate enough to lose her balance. It was only for an instant, but it was an instant too much.

" The wo-rld is mine!" fervently announced the future Monte Cristo. And at that juncture, as though the component parts of Nature had taken umbrage at his boast, down fell the rock flat upon the stage, raising considerable dust from Neptune's bed, and displaying not only a prostrate young lady grovelling over a pan of salt, but the box which supported the hero, and which was labelled in large black letters, " Babbitt's Best Soap."

The language used by the manly Corsican, when the curtain had mercifully come between his humiliation and the ribald shouts of the audience, would be as unfit for publication as it was for the poor culprit's horrified ears. Such blankety blank, blank stupidity he had never seen, blank him if he had. Monica was

indignant at his ingratitude for her well-meant and fa-
tiguing efforts, and enraged at his vulgar profanity,
the like of which had never before been uttered in her
presence. But the sense of her own shortcomings, and
her somewhat increasing awe of him in his business
capacity as stage manager, quelled her for a moment.
Whether she would eventually have burst the bonds
which held her tongue a slave, and withered the man
with her condemnation, was left uncertain, as a cham-
pion made a sudden and unexpected appearance.

"Oh, hold your jaw, can't you, Montgomery?"
growled Crawford, under the very nose of Mr. Ambler, who had stood by, an interested though non-in-
terfering spectator of the little private scene. "You
ought to be ashamed of yourself. Do you suppose
she did it a' purpose? Come on, wipe that scowl off
your face and put it in your pocket. It's time you
got dressed for the next act."

Perhaps Mr. Montgomery began to realise, with
the cooling of his temper under this judicious mingling of delicate badinage and reproach, that he had
been too warm. At all events he departed, grumbling
like distant thunder, to supersede those tights with a
costume suitable to a millionaire in gay Paris, and
Monica was left to await, with sinking heart, the coming of her own ordeal.

As an amateur, she had never been nervous in the
least, but had been buoyed up in *rôles* which might
well have daunted an experienced actress, by a joyous confidence in her own ability. Now, as the time
approached when she must make her first professional
appearance, even the fact (of which she frantically reminded herself) that audience and actors alike were a

parcel of bumpkins and boors, could not restore the courage which seemed to ooze from her fingers and toes.

Certainly the beginning of the evening had not been promising, but she must retrieve herself—she must—she must!

She had been dressed for a long time, but at the last moment she flew back to her corner behind the wash-stand, dabbed on a little more rouge and powder, and attempted to blacken her long soft lashes with some cosmetic heated on a hairpin, as she had seen the others do. Splash went a small shower of smudge over marble nose and brilliantly roseate cheeks. The whole " make-up " had to come off again with hasty application of cold cream and a towel, and then, to her horror, there was not time to restore its pristine beauty. She had to run out in response to a shout from the property man, who in this instance did duty as call-boy.

"Mademoiselle Danglars! Come along, for the Lord's sake! They're waitin' for you, and fakin' some nonsense till you come on the stage."

Poor Monica! Her face, which should have been a triumph of art, was shining with cold cream. Her head swam, and she was overcome with a sensation as of sea-sickness, added to a strong conviction that caterpillars were walking in slow procession up the marrow of her spine.

Mr. Todd, who had slipped round from the " prompt box," where he had been holding the book of the play, encouragingly gave the quaking culprit a slight push, which sent her out upon the stage.

It was true. They had been waiting for her, and,

as Mr. Todd had classically observed, been engaged in
" faking " speeches to the best of their ability till she
should appear. She heard her own voice speaking at
last ; it sounded far away, weak and metallic. She
seemed also to have lost control of her arms and
hands, which flourished about in gestures which would
have done credit to a " wooden doll dancer " in a
pantomime. All the pretty waving motions practised
before the mirror were forgotten, and when Monica
afterwards pictured herself as she must have appeared,
it seemed to her that her antics must strikingly have
resembled those of a chicken, which, though decapi-
tated, refuses to consider itself properly dead.

She did not, however, as she had feared, miss any of
her lines. Somehow the words would come back to
her when needed, suggested by the cue and the preceding speech. Even for this small favour from the
gods she was thankful, and for the fact that, though
she received no compliments upon this, her first performance, neither were any more reproaches heaped
upon her humbled head.

She went to the pandemonium of the dressing-room,
when all was over, dazed, and wondering at herself.
"Oh, the difference," she thought sadly, " the difference between being an amateur on the grandest scale
and a professional on the smallest."

It might have comforted her a little, perhaps, could
she have known how many other ambitious ones had
worked this puzzle out with sweat and tears of experience.

CHAPTER IX.

*"By the pricking in my thumbs
Something wicked this way comes!"*

"I WANT to drown my sorrows in drink," said Monica, gloomily. "Let's have some lemonade, and get *real* devilish!"

Della Thomas smiled, and took from the mantelpiece a lemon and a brown paper cornucopia of moist sugar, which the girl's provident forethought had that morning provided.

They had come home tired from the theatre, and had had rather an unpleasant little adventure by the way. Monica had been longer about taking off her "make-up" and packing her impedimenta than the others, more experienced and less fastidious than she; and Della had waited for her, having given one long, wistful glance after Nick's obstinately retreating figure.

Every one had gone, even Mr. Crawford, who, though somewhat resentful, had hoped against hope that the unwilling fair might prove repentant. The girls had been shouted after by boys as "the show actresses," and addressed in offensively affectionate accents by ambitious striplings. They had nearly fallen over the soft mass of a recumbent drunkard's form while fleeing round a dark corner, and then at last had run plump into the arms of their landlord on opening the door of the hotel.

"Say, girls, I was kind of layin' in wait fur you," he said. "I seen you hadn't come back yet with the other folks. Say, can't the gents in your show do better by you than this? Two sweethearts like you trapsin' the streets alone this time o' night! I'm darned if it ain't a shame. Come along into the bar-room with me; there ain't nobody else there, and I'll stand you both some beer and crackers, for I'll tell you what it is, I guess you two are the stunningest gals in the show."

Monica looked him slowly over, beginning in a peculiarly contemptuous manner with his far from de-sirable boots, and not releasing him from the hot pincers of her scorn until her eyes had reached the place where his necktie ought to have been and wasn't.

"Creature!" she murmured beneath her breath, and this not being taken entirely in the way it was meant, she drew her skirts aside with a delicate shud-der. "Kindly allow me to pass," she commanded, "and do not attempt to annoy us any further."

"Good gosh!" ejaculated the man. "My *saikes!*" Then, as their dresses brushed haughtily against him on their way toward the stairs, "Will *you* kindly ex-cuse *me* while I continner to live? Or I'll stop breathin' if you've anything partickular agin' it, an' let you dig a hole in the ground with me if you wanter."

"Oh, dear, we've made an awful enemy of him!" said Della, when they had closed the door. "Luckily we've only got to-morrow to stay or we'd starve. I don't believe he'll let us have anything more to eat in his house."

"Perhaps he'll put spiders in our soup, and ask us

if we expected 'canary birds' in his sort of hotel,"
returned Monica, making the threatened lemonade,
and cheerfully defying the wrath of the Ryder House
proprietor. But then Monica did not know of what
revenge some landlords in the soft coal region were
capable.

They had been invited to join the after-theatre
revelries in the stage manager's room, but had refused
to do so, and already it was being whispered about
in the company that Miss Nairne was an " awful unsociable gurl." She couldn't act much, either. At
least, that was the verdict to-night among the barn
stormers, who considered themselves, if not each
other, past masters and mistresses of the histrionic
art.

Unconscious of the criticisms of their neighbours,
Monica and Della sat up late, Della trying to pretend
that she was happy and cared nothing for the defection of her lover. Even the assemblage in the
Montgomerys' room had broken up, and still the
girls' light burned, and still their voices chattered,
Monica reciting her latest part, that on Monday night
the words might fall the more trippingly from her
tongue.

Suddenly a terrific noise sounded upon their door,
blows that well-nigh cracked the fragile panels.

Monica sank on the bed, horrified and startled; but
Della, with a new instinct of protection, flew toward
the door, to fling her weight against it, and prevent
further treachery on the part of that fatal broken
bolt.

" What's the matter? " she cried, sharply.

"Stop your row in there, you show women, you!"

roared the savage voice of the landlord. "I'll let you know this is a decent house, and I won't have such disturbances goin' on at this hour o' the night. What do you mean by it, you—hussies, laughin' and carryin' on in there?"

The knob rattled and turned, and Monica, trembling from head to foot, rose to assist Della in the defence of their citadel. Both girls were in their dressing-gowns, with hair streaming down their backs; and Della, possessing no dainty slippers such as clothed Monica's little feet, wore over her stockings what she would have called her rubbers.

Realising at last that the bolt offered no obstruction, and that he had but the combined weight of two slim young women to push against, the bully, who had come to wreak his vengeance, forced open the door, despite the terrified girls' resistance.

"How kin I tell who you're monkeyin' about with in here?" he yelled. "But I'll soon know that! This is a decent house for decent folks, and I jest tell you, a little more, and out you're pitched into the street."

"We were making no disturbance whatever—simply talking together in a low voice," desperately remonstrated Monica. "How dare you try to come into our room? Della, call for help."

"I reckon I'm master in my own house," the brute bellowed. And flinging the door so violently backward that the girls were swept staggering away from it, he would have leaped into the room had he not suddenly been seized from behind.

The rescuer was not the manager of the company, who might have been supposed to stand ready for the protection of its members' interests, nor was it the stage manager, who stood with abjectly hanging braces, judiciously peeping through the crack of his own door.

Two dishevelled young men, one of them looking far more attractive than in his attire of every day, had caught the big fellow, and between them were hurrying him, swearing and protesting, toward the head of the stairs.

Small as he was, Nickson was a young man of uncommon strength, and in reality his efforts did far more toward the undoing of the landlord than Crawford's picturesque proceedings. It was little Nickson who, by a wrench of the big man's arm, gave an impetus in the desired direction. But as Crawford had made a grab for the coat collar and seat of the trousers, with a motion as of casting a rag-bag into space, it was he who received all credit from the half horrified, half guiltily admiring Monica.

Down went the furious wretch, with a clattering of dilapidated balusters, and a crashing of cow-hide boots; but scarcely, it seemed, had he reached the bottom stair, than he had begun stumbling up again, roaring imprecations and foul words.

Monica knew that the only proper course of procedure, under the circumstances, was to retire out of harm's way with Della, and religiously to guard the door. But the sight, though it sickened and even alarmed her, held her powerless to move. Della, too, stood clutching the door-post, and staring, with parted lips; but all her thoughts and all her fears were now with Mr. William Nickson.

No one else appeared "to warn, to comfort, or com-

mand," though the landlord had reached the top of
the stairs again, looking—with his shock head held
down between his great shoulders—like an angry bull.

Heads were at all the doors along the passage; but
it was Mr. Ambler's policy never to offend a landlord,
and where Mr. Ambler led his stage manager followed.
Young Mr. Todd would have shown himself in defence of the Human Flower, but did not now care to
excite that blossom's jealousy, and considered that Jim
and Nick could do very well by themselves.

Poor old Mr. Wilts chirped sage advice from his
fastness; and Mrs. Patton (awful in an unbleached
cotton chemise and curl-papers) lamented the leonine
courage of her recreant husband, who would have
been ready to give battle, even inadequately armoured
in the famous spangled tights.

Monica could not repress an occasional cry as the
three figures struggled together at the top of the stairway, and then went noisily down together in a heap,
bumping on every step until they had reached the
bottom.

A sound of continued scuffling arose from below,
and presently followed the loud slamming of a door.

"We've locked him in his room," panted Crawford
breathlessly, as he and Nick triumphantly reascended
the stairs. "I guess he's tired of fighting for a little
while; and, ladies, you're safe for the night."

He said it with the air of a conqueror, and Monica
felt honestly grateful to him. She scarcely thought
of poor little Nick, with the dog-like eyes and the pic-
ture-frame legs, for he was such an insignificant as well
as slovenly fellow, and at best he had played but a
secondary part.

"If it hadn't been for *you*," she said, impulsively, "I don't know what we should have done. Nobody else " (in a slightly raised voice) " seemed inclined to help us—except Mr. Nickson, of course."

"It was a pleasure to do anything for you," responded Crawford ; "you' and Della. Jiminy Christmas! I'd have liked to o' killed the beast for darin' to insult you."

He certainly did look very handsome and manly as he spoke, his great white throat bare, and the black hair, so hatefully sleek in the day-time, ruffled into short curls all over his round head.

It occurred to Monica, with a self-reproachful thrill, that she had misjudged the poor fellow, even been rude to him, perhaps. He was a rough diamond, and if she had met him in a book, instead of in real life, she believed that she might have admired and respected his qualities immensely. It was a great pity that he was so dreadfully common ; but, perhaps, if looked at rightly, that fact might render him only the more picturesque. And besides, she might step down from her pedestal and help him a little, as she meant to help Della Thomas. Surely now she owed him so much for his courage and championship in this sordid crisis. Of course she could not exactly *associate* with him as though they had been on an equality, but she could be *kind* to him. By way of making the first step in this direction she held out her hand. " Thank you—for us both," she murmured. And when Monica was grateful, her eyes were apt to say, with the very best intentions, a great deal more than they actually meant.

CHAPTER X.

"Heaven prosper our sport.
No man means evil but the devil, and we shall
know him by his horns.
Let's away."

THE landlord, unlike the baffled villain of the shilling shocker, did not return to the attack, though he could very easily have released himself from durance vile by springing from his ground-floor window. He had other revenge in view, and though, for fear of developments prejudicial to his own moral character, he would hardly have appealed to the police, he had it in his mind, no doubt, to render the remaining stay of the Ambler Company a disagreeable one.

He was thwarted, however, in the accomplishment of any dark scheme for starvation, "freezing out," or other persecution, which he might have entertained, for by the first grey gleam of morning the barn stormers were quietly astir.

Mr. Ambler was a general who objected on principle to open warfare, no matter how glorious the cause. It was bad for business, and "queered the show" along the route; and scarce any insult (to another than himself) was worth fighting about. He was vexed at the occurrence which rounded off the Bagra engagement, and unreasonably angry with Monica and Della, though if asked wherein lay the head and front of their offending, he would only have spluttered and drowned the voice of the querist by shouting, "Don't you talk up to me!"

The affair had happened, however, and the only thing to do was to engineer a triumphant escape from attending disasters. There was shame in remaining; there might be glory in departure. Therefore it was that Monica and Della were startled from sleep while yet it was dark. Some one was softly tapping at the door, and the voice of the property man was heard in the land.

"Girls! girls! get up and do your packin' as quick as you can. We're goin' to be away from this house in an hour."

Della crept out of bed shivering. Only two or three days ago it would have been Nick who stole to the door, telling her to slip on a wrapper and let him in to make up her fire. He would have returned, too, when she was dressed, to give any help in packing which she might need, to strap her trunk for her, and pull it into the passage outside.

But Nick would not come again unless she humiliated herself to beg that he would do so, perhaps not even then, for he was obstinate as well as sensitive, and she had begun to realise how deeply she had wounded him. Still, as she stood with chattering teeth, lighting the kerosene lamp, and glancing across at the little dark head that lifted itself from the pillows of the other bed, she regretted nothing that she had done. The dumb gratitude of a dog was in her heart, and she resignedly took up the burden that she had to bear.

It was right that she should sacrifice all she loved best for the girl who had been such an angel to her.

It was right that she should work for her, too, and
shield her so far as she could from the hardships of
the rough life in which an angel appeared so strangely
out of place.

It seemed natural and proper to Della that she
should be the one to crawl out of bed in the cold,
grey dawn, light the lamp and kindle the fire, and
make things comfortable for her dainty room-mate.

" Don't you get up quite yet, Angel," she said, between teeth that would chatter together as she spoke
like castanets. " I—I—don't mind the cold a bit ; I'm
so used to it, I like it, and you'd only be in the way."

She hated to soil her pretty hands with the lumps
of soft coal which had to be laid, bit by bit, on top of
the sticks and crumpled newspaper, if the fire was to
be induced to burn ; but there was no hope that the
grumpy, coloured porter would come up at this time
of the morning, as he usually did, to make the fire,
while they hid their heads under the bed-clothes, and
pretended to be haughtily unembarrassed by his presence. It was for Monica that Della performed the
grimy task, and thus there was even a certain pleasure
in blackening the pink filberts of her nails.

Monica felt a sense of guilt in taking advantage of
her new friend's unselfishness ; but she was conscious
that she could not have built a fire, and possibly there
was a vague conviction of her own superiority in the
thought.

Hurriedly they performed such curtailed ablutions
as time allowed, scrambled into their clothing with a
miserable feeling of being unkempt and unworthy to
face the pure light of morning, when they should find
it out of doors.

•

Then came a wild rush over their packing, during which half Monica's things would have been forgotten had it not been for Della, who, like an "old faker," conscientiously went the rounds of the room, peering into every drawer and cranny where stray belongings might lurk concealed.

"Mrs. Montgomery put me up to that," she said proudly, when Monica complimented her upon her prudence. "She always looks into everything when she first takes a room at an hotel, and when she leaves it also, and so do I after the awful things she told me. I can't be easy now until I've searched. What do you suppose she once found in a bureau drawer?"

"Oh, I don't know," responded Monica, awed at the other's tone.

"Why, a nest of little young mice, all pink and naked and squashy, with great flashing black eyes, and tall, waggly ears. But don't look so dreadful! I guess it won't happen to us; and, anyhow, I'll always open everything first."

The flitting of the company had been accomplished with remarkable speed and stealth. The three members best provided with muscles, Nickson, Crawford, and Todd, carried the luggage downstairs, depositing it softly in the lower hall, while the landlord's bell-toned snoring melodiously floated through his key-hole to their ears. Arrangements were hastily made for the conveyance of the trunks and meagre rolls of scenery to the railway station, and it was not until the ladies had started away, carrying their handbags and satchels, that Mr. Ambler thundered on the land-lord's door an intimation of their departure. He was

ready to make a virtue of necessity now, remarking
that, after what had taken place the night before, he
preferred to shake the dust, or rather the mud and
snow, of Bagra from his feet without unnecessary delay. What he wanted was the bill, and he wanted it
mighty quick, too. He'd a train to catch, with his
folks, but no fool of a landlord should say he wasn't
always ready to do the square thing. He paid cash,
he did, right on the nail.

Mr. Ambler could be pleasant enough when he had
an object to serve, such as making himself agreeable
to a new member of the company, before her pretty
face had ceased to be a novelty, and she had become
identified in his mind merely as one of his troublesome "folks." But he seldom had an object ; and if
Mr. Ambler, under ordinary circumstances, was not
exactly a specimen of ideal manhood, Mr. Ambler,
cold, sleepy, and breakfastless, was much (as the
Human Flower expressed it) like a "mouldy old bear
with a sore head."

Nobody else had had any breakfast ; but that, comparatively speaking, was a detail. If Miss Nairne and
Miss Thomas had only had a cat's sense, the row
would never have happened, and they would all have
been comfortably asleep in their beds. Their advance
man wouldn't have engaged their rooms at Poddiwiski, the next stand, until the following day, and it
would be only a fluke if they hadn't all to sleep in the
hall that night.

Every one crowded round the stove in the station
waiting-room, gloomily keeping silence while Mr.
Ambler grumbled, or whispering, and pretending not
to hear. All Monica's wretchedness on first joining

the company had returned to her, and had it not been
for poor Della, she told herself, she would not remain
an hour longer to be brow-beaten by this vulgar pos-
sessor of "a little brief authority."

There was a Della, however, a Della who sat close
beside her, in a shabby frock and inadequate jacket,
throwing loving glances at her from time to time.
And so Monica stayed, and got into the small local
train with the others, who waxed merrier as breakfast
and the next stopping-place grew probable, and
amused themselves by throwing peanut shells across
the car. It mattered nothing to them what the few
other early Sunday morning passengers might think
of them. They were "the show folks," and were a
law unto themselves. If people stared at them, surprised by their antics, or pricked up their ears at the
crude jokes shouted from one end of the long car to
the other, they took it for granted that all the glances
directed at them were prompted by admiration and
delight in their witty ways.

It was after nine o'clock when they arrived at Poddiwiski, which appeared to be a town of somewhat
more pretentious style than Bagra, to which they had
lately bidden good-bye.

There were no carriages or hacks at the station,
however, and the company set forth in a straggling
procession to find their hotel, the luggage following
after them on trucks. Monica felt ashamed of her
own shame at being identified with these people by
the sober, Sunday-faced folk who passed them staring, and whispering, perhaps, what the more youthful
population of Bagra had shouted aloud.

She and Della walked decorously behind, Della trying not to let her eyes wander towards Nick, who swaggered along, far ahead, with the Montgomerys. They had not gone far, however, when they were approached by Crawford.

"Say, your satchel's too heavy for you, Miss Nairne," he remarked. "Won't you let me carry it?" Then, with a certain condescension, "I can take yours, too, Della. You know this ain't the kind of show that says things if a gentleman carries a lady's satchel for her."

Monica, remembering last night with gratitude, and unwilling to deserve the reputation of being stuck up, which Mrs. Ambler's criticism had bestowed upon her, unwillingly surrendered the bag, while Della slowly followed her example.

"Why, what could any one say," the amateur inquired, with an effort to be affable, "except that the man was very kind to take so much trouble?"

Crawford grinned, and looked at her rather shamefacedly out of the corner of his eyes.

"Say, don't you really know?" he inquired. "Well, then, if you don't, I'd better not tell you. But this company's all straight enough that way; and, besides, *you* ain't the kind o' young lady that such things is said about."

Monica would have been glad to snatch her bag away; but, if she were not to put up with this man's boorishness, how was she to begin to help him, as she had virtuously made up her mind to do?

Mr. Ambler's gloomy prognostications, which had somewhat frightened the newcomer, were destined not to be fulfilled. There was accommodation for all at the hotel, with the usual "doubling," which was done

to save the purse of the management. The environment was even rather superior to that at the Ryder
House, for, at all events, the window blinds were in
working order, and the stove in the girls' bedroom
did not smoke.

The eggs at breakfast were certainly rather suggestive of the Renaissance or some other remote period
of history. The coffee was burnt and sharp with an
admixture of chicory, and the hot biscuits were
freckled with soda ; but Monica's fastidiousness was reduced by hunger, and her spirits began to revive after
food.

As she risked the future of her complexion on reek-
ing fried potatoes and ham, a jovial old landlord appeared in the doorway.

"Say," he prefaced, in the manner to which Monica
was becoming accustomed, "any of you good girls
answer to the name o' *Nairne ?*"

Monica flushed brilliantly. She certainly *was* a
girl, and, though she prayed to be forgiven her sins, in
the abstract she was in the habit of considering herself
good. Still, to be called in so many words a " good
girl," seemed to be placing her on a level little higher
than the beasts of the field, and she resented it.

"My name is Nairne," she grudgingly vouchsafed,
when every one turned, with his or her mouth full, to
gaze at her. "But—" it was on the tip of her tongue
to say "I am *not* a good girl," when a fear that her
reproof might be misunderstood restrained her.

"Then there's a box for you, a whackin' big one.
Come by express las' night."

Monica's fork clattered down on her plate, bounding
spiritedly off again into the nest of little dishes that

surrounded it like an earthenware halo. The landlord's news seemed to her incredible. Nobody in the
whole wide world knew where she was. It would be
impossible for any one to write to her, or send her
boxes, even if there existed a being who might have
been desirious so to do.

"I think there must be some mistake," she objected,
meekly.

"Nary mistake; that is, if you spell yourself
M-o-n-i-c-e-r, or some outlandish front name o' that
sort. The box is directed care o' the Ambler Comedy
Company, Hotel Mars, Poddiwiski, Ohio. I guess I
can spare a boy to tote it up to your room fur you, if
you want."

The fried potatoes had lost their greasy fascination
for Monica. She was now in much the state of excitement which must have transported Cinderella when
told by her fairy godmother that she was to go to the
ball. Following her informant into an adjoining
apartment labelled "Office" and resembling the shab-
biest of bar rooms, her eyes actually beheld the mysterious article in question. It was certainly a box,
and it was certainly addressed to "Miss Monica
Nairne," in a large, firm-looking handwriting which
was strange to her.

Notwithstanding the landlord's generous offer, it
was Crawford who carried the heavy burden upstairs
for her, depositing it in her bedroom. His, also, was
the hand which wielded the hammer, wrenching out
the nails, and tearing up the boards which formed the
cover, not without considerable battering and bruising
of blunt finger ends.

After such valiant service, Monica could hardly request the poor wretch not to stand upon the order of his going; and therefore it came about that what her eyes beheld, Mr. Crawford's privileged orbs took in simultaneously.

Somebody appeared to have bought out a confectioner's shop or two, in his anxiety that the big packing-case should be crammed to the brim. There were oranges and bananas, and fancy boxes of chocolates, and various other sweets. There was a frosted plumcake, and a "layer cake" all pink and white; there were salted almonds and sugared almonds, a jar of olives, a roasted partridge rolled in a damask napkin, to say nothing of several bottles of port wine neatly packed at the bottom. And underneath all reposed a card, on which a line or two had been scribbled in pencil, evidently by the same hand which had addressed the box.

Monica, on her knees among the débris, and forgetful of Mr. Crawford, eagerly snatched up the bit of pasteboard, while a pair of curious, jealous eyes searched her face, and then surreptitiously turned toward the writing on the card. "Compliments and regards of *Dinah*, who, though missing her mistress, and anxious for her continued health and happiness, is otherwise content," were the words which he who ran might read.

"Oh, that Marquis of Carabas!" cried Monica, laughing like a released schoolgirl. "What will he do next? and how on earth did he find out where I was?"

She checked herself suddenly, remembering that she was not alone, and then, brightly blushing, looked up to find Crawford's eyes gloomily fixed upon her.

He had never read " Puss in Boots " (indeed, there
had been no fairy stories in his sordid childhood, the
only fables he knew being of his own invention, and
crudely known by a less lenient name). To him the
Marquis of Carabas took shape at once as some titled
lover in the English girl's own land, and while he felt
a certain awe of her for possessing so magnificent, as
well as so generous, an appendage, he grew sullen, and
injured, and sad at heart.

"Do you happen to know," Monica asked, eagerly,
" whether the places where we play are mentioned in
any of the dramatic papers ? "

"That they're not," responded the clouded Crawford. " We ain't of enough importance for that, nor
yet the towns we go to."

" You're *quite* sure ? "

" Quite sure, Miss Nairne."

" Then *how*—" Monica bit her lips. She had already had cause for anger against the Marquis of
Carabas, and she ought now to be very seriously dis-
pleased with this second liberty that he had taken.
What right had he to force money upon her and send
her presents? It was her duty to be deeply vexed.
But she was not vexed. She was, on the contrary,
almost childishly overjoyed. She felt as she could
remember having sometimes felt at Christmas, when
there had been a dear Santa Claus for her, as for other
happy children, so long—so very long—ago. It was
beautiful to see the pretty, dainty boxes of sweets,
and the brightly-colored fruits in this dreary room ;
and there had been a thrill of delight ineffable that
came with the sheer surprise of it all.

Her heart beat fast, and her face was wreathed

with smiles. Every one in the company should have something from her store. Yet, again, *how* had he found out? He had said he should follow her route in the dramatic papers; but she was not in the dramatic papers, it seemed.

An air of mystery seemed to exhale illusively from the very card she held.

There was great rejoicing among Mr. Ambler's comedians that night, for Monica and Della gave a reception, which returned Mr. and Mrs. Montgomery's hospitality, and, at the same time, afforded the opportunity for a feast such as the company had never known.

Monica's popularity was in the ascendant. Crawford, despite his jealousy, had not been able to refrain from mentioning the name of the distinguished donor of the box, and she was, consequently, looked upon with greatly increased respect, even by the bumptious manager himself. As Mr. Ambler gravely swallowed Monica's chocolates, he was seized by an inspiration which bade him to bill his new member as " *Lady* Monica Nairne, the English Professional Beauty." Perhaps she *was* Lady Monica for all he knew. There was assuredly something queer about her past, and, anyway, whether it was the truth or not didn't signify in the least. The thing was, that, without any extra outlay, immense *éclat* would be added to his show.

CHAPTER XI.

"What shall I do with my doublet and hose?"

"DEAREST, do you remember what is going to happen to-night?" asked Della.

Monica sighed, rubbed her eyes, and awaked to realise that it was Monday morning, and that her friend was kneeling beside her, in the purple wrapper, with a tragic face.

"No, I don't remember—yet," she responded, sleepily.

"I've got to play Weenty Paul." If the girl had had to announce that she was to suffer capital punishment, there could scarcely have been a deeper note of anguish in her voice.

"Oh, dear!" Monica tried to rouse herself into sufficient sympathy, for she had been dreaming, and the scent of May, that had blossomed and perished in the spring of a year that was dead, still steeped her senses. "Why, we—we haven't even rehearsed 'The Octoroon' yet. Surely we can't play it to-night?"

"Yes, we can," despairingly. "We never have more than one rehearsal of anything. We just study our parts one day, rehearse next morning or afternoon, and put on the piece that evening. That's what we're going to do with the 'The Octoroon'; and, besides, everybody but us has been in it before.

Didn't you hear Mr. Ambler say so when he was picking your bones—I mean your partridge bones—last night?"

" I'm afraid I was thinking of something else," said Monica, guiltily. (She had been puzzling over the mystery of the box.)

" Well, you know, we weren't to have played it till the end of the week; but Mr. Ambler said the manager of the hall had been around to call, and thought it would be the best piece to open with. *I* believe, though, he's just doing it out of spite on me for staying. It almost seems as though I'd rather die, or—or 'most *anything* else, except not having *you* any more."

" Oh, it won't be so bad, dear," Monica consoled her. " Just think what lots of great actresses have had to dress in boy's clothes. Why, as for *me*, I'd rather play Rosalind than anything in the world."

Della mournfully shook her flaming head. " I don't know who Rosalind was," she confessed, dolefully. " But I *do* know that you're different from me. You've got *legs*."

" Haven't you?" laughing involuntarily.

" I've got—things. Look!" With a tragic gesture which would have done her considerable credit on the stage, Della swept aside the unbuttoned wrapper, revealing a certain sketchiness of toilet calculated to show off to the best or worst advantage those terminations of her body to which she had so feelingly alluded.

" They are certainly—er—rather *slight*," admitted Monica, reluctantly. " I'm afraid, if you took to going about in short frocks, you might be arrested, you poor dear, on the ground of having no visible means of support. But, then, you told me the other day that Weenty Paul is supposed to be a little mulatto boy, only about twelve or fourteen years old. It would be ridiculous for him to have legs like a chorus girl's. Why, yours will be exactly right, most artistic for the part."

"I don't mind about the part of Paul. I only mind about that part of *me* I've got to show," wailed Della. "I have to play it, I know, and I ain't goin' to back out at the last minute, only to be fired again, and have to leave you. But—I've prayed to the Lord about this thing, Angel, and perhaps there'll be *some* way found out of it."

"If only there might be a ram with his horns caught in the bushes!" Monica said, fervently. "But then, even if there were, it isn't very likely they'd let him go on and play Weenty Paul."

It would have been pleasant to rise late on these bitter mornings, and would have seemed more in accordance with the life of an actress, as Monica had, before joining the barn stormers, fondly fancied it to be. But the regulations of these little country hotels were unbreakable as their own soda biscuits or the laws of the Medes and Persians.

It didn't matter so much when you got up. You could be mad enough to rise at seven and bathe in the cold if you liked (was the landlady's point of view), or you could tumble out of bed at ten minutes to eight, twist up your hair on top of your head with three hairpins, and huddle on your clothes, there being no necessity to "wash for a low-necked dress" when you were going to put on a high one. But whichever course you selected (let it here be said that the ver-

dict of the Ambler Company, with two or three not-
able exceptions, was singularly unanimous on this
point), you must be down in the dining-room by eight
o'clock or you got no breakfast. Servants in the
Ryder House and the Hotel Mars, and others of that
ilk, were few and far between, and they had something
else to do beside trotting up and down stairs with
trays for "shif'less show folks."

Della, to be sure, would gladly have fetched the
best that was procurable to her adored one, who
might thus have slumbered on as long as she liked;
but Monica was only selfish when she was absent-
minded, and would not be lapped in luxury while another slaved.

Poor Della was melancholy at breakfast, and melancholy on the way to the theatre, though she brightened suddenly with the discovery that the temple
devoted to Thespis could on this occasion boast a
plenitude of dressing-rooms.

"If I'm to play Weenty Paul to-night, I must have
a dressing-room all to myself," she said, with deep
contralto earnestness, to the stage manager. "Oh, do
let me have it! I know it isn't an important part, and
I'm no actress; but I don't know *what* I'll do if you
say no."

As the Poddiwiski Hall was a great barn of a place,
which gave a timid observer from outside the impression that the present might be its day for falling down,
and was provided with a long row of little stalls, par-
titioned off, for the toilet of the performers, Mr. Montgomery allowed his heart to be melted by the pianist's
appeal; and a separate dressing-room was duly allotted to Miss Thomas.

Monica also had one to herself, next door to Della's; but when, on her arrival at the rehearsal, she would have visited it, Mr. Crawford planted himself outside the door, and barred the way.

"Don't you go in there yet, will you?" he exclaimed. "Now, don't; there's a good girl! You'll know my reasons by and by, and you can bet they're solid. Go into Della's room if you like."

Monica did accordingly go into Della's room, curious and eager for her first sight of a theatrical dressing-room, even in such an environment as the present.

It was a disappointment, of course; but she had bidden herself to expect that. The partition which divided the little den from its fellows in the long row was about seven feet in height, and by standing on a chair, she could have peeped over into the apartment at present forbidden by Mr. Crawford.

Possibly it would be more precise to have said *the* chair, for there was but a solitary specimen of that style of modern convenience, and it was a rickety one, the upper portion of which seemed to be contemplating a speedy divorce from its own legs, on the ground of infidelity.

The floor was carpetless, and incredibly dirty. Round two sides of the partition ran a shelf of rough wood, upon which a small lamp dribbled kerosene oil. What had once been a mirror, and now remained a sheet of tarnished mercury, with a shimmer of glass at one end, leaned blindly against the wall, while the shelf underneath displayed reminiscences of the last incumbent, such as buttons, curl papers, bent pins, and a few worthless ends of vari-hued grease paints. Other furniture there was none, unless a battered tin basin, standing on the floor, and half filled with water, on which a scum had risen like cream, could be called such. Three or four nails had been driven into the bare pine, of which the partitions were composed, and scarcely an inch of space on the walls was free from scribbling or hieroglyphics of some description, much of the writing being profane or worse.

Names were everywhere, and a favourite inscription was, " Mr. So-and-So, or Miss So-and-So, leaves best regards for Mrs. Somebody-else, should she come this way." The date followed, with the name of the departing company ; and Monica would have taken considerable interest in this curious little chronicle of tenth-rate theatrical events had she not been so startled at some of the things she saw, that she determined to search the archives of the walls no further.

This rehearsal was widely different from her first, so far as Monica was concerned. She had been assigned the *rôle* of Dora in " The Octoroon," a part of some importance and some length. But though she was kept constantly on the alert, and, as a newcomer who had to be watched, was made to act while all the others were allowed to " walk through " their most telling situations, she had an eye of sympathy for the unfortunate Weenty Paul. No one more unsuited to the presentment of the merry little mulatto boy than the tall, thin, solemn, near-sighted Della could be conceived. But the soubrette, to whom the part should have been assigned, had refused to play anything unless she could have Zoe, the lead, which, as she excitedly impressed upon everybody, she had played with brilliant success when she was a star.

With the air of a virgin martyr being led round

and round the stake, where she was later to be bound
and burned, Della spoke her lines, and was put
through her stage business by Mr. Montgomery. Her
face was a study of varying moods, and as the long
hours of rehearsal dragged on, a certain look of dogged
resolution grew upon it.

"You've been making up your mind to something,
haven't you, dear?" inquired Monica, as they walked
back to the hotel at the early dinner-time, having
been told that the rehearsal would be continued, like
a serial story, after the completion of the meal.

"Yes, I have; I've got a plan," Della answered,
gravely. "It isn't very good, perhaps; but it's better
than nothing. I was in hopes, when they saw me rehearse, they wouldn't let me play; but they don't
seem to mind *how* bad Paul is, so there's no hope that
way. I must just do the best I can."

"Won't you tell me what your plan is, and perhaps
I can help you with it?" pleaded Monica, who,
though pleased that she was to have a dressing-room
quite to herself throughout the week's engagement
at Poddiwiski, was yet rather hurt at her adorer's
desire to be alone, and this new attitude of sober reserve.

"You couldn't help me; *nobody* could help me,"
Della returned, with resignation. "I should be
ashamed to have even you see me—er—getting into—
them to-night. That's why I want to dress alone."

Monica was silenced, but began looking forward to
the appearance of Weenty Paul in costume with a
species of guilty curiosity.

The continuation of the rehearsal lasted until four
o'clock, and, as the stage manager was dismissing his

weary puppets, he turned to Della with a sudden thought.

" By the way, Miss Thomas," he said, " I've been so busy, I forgot to ask you. Have you got any clothes to wear as Weenty Paul to-night?"

Della grew pale. " I've got a loose brown corduroy jacket," she replied. " I thought, over a blue flannel blouse of mine, it might do for a kind o' shooting coat."

" That's all right. But how about the——"

She hurriedly cut him short. " The *other* things? Well, I haven't got any. So *there!* "

He grinned, for there had been some talk as to the reason of Della's unwillingness to undertake this part (when Nickson's back had been turned), and certain speculations had been made as to the precise degree of the pianist's thinness.

" Nobody supposed you had got any," he retorted. " But you'll have to *have* 'em, you know. What did you intend to do?"

" I—I intended to make some things out of an old skirt," said Della, standing at bay.

This then, had been her plan, Monica thought. She had intended clothing her abhorred limbs in garments more concealing to their proportions than the ordinary ones in vogue among the opposite sex, and then appearing from her dressing-room when too late to effect a change. But if this were the case, the poor girl's hopes were destined to be shattered.

Mr. Montgomery openly laughed. " Oh, I guess we'd better not trust you to do *that*, as there's so little time for alteration if the things weren't right. Let's see—who's the smallest man in the company, and the slimmest in the waist and legs? Why, *you*, of course, Nick. 'Tain't generally until after a fellow's married he lets his girl put on the breeches; but I guess you'll have to begin now, and lend yours to Miss Thomas."

A giggle went round the assemblage, for the late *penchant* of Mr. Nickson for the pianist was as well known as his defection.

"Anything to oblige," he mumbled, darkly flushing to the roots of his unkempt brown hair; and then, hurrying from the stage with the idea of relieving Della's painful embarrassment, he repaired to the region of the dressing-rooms, to complete certain alterations he had been organising there.

Monica had expected a burst of indignation from Della on the homeward way; but, to her surprise, the girl walked along without speaking, and Monica could see, even in the deepening twilight, that her lips were compressed and white.

It would be wiser, perhaps, not to refer again to the dread topic, since the torture of anticipation doubtless surpassed what the reality could bring. Thinking thus, Monica spoke no more of Weenty Paul, but engaged Della's attention and services in the alteration of a frock which was to do duty as a riding habit in Dora's great act that night.

The two girls returned to the scene of their labours earlier than actually necessary when evening came, rather than endure the ordeal of passing through a gaping crowd. But, though a full hour would intervene before the ringing up of the curtain, already the street in front of the theatre was populous. Poddiwiski was supposed to be a " good town for the show business," and Mr. Ambler had lavished a few dollars on the hiring of a local band, which played before the door of the hall.

In *some* companies, he severely impressed upon the privileged members of his own flock, the gentlemen all had to parade, immediately after their advent in a town, in uniforms, and with loud-tongued instruments of brass, while the ladies swelled the procession in their best dresses. He had found in previous experiments that the acting qualities of his show suffered in proportion to the musical accomplishments of the members, and had therefore abandoned that plan of procedure the season before; but he wanted his people to be properly thankful to him for their immunity from such duties, as though the change had been made in their interests, and not his.

It was considered a sign of great superiority in a dramatic combination when the band was engaged to play the audience in, and the inhabitants of Poddiwiski, pricked to eagerness by the inspiring music of a cornet, a flute, and a drum, were preparing to turn out in vast force for the first performance.

Della's heart sank at the thought of the crowd which would presently witness her humiliation; but she no longer gave vent to her feelings in speech.

"Hello, young ladies," remarked the local manager, as they passed him going into the hall. "We're goin' to hev a big night, I guess. The town's turnin' out well, and not only that, but *one of the stage boxes is engaged.* The feller's paid *four dollars* for it. Say, what do you think o' that? It ain't happened before in my time fur any show, except the *amatoors.*"

The future Weenty Paul shivered.

Monica had not yet seen the inside of her own dressing-room, and now, as she opened the door, she uttered an exclamation of surprise.

The lamp, which was already lighted, showed an interior very different to what Della's had been when she had visited it in the morning. The dirty floor had been carpeted with crisp newspapers, and the partitions were fully covered with the same. The long shelf had an ambitious adornment of snow-white paper, roughly scalloped at the edges. There was a whole mirror, and a cake of bright pink soap blushed beside a new tin hand-basin, filled with clean cold water.

"Oh, Della," the girl cried, "do come here!"

But Della had already gone out "in front" to try her piano, which even the terrors of the future had not caused her to forget.

Monica stepped outside her door, and confronted Mr. Crawford perambulating the passage in his shirt sleeves. A conscious grin was on his handsome face, and she knew in a moment whom she had to thank for the transformation scene.

"How do you like your dressin'-room?" he enquired, sheepishly.

"Oh, it is so nice!" she responded. "It will seem like being in a dear little band-box. I am sure *you* did everything. I can't think why you should have been so kind; but, at all events, I thank you very, very much."

"Oh, it wasn't anything. I've slicked Della's a bit too. Since you and she were such friends, I thought you wouldn't like it if she wasn't fixed up as spick and span as you," Mr. Crawford airily returned.

He neglected to mention that Nick had done more than half the work, and had refused his services unless the pianist's room were to share the proposed improvement. It was quite safe, he knew, to keep this fact to himself, as Nick had been ashamed of it, and would suffer much rather than make public his part in the transaction.

There seemed something pathetic to Monica in this labour that the poor, common, handsome fellow had undertaken for her comfort. The very cake of soap and the shining tin basin, which he had bought with his hard-earned money, were pitiful in her eyes, and she could well-nigh have watered them with tears. She hardly knew in what words to express her appreciation of all his trouble and thoughtfulness; but what she did say emboldened him to follow her inside the dressing-room.

" 'Twas just nothin'," he repeated. " But, see here, Miss Nairne, I'd do anything fur you. I never seen a gurl like you before. You're as different from the sort I've always know'd as the day is from the dark. Not that they ain't good of their kind; but they ain't like *you*. It kind o' doesn't seem right that you should hev to rub along in our rough sort o' life; and if you'll let me, I'd be so awful glad to smooth things fur you as much as I could. Say, *will* you?"

"I—why, I do very well," Monica faltered, tears rising in her eyes. She could scarcely have told what brought them there; but, perhaps, had she fully dissected her own feelings, she might have realised that her emotion sprang partly from self-pity, stirred into new life by his appreciative eulogy of her, and partly from a quick, romantic sympathy, which answered to such words spoken by so fine a specimen of the rough diamond.

"You say you do, because you're a brave gurl; but there's things I *could* do to help—lots of 'em. I could take you home from the theatre nights, even if you won't let me walk with you when you're goin' there. I could see that your fire's burnin' warm and bright for you when you get back; and plenty of other little chores. It would make me awful happy if you'd say 'yes.'"

"Well, then, yes!" cried Monica, laughing off the solemnity of the occasion. It would have seemed almost brutal not to consent, standing on the very threshold of the room which he had taken such pains to fit up for her. But, even as she answered, she was fully conscious how shocked she would have been at the bare thought of making such a concession only two or three days before.

Other people were coming in now; and, having committed herself to a course which she was to regret in bitterness, Monica gave her lowly admirer a grateful smile, and shut herself into the renovated dressing-room. She could faintly hear the sound of the young pianist's really charming playing from the other side of the distant curtain, and then it ceased, and Della's dressing-room door opened and closed sharply.

Every one had arrived by this time, and a buzz of excitement filled the air. This was the first performance the Ambler Company had given of "The Octoroon," and even with these seasoned barn stormers, who were accustomed to "putting up" a heavy new piece (which many others would have rehearsed for a couple of months) at a few hours' notice, there was a certain nervous exaltation that most of them would have been ashamed to confess, and unable to explain.

The ladies called back and forth to each other across the open tops of the partitions, and two or three of the men "ran through their lines" together, in some difficult scene, in the same fashion.

Suddenly Della's voice rose loud and clear and agonised above the others.

"Mr. Montgomery! Mr. Montgomery! I *can't get them on!*"

"What?" roared the stage manager from one of the stalls at the farthest end. "No! you don't mean to tell me you can't get on Nick's pants?"

"I can't"—(very distinctly and reproachfully)—"get —on—the—trousers that were lying over a chair in my room."

"Those are the johnnies. Nick asked me to put 'em there for him. Too modest, I guess, to do it himself. They ain't too *small* fur you, are they?"

"Yes, they *are*, I tell you."

"Great Jehoshaphat! who'd have thought it?" Mr. Montgomery could be heard muttering. "Well, the next smallest man is Pa Wilts, I reckon. Pa, your room's close to Miss Thomas's. Fling her over a pair of your unmentionables, will you?"

After a moment's mumbling and delay, the soft sound of a heavy article being thrown through the air was distinctly audible.

All were now deeply concerned in the progress of Della's toilet, and short guffaws of stifled laughter followed whispering in the rooms occupied by the men. It began to be the general opinion that the conformation of Della's body above the waist could

give no adequate impression of the proportions below.

Five minutes elapsed, and then Della's voice rang
out again.

"These won't do either; I shall have to have 'em
larger yet, if you want me to go out on the stage to-
night."

"By—*J-i-n-g-o* ! " ejaculated Mr. Montgomery.
"Well, if I ain't jizzled! That gurl's a giraffe above
the belt, and—and—a hippopotamus below! Here,
you shall have a pair of Mr. Ambler's pants. He's
the widest man in the show."

The last-named garments were duly tossed over
Della's partition, while all (with Monica as keen as
any) waited in breathless interest for the verdict.

"These will do, I think," announced Weenty Paul,
gravely. And a general sigh of relief arose.

It was now time for Mr. Montgomery to rush out
from his dressing-room, and see that Mr. Todd and
the local "stage hands" had set the Peyton's lawn
and breakfast-table, with due regard for his directions.
There were also a number of little darkey boys, hired
to act as supers, who must be collected and made to
understand, for the seventeenth time, exactly what they
were to do. The audience prematurely defrauded of
their piano overture, were impatiently clamouring with
cat-calls and stampings for the curtain to go up ; and
altogether, not only Mr. Montgomery but all the
others concerned in the first act, had as much as they
could think of without keeping Della Thomas's affairs
in mind.

Still the pianist's door remained obstinately shut,
and it was only at the last moment, when Mr. Todd,

(as the gaudily painted red Indian) impatiently awaited
the arrival of his little mulatto friend, that Della answered the loud call which summoned her to duty.

Monica was expecting her own cue, and was standing
with Mr. Wilts (her parent *pro tem.*) on the opposite
side of the stage. She had not heard Della go on,
but, startled from a nervous conning of her lines by a
wild shout of derisive laughter from the audience, she
hastily peeped out from the wings.

Weenty Paul had just run on to the stage, making
a fine "centre entrance" with the Indian, in his
home-sewn war bonnet of turkey feathers and red
flannel cut from an old chest protector.

Monica gasped; and then, covering her face with
her hands, laughed till she cried. It was cruel, but
she could not have refrained had it been to save a life
she loved; and every one on the stage—even fractious
Mrs. Ambler—had fallen into convulsions of hysterical mirth.

Della had tucked up her long, red hair under a wide,
soft felt hat, and had disdained the fuzzy black wig
which had been provided for the part. Not being
accustomed to the use of grease paint, her features
were irregularly darkened, with here and there a big
brown spot, which might have been a "moth patch"
or a bruise. But, strange as was the appearance of her
face, in the perspective of the goggling eyeglasses
that she had forgotten to take off when her make-up
was complete, the gaze of the beholder did not linger
there, travelling quickly to her legs.

What legs they were! From the hip to the knee
they were Falstaff's—Falstaff afflicted with elephan-
tiasis!—below they fluttered within the loose folds

of the trousers in all their pitiful native frailty. Irregular wads and bunches rose like convulsed muscles under the nether garments of Mr. Ambler, which, from the waist, halfway to the feet, were filled wellnigh to bursting.

"What under the everlastin' canopy!" shrilled Mrs. Patton, "*has* the gurl bin and gone and done?"

What she had done, prompted by modesty and the fatal wish to conceal her attenuation, was to stuff two or three thick winter petticoats inside her trousers, kneading them here and there into shape, and tucking them as far down as, in the nature of things, they could be induced to go.

Uncertain of herself, though feeling she had done her conscientious best, Della came sidling on, holding the edges of her long corduroy jacket gingerly together in front, and in deadly fear of revealing the rotund vision of her back to an unsympathetic world.

"Run her off—somebody—*quick!*" commanded Mr. Montgomery, in a choking voice.

Thus it fell to the lot of Nick to take his lost sweetheart by the hand, and, covering her retreat with the long tail of his Yankee overseer's duster, trot her rapidly from the scene of her brief, inglorious career as Paul.

Weenty Paul did not appear again that evening. Everybody else spoke his lines when they happened to be necessary as cues; and the most knowing of the little black supers was told off to die ("without any frills" by way of acting) in his place.

Nick was the only man among actors or audience who did not laugh, but never a smile curved the corners of his sensitive, thin lips.

Scarcely was the excitement over when Monica heard the cue which called her to the stage. She had hoped that, after the entering wedge had been put into her nervous system with the performance of the slight part of Mademoiselle Danglars, she need never experience the horrors of actual stage fright again.

But now, as she opened the door which was supposed to lead out from Madame Peyton's house upon the lawn, where the distinguished family were breakfasting, everything swam for an instant before her eyes. Her foot caught in the simulated door-sill, and, stumbling forward, she involuntarily made her entrance with a hop, skip, and a jump, which carried her across the whole length of the stage to the other side. There she only saved herself from an ignominious tumble by clutching at the projecting ledge of the stage-box, a luxury unknown in most country theatres, and, looking up, startled, her eyes met those of the Marquis of Carabas.

CHAPTER XII.

"Fetch him off, I pray you. . . . Fie on him! I am sick or
not at home. What you will to dismiss him."

IF only Monica could have engaged a little private
trap-door through which to disappear, she would have
been thankful. That he, who had seen her first, and
last, in the heyday of her hopes, and had heard her
foolish boastings of expectations never to be fulfilled,
should look upon her now !

It was too galling—too unbearable. Even poor
Della's humiliation seemed not so deep as this; for the
shame which had been Della's now became Monica's,
and she blushed for the shortcomings of Weenty Paul
and the whole company of barn stormers, with whose
fortunes she had joined her own.

She knew exactly how much money he had spent
for the pleasure of coming to laugh at her. *Four
dollars !* That was the sum mentioned by the manager of the hall. She wished he had put it to almost
any other purpose. What should she do if obliged to
meet him after the play was over?

Of course she must speak about the thirty pounds;
but how could she with dignity reproach him for what
he had done, when already she had spent a fifth of
the amount, and, as yet, saw no means of replacing
it ?

Her head whirled with contending thoughts, and it

was a difficult task to subordinate her own identity to "Dora's." She was in a fever of anxiety not only on her own account, but on that of others. She wanted every man to be an Irving, every woman a Terry, that they might favourably impress the owner of those grey eyes that twinkled even in the shadows of the stage-box. The poor make-shifts of scenery and costume, contentedly flaunted by Mr. Ambler's comedians, and applauded by an unexacting audience, fretted her far more than they had done on the first night ; for then amusement had mingled with her scorn.

It had not occurred to her on their previous meeting that the Marquis of Carabas was a handsome man. But whether it was merely the force of contrast between him, in his immaculate evening dress, and the country clod-hoppers in the audience, or whether she had not earlier done him justice, the fact remained that the occupant of the box assumed an almost irritatingly desirable appearance in her eyes.

She tried not to look at him, to forget his presence and his very existence in her part ; but the *rôle* of the volatile Dora was scarcely absorbing enough to produce the prayed-for effect. Besides, even Della's fiasco was forgotten by her fellows in the excitement of speculation regarding the magnificent unknown, who had paid *four dollars* to see them act. The prevailing opinion was that he must be a New York or Chicago manager, whose ears had been reached by the fame of some particular member of the company, and who had journeyed many miles in the hope of securing new talent.

Each man and woman believed that he or she was

the lodestar, and one and all played to the box with
such undisguised nods and becks and wreathed smiles
as disgusted and shamed the only person who could
partially have solved the mystery.

The Human Flower, who, though she had availed
herself of her privileges as spoiled beauty and stage
manager's wife to refuse to act, nevertheless skipped
about behind the scenes making herself generally useless, and was now ready, as she confessed, to gnash
her expensive teeth, in that her genius must go un-
recognised by the theatrical autocrat. She was almost sure that she remembered his face in the *Clipper*,
and the chances were that he had come especially to
admire her acting.

Monica alone said nothing. She did not know
what developments might be pending, and she felt,
beside, that she owed no one any explanations.

When her great scene came, and, in her improvised
riding-habit, she had to run on the stage and outbid
the villain, who would make the hapless Zoe his slave,
it was the Marquis of Carabas who led the applause
from his box. He leaned forward, looking very distinguished, smiling and enthusiastically clapping his
hands together. So evident did it then become that
his approval was for the actress and not for the lines,
that every woman in the company (save poor Della,
bravely sitting at her piano, clothed and in her right
mind again) hated the leading juvenile with a bitter
hatred.

When it was all over, and Monica had gone to her
dressing-room, she realised, as she had been doing at
intervals throughout the evening, that the real embarrassments of the situation were only about to begin.

It did not appear very probable that the Marquis of Carabas, having taken the trouble to come to the theatre—from how great a distance she did not know —would go away without seeking speech with her, and obtaining it, too ; for he was a man of masterful as well as determined mien.

She had promised Mr. Crawford that he might walk home with her. To be sure, Della would be there ; nevertheless, Monica now more than ever regretted her condescension. What would the Marquis of Carabas think if he saw her thus deliberately placing herself on terms of equality with a man of the Crawford calibre ? *He* could not guess the reasons, which she believed to be generous ones, for what she was doing, and he would only misunderstand. She told herself that she was both snobbish and conceited to care as she did, and to feel such shame in being seen with the humble companion from whom she had consented to receive favours. But the snobbishness would not be exercised, and she was in no enviable mood as she dressed to leave the theatre. Her last thought, on viciously stabbing the pins into her hat, was that of all things she hoped and intended to avoid a meeting with the Marquis of Carabas. But, even so, she critically peered at her reflection in the wavy surface of the mirror, smoothed the little love locks which strayed across her forehead, pulled her Tam to a becoming angle, and dabbed the end of her nose with the powder puff. It was always as well to be prepared for emergencies was a motto she had been taught by the good nuns at the convent in France.

Della, looking white and tired, was waiting for Monica in her own dressing-room.

"Don't say anything to me about *that*, Angel," she implored, piteously. "I can't bear it; I feel as though, if any one just pointed a finger at me, I'd burst out crying. Oh, dear!" sinking her voice to a whisper, "here's that Jim Crawford hanging around. I *did* hope everybody'd gone."

"He—I—that is, he asked if he might walk home with us, and—I said yes," Monica stammered, her confusion increasing with the surprise on Della's face.

With this Crawford joined them, his face shining from the soapy water which had washed away his make-up. A modicum of black paint still clung to his long lashes, and was streaked beneath his eyes.

The jaunty remarks he had to make as they passed out (crossing the stage, descending thence to the auditorium by four or five ladder-like steps) jarred upon Monica's ears, and she could scarcely reply. Though her eyes were downcast, she could yet, after the fashion of women, see every corner of the big empty room, where only a sleepy employé remained to put out the lights. No one else was there. The Marquis of Carabas would probably be found waiting to speak to her below.

But no figure started forward out of the darkness, as Monica had expected, when their feet had ceased to echo on the iron-shod stairway. Even the youths, who made a point of lingering till the "show actresses" came out, had departed, and the dark streets which led to the Hotel Mars were quiet and deserted.

There was still a chance that the Marquis of Carabas might be seen pacing impatiently up and down before the door of the one hostelry of Poddiwiski.

Indeed, he might even be stopping there for the night, since, so far as Monica knew, there was no other temporary accommodation to be had in the town.

Mr. Crawford gallantly pushed wide the door of the hotel for the ladies to pass in, and again Monica's veiled eyes were alert. But no other door opened. No one was pacing up and down. Sounds of revelry proceeded from the office, the voices being easily recognisable as belonging to certain male members of the Ambler Company, and Della morbidly assured herself that they were discussing her appearance as Weenty Paul.

Having refused Mr. Crawford's eager offer to see to the condition of their fire, they bade him good-night, with civil thanks for his escort, and left him wistfully looking after them as they moved with maidenly dignity up the stairs. They had two flights to climb before reaching their room, and, having accomplished the first, they must pass the door of the public parlour before beginning their second ascent.

The door was ajar, and Monica could not resist the temptation which assailed her to push it open and peep in. This was strange, as her one desire had been to avoid a meeting with the man whom she only knew as the Marquis of Carabas. It was strange, too, that when the two girls had shut themselves into their bed-chamber, and all hope—or rather danger—of such a meeting was over, instead of rejoicing in her escape, Monica's heart was heavy in her bosom.

CHAPTER XIII.

"I could not stay behind you. My desire, more sharp than filed steel, did spur me forth. . . . Jealousy, what might befall your travel, being skilless in these parts."

"SAY! here's a note for you!"

The "say" prefaced the announcement to save the ignominy of adding "Miss" or "Madam," as a servant at an hotel or lodging-house slavey would naturally have done in England.

In the country towns of the soft coal district all was different. Mary Ann was not only convinced of her own perfect equality with the guests of the hotel where she condescended to help, but would have been surprised as well as indignant had any one suggested that she did not stand upon a far higher social level than a parcel of show-women.

This particular "Mary Ann," who signed her name Decildia Platt, was a relative of the hotel proprietor, and one of the belles of the town. It was, therefore, with an air of extreme condescension that she handed Monica the letter which she had been induced by a strong motive of curiosity to bring.

The girls had returned to their room after breakfast, and finding it in the same state in which they had left it, had begun to render it more habitable by making the bed and brushing up the coal-powdered piece of zinc laid under the stove.

Miss Platt flung herself comfortably into an easy-chair, her eyes flashing from Della, who patted up the pillows, to Monica, who, blushing with surprise, opened the envelope that was branded with a very exact impression of Decildia's thumb.

"Your feller writes a pretty hand," the young lady vouchsafed, taking up a framed photograph which stood on a table close by, and wiping off a speck of coal dust with a finger moistened from her tongue.

Monica looked up—a look that was intended to freeze; but it was wasted upon Miss Platt.

"Kindly go down and say to the messenger that the answer is 'yes,'" directed the former with severity.

"Oh, my! I guess I ain't in any hurry," retorted the niece of the Hotel Mars's proprietor. "You kin go yourself. I ain't nobody's messenger."

Monica walked in stately fashion out of the room. In the passage, she re-read the note, which contained a request that the writer might be allowed to call at eleven o'clock. "Yes" or "No" to the bearer would suffice as an answer; and her correspondent signed himself sincerely hers, John Randolph, alias the Marquis of Carabas.

The girl ran downstairs, to find one of the smiling, white-eyed black men who had waited on her in the Marquis's private car.

Hardly had he got away with his answer than she remembered that there was to be a rehearsal for her at eleven, and she was obliged to run breathlessly out into the street, panting forth the request that his "master would come by ten or half-past ten instead."

"I ain't got no *mahstah*, missy," corrected the darkey, grinning good-naturedly. "De days fo' dat is ober. But I'll done tell *Mistah Randolph* w'at yo say."

It was Monica's second lesson that morning in American independence.

Miss Platt was still in the one easy-chair when Monica returned to the bedroom, but had apparently forgotten her late huffiness. She was talking to Della, to whom such manners as hers were no novelty, and scarcely looked up on Monica's reappearance.

"I always say I'm so sorry for you poor show actresses," she patronisingly remarked. "Folks *is* so down on you, ain't they? Ma'd be as mad as fire if she know'd uncle let me associate with show people, and I bet she'd fetch me home mighty quick. But it don't do *me* no hurt, and your lot's a good heap decenter than some that's bin here. The Lady Minstrels, now, that come last fall—well, they *was* rank! We had to turn 'em out o' the house; but I ain't see'd you do much harm yet. Say, is it true that the men in your show give you all your nice clothes fur the stage and off? That's what ma lets on, and *worse*, too; but I wouldn't like to hurt your feelin's. That's what I says to her. I guess you're *human*, says I, if you *is* show women, and I shouldn't mind if you introduced me to that handsome gentleman that sits next the manager at the dinner-table. You know, the feller that's sweet on one of you two gurls, and brought you home last night."

"Oh, *oh !* " gurgled Monica, between laughter and futile indignation, "*would* you mind going away before we do you a mischief?"

"Is she practisin' some of her stage words?" queried Miss Platt, turning to the grave Della, who seemed to her far the more reasonable of the two.

"Perhaps," said the pianist hastily, anxious to avert a storm. "We have to practise a good deal. We've got to do it now, so maybe you'd better go."

"All right, I've got plenty to do!" tossing the bristling curl-papers. "I thought you might like to have me set awhile with you, and show you I wasn't proud. But say, you was funny last night when you come on the stage and them pants all bagged out. I *wish't* you hadn't run off so soon. I just *love* a good laugh, and my beau that was along with me, he was tellin' me about the clown in the last circus he was to. He——"

She got no further, for certain glances and gestures showed her that she had outstayed her welcome, and Miss Platt, chambermaid and belle, was not one voluntarily to intrude.

Once rid of Decildia, Monica's first impulse was to change the neat little grey cloth travelling-frock, which she had continually worn since her advent among Mr. Ambler's comedians, and change it in haste, that she might be ready when the Marquis of Carabas should appear. But hardly had she begun unfastening the buttons, with a mental vision of the smart blue blouse she would don instead, when she stopped, in altered mood. No, she would *not* dress for this stranger, to be stared at by the company, who had seen her in grey at breakfast, and must see her in blue (if she wore it) at rehearsal. She severely fastened her gown again, and vouchsafed a few casual explanations to Della.

"Oh! will you have him up *here?*" asked her friend, with sparkling eyes.

She longed for the answer. If the Angel could have callers in her room, why, perhaps, if *she* could only make it up with Nick— But she progressed no further in her cogitations.

"*Here ?* " Monica echoed, in horrified dissent. "*Certainly* not. I shall see him, for the few minutes he is likely to stay, in the drawing-room—I mean, in the parlour."

"I guess you've hooked a pretty fine beau," commented Miss Platt, when she had volunteered to carry to Miss Nairne's room the news of Mr. Randolph's arrival. "Say,"—ingenuously perusing for the second time the card which the visitor had sent up in the American fashion—"I don't know that name, no more'n I know'd his face, around anywhere in these parts."

She then, having watched Monica from the room, proceeded to smooth the dark fringe, which she called her "bang," and from which, in Mr. Randolph's honour, she had hurriedly untwisted the curl-papers, with Della's hair-brush and comb. A little later she decided, having listened at the keyhole to assure herself that nothing improper was taking place, she would make a point of sitting in the parlour, and playing "one of her new tunes" on the piano.

Monica went down sedately, but, though she could compose her features and her manner, she could not subdue the tell-tale colour which mounted from throat to forehead. In her pocket burned all that was left of the fatal thirty pounds. She had meant that the meeting should be eminently decorous, but scarcely had she opened the door marked "Parlour" in large black letters, than she found both her hands being enthusiastically shaken.

"How *do* you do, you brave little lady?" inquired the "rather nice voice for an American," which, somehow, she was gladder to hear than she had thought she should be; and she was looking up, smiling and blushing, into the keen, grey eyes. They were not twinkling now. If they had been, with comprehension of the humorous side of her situation, Monica felt that she must have run out of the room.

"How do *you* do?" she echoed, demurely.

"All right, thank you. Now I see it wasn't only stage rouge that made you look so well last night. Good Lord! I hope you'll excuse me, Miss Nairne; but you've got just about as much right to be in this place as a rose has to fall into a pig-sty."

"The pigs haven't eaten me up yet," she responded. "Shall we sit down?"

"Yes; and talk things over."

"There are several things I want to 'talk over' with *you*," Monica said, quickly and meaningly. "I think I had better do it before we begin upon anything else." She subsided upon an uncompromising sofa covered with well-worn rep, and motioned him to a rush-bottomed chair at her side. "I daresay you meant well, Mr. Randolph; but, do you know, you—you did very wrong, and you hurt my feelings *very* much."

His dark, clean-shaven face flushed like a schoolboy's.

"I *didn't* know it," he defended himself; "but I'm sorrier to hear you say it than most anything else could make me. Will you just fire away, please, and tell me what I've done?"

It was harder to explain, under the steady gaze of

his eyes, than she had fancied it would be, for, after all, there was nothing in the explanation for *her* to be ashamed of. It was *he* who had done the wrong.

"Why," she faltered, "that—that *money*, you know."

"By Jove, I *don't* know."

"That day in the train. It—you put it in my purse—thirty pounds." Monica's hand went to her pocket. What excuse she should make for having dipped into the amount she had once vowed to starve rather than touch, she had not even yet had time to decide. "Of course, you intended to be kind. . You thought I was poor, and—it was quite true. I *was* poor, but not poor enough to accept charity from you, or any one else on earth."

Mr. John Randolph continued to look at her, with an expression in which complete innocence vied with mild reproach.

"I—*I* put money into your purse?" he repeated, solemnly. "Upon my word, Miss Nairne, I guess I must be stupid, but I can't seem to understand."

For the first time the thin wedge of doubt entered her mind, and yet—there had been no one else. He *must* have done it. With much stammering, and very red cheeks, she floundered through the explanation which she could not refuse, far as she was from believing it to be necessary.

His face might have served as a model for an artist who wished to paint a guiltless man, surprised by the false accusation of a crime.

"Well, now," he slowly said, when she had finished, "you must have a pretty low opinion of me. I wonder what I did to give it to you? There must have been *something*, I reckon, or you'd never have been thinking all this time that I'd be mean enough, sneaky enough, to go into a young lady's satchel, and open her portemonaie."

So poignant was the reproach in his voice that Monica began to be actually frightened. She was struck dumb, and unable to answer for the moment his counter accusation.

He hastened to seize upon his advantage. "I suppose you English ladies think there aren't any gentlemen in America, or you never would have suspected me of doing such a thing—for no gentleman *would* have done it, you know. So that's what it comes to! Well, I'm sorry you've so poor opinion of me, Miss Nairne ; that's all I can say. But since you have got it, I suppose the sooner a fellow you think of like that takes himself away, the better you'll be pleased."

He made as if to rise, but Monica, with tears of shame and remorse in her eyes, laid a small impulsive hand upon his coat sleeve.

"Oh, don't go!" she exclaimed. " Do, please, forgive me! I never dreamed of insinuating such dreadful things. You see, a girl doesn't quite understand the way men look at such matters. I—I thought it a mistake to have put the money there ; but I didn't know that a man would consider it an ungentlemanly act. He might have wanted to help a girl who had just told him she was friendless, and whom he might easily have guessed was far from rich. I fancied that was the reason you didn't tell me your name, and—and all. But now that you have talked to me, I see, no matter how mysterious it is about the money, that you never could have put it there. Or—or you couldn't have got anybody *else* to put it there, *could* you ? "

"Not a *human being*," asseverated Randolph. "Of *that*, I'll take my oath. Now, do you believe me?"

"I do," said Monica. "And—will you forgive me?"

"I will. Will you shake hands?"

She put hers out, and they shook hands solemnly for the space of full half a minute. Then Monica was obliged to draw her fingers hastily away, for the door opened, and Miss Platt bounced noisily into the room.

"Guess I'll practise on the piano a little while, if you folks don't care," she announced.

Monica bit her lip. There had been so much to say. In half an hour the rehearsal would commence. Yet it would look very strange if she told the abominable girl to go and leave them alone.

Randolph rose, and sauntered over to the piano in the wake of the fair Decildia, who bridled over her pile of music, patted her foot, and moistened her plump lips with her tongue.

"I wonder if you've got a piece called, ' Darling, Kiss my Eyelids Down '?" he questioned, in an interested way.

"No, sir, I ain't," the maiden responded.

She would rather have perished than address any living female as " madam," or even " ma'am "; but a man, and so " elegant a gentleman," was different.

"That's a pity. Judging from your way of speaking, it would just suit your voice. It's a very pretty song, and I should like to hear you sing it."

"Oh, law !" said the girl, simpering.

"Yes. And I might have that pleasure, too, if only you had time, and felt like fetching a book full of songs from the piano on my private car, which is switched off on to a side track down close to the railroad depôt. I wouldn't trust everybody to go looking among my papers and books and things, but I might trust *you*. And it isn't very far, only half a mile or so. If you'd care for it, you might keep the book, and I should be certain to give myself the pleasure of waiting in this room till you get back and sing the song for us. What do you say?"

"I say I'll go, and be home again in a jiffy."

It might be that he was "playin'" her, but the chance to see the inside of this magnificent person's real, live, private car was one not to be missed on any account, as it was probable that it would never occur again. Miss Decildia Platt shut down the lid of the battered hotel piano with a slam, and started forth.

Randolph smiled. "She can't get back for three quarters of an hour, if she runs both ways," he said. And then he resumed his chair by the sofa. "You've got no more doubts of me about that miserable money, have you, honest Injun, now?" he asked.

Monica hastened to protest that she had not. She was thoroughly perplexed by the new complication in the affair, which she had believed to have been all too simple of explanation. But not to accept the evidence of this pair of frank and anxious eyes would have been impossible. And then, besides, that dark and baffling mystery was not without its compensating gleam of brightness. She would not have to account for the money that was gone, and the rest she might spend with a clear conscience. She looked into the Marquis of Carabas's face and smiled.

"Thank you, Miss Nairne. Now, then, that I've

braced up a little, let's go on to the second indict-
ment. Well, what's the next black mark you've put
down against me? Perhaps I can explain that away,
too."

He was certainly rather good at explaining things
—and people who were not wanted—away.

"There's nothing else, indeed; except that you
were too kind about that huge box. You oughtn't to
have sent it, really."

"Oh, I didn't. Dinah sent that." He checked himself suddenly as he spoke, and glanced at her, with a
certain quick anxiety; but her face was calm. "And,
by the way," he hurried on, "Dinah sends her love.
She's been adopted at my place in the East, and is a
spoiled favourite already."

"Does your wife like her?" Monica innocently
asked.

One would have thought, who heard her speak, that
she quite took for granted the fact that a man of Mr.
Randolph's age must have given hostages to fortune.
But even the most candid young women are not without guile. Monica did not believe that the Marquis
of Carabas had a wife. He did not *seem* or *look,
married ;* but her desire was to find out for sure.

"She would like Dinah, if she—if there were such a
person, which there isn't."

"Not married?"

Monica's face was sweet and child-like as she looked
at him.

"Never was. Never *will* be, I used to say; but I
was opinionated then. One gets beyond having
opinions when one is my age. I'm nearly forty. And
you, I suppose, are eighteen. What a difference!"

"I'm twenty-one," said Monica.

"Poor child! May I call you that? You see, my adopting your cat seemed to make us such old friends, didn't it? And, look here, I wonder if you'd be offended if I told you straight out why I've come? I'm kind of afraid of you now."

"If you say that," exclaimed Monica, "I shall believe you haven't forgiven me."

"Well then, here goes, and may you have mercy on my soul! I kept on thinking and thinking about you since last Friday. You got right in between me and some business deals I had to make in Buffalo. A young girl, beautiful—(I beg your pardon, I didn't mean that! Yes, I *did* mean it, but I oughtn't to have said it—*that's* what I meant!)—all alone, going to meet an awful disappointment, and having to face it without a friend, without a chance of getting away, perhaps. That's what went on repeating itself in my head. 'Jack Randolph,' said I to myself, 'you were a blackguard to sit there and let that girl go off without a single word of warning. Perhaps she wouldn't have thanked you for it—perhaps she would have just turned up her pretty little nose at your advice.' (I beg your pardon again, I'm sure!) 'But never mind that, you ought to have done your best.'

"Well, the long and short of it was, I couldn't get a minute's peace. I felt like a sort of murderer—as though I'd killed you, and buried you under the leaves somewhere, where nobody'd see but myself. So I just hitched my old car on to a train, and ran out west, that's all."

"Oh!" ejaculated Monica. She could say no more. There seemed nothing, as yet, to be said. Or else there was too much—more than she knew how to speak. Therefore she compromised with a long, soft, cooing "O-oh!" breathed only as an English girl could have breathed it.

"I knew I'd be too late for Bagra by the time it would be possible for me to get away, and that was the only town on the route you gave me. I bought the stage papers, but they didn't seem to have the pleasure of Mr. Scott Ambler's acquaintance. So I just wired to the manager of the Bagra theatre for the company's next date, found a man who knew the place, and he gave me the name of the only hotel. I talked the matter over with Dinah, who decided to send you the box, as a kind of preface, and then I rambled on myself. Are you very angry with me?"

"Not—very," smiled Monica; "though I am almost sure I ought to be."

"No, you oughtn't. See here, Miss Nairne, I put it to myself as though you were my own young sister. (Not that I've got one. I wish I had!) As soon as you told me you were going to join a company at Bagra, Ohio, I had a pretty good idea of the sort of thing you'd be let in for. I felt kind of delicate at the time about saying anything, though I was mightily tempted to, even if I got snubbed for my pains. But, afterwards, I saw how I'd failed in my duty. You honoured me by confiding your plans, and since I didn't help you then as I ought, I've tried the next best thing. I hope you didn't mind my looking in at the theatre last night? I wanted to make quite certain how matters were ; and I tell you I just tingled to see a girl like you among those—cattle. I wouldn't try to speak to you last night, though I'd have

given my head to do it. But what I want to say
to you now is, won't you make tracks out of this, at
once?"

Monica looked at him thoughtfully. She could not
help liking and trusting him, as, indeed, she had instinctively done more or less from the first. But she
could not quite understand this typical product of a
new country, and she wanted him still further to
explain himself and his plans.

"I guess you're wondering what business it is of
mine, anyhow," he said, rather uncomfortably. "But
we Americans think it's every man's business to look
after a woman, old or young, who's in any difficulty or
trouble. Say, let's play you're my sister, will you?
I might call it daughter, so far as the years go; but,
somehow, I confess I don't want to do that."

"What would your advice be if I should be willing
to play at that game?" Monica laughed.

"You're a prudent young lady. You don't mean
to put yourself under a brother's authority till you
know how he wants to use it. Well, I should say,
'See here, small sister, if you're such an independent
little girl, and are bound to earn your own living,
your brother is the man to help you do it. What influence he has—and he has a little in several quarters
—he'll use for you. And when you've got a good
position, bringing you in a pile of dollars, why, you
needn't think you owe him gratitude for what he'd do
for anybody; and you needn't even be bothered to
see him again, if you don't like.' There! that's what
I'd say, if I was your big brother."

Monica was serious enough now, and when he
finished she looked up with that before-mentioned

dangerous light of gratitude in her soft, long, violet eyes.

"You would be a very good brother, I think," she answered, " though we know each other so very little, don't we? and I thank you as much as though I could accept your kindness. But I can't do that, really. Do you remember the old proverb about 'making one's bed, and then lying on it?' Well, that's what I must do now. And the bed really isn't so dreadfully hard as you might think, or as I thought when I first had to try lying down on it. I suppose I'm kept up in the midst of wild and weird experiences by the spice of queer novelty and adventure there is in them ; and, besides, there is a girl in the company whom already I've grown to love. I wouldn't desert her for the world." And then Monica found herself pouring forth the story of her quick-springing friendship with Della (missing out only the grim incident of the pocket-book) exactly as she had vaguely wished to tell it to this man, when there had seemed no probability that she ever would do so.

"She might go, too, if you liked," persisted Randolph. " There are lots of things you could do. I'm a sort of cosmopolitan, you know, or, at least, I trot about over my own country a good deal, and have got a place that does duty as a home in New York State, and another in Colorado. There's a couple of mines or so out there, that kind of think they belong to me, and some newspapers, east and west ; so, you see, I'm bound to know a lot of people in all sorts of businesses and professions. You could write stories for my papers, and for others, too (I'd choke the fellows if they didn't take 'em !) ; or you could recite, or be something under Government. *I* wouldn't be in it at all. Don't you believe me when I say you needn't even bow to me in the street?"

He leant forward very earnestly, his elbows on his knees, and Monica, too, bent toward him with a certain *empressement* of manner. It was possible that their heads were somewhat closer together than there was any actual necessity for two people's heads to be, which had been at opposite ends of the earth only a few short weeks ago. But it was at that moment that the half closed door was noisily flung back, and Crawford came jauntily into the room. When he saw how it was occupied, he stopped almost as though he had been shot.

He had run up to the room shared by Miss Thomas and Miss Nairne to enquire if they were ready to go to rehearsal, and if he might walk with them to the hall. Della, who did not approve the new understanding between her beautiful white Angel and the man so much beneath her, not only in station but in nature, confined herself to remarking that "Miss Nairne was in the parlour." She did not go on to mention that her adored one was engaged with a caller. Indeed, it gave her a certain pleasure that Jim Crawford should be put to the pain of finding out the fact for himself.

And he did find it out, with a sense of shock and personal injury that was like a blow between the eyes.

His face fell, almost in the literal sense of the words, until it seemed elongated, and the length of his upper lip increased by half an inch. Had the man in such earnest conversation with Miss Nairne been one of his own sort, the effect upon Crawford's mind would have been less intense. But though he would ever have been ready to assert that he was " as good as anybody else," he yet instinctively recognised the difference between himself and the other man—the stranger who had excited everybody's curiosity in the box at the theatre last night. The very clothes of the newcomer, so unassuming, yet so perfect in their way, seemed to Crawford a species of gratuitous insult to him. He would have liked to kick the neat brown travelling hat from the table, where it lay, all the way downstairs, as he and Nick had done with the landlord when they had enacted the *rôle* of knights-errant the Saturday before.

He moved his blunt fingers awkwardly up and down the pea-green door-post, breathing short and hard.

"Excuse me for *intrudin'*," he said, clumsily, "but I come to see if you'd forgotten there was a rehearsal. Everybody but you, Della and me has gone on to the hall."

"Oh, thank you!" exclaimed Monica, blushing faintly. "Please tell them that Della and I will be there almost at once—will you, Mr. Crawford?"

He slunk away, his lips pouted out like those of a sulky child. He would have liked to wait for the girls and discover from the lips or conscious glances of the one whom he had chosen to be his own whether this were the Marquis of Carabas, and what the Marquis of Carabas might be to her. But affairs had not yet gone far enough between the new juvenile lead and himself to make such disregarding of her request prudent. He went on to the theatre, therefore, as he had been bidden to do, slowly, turning his head from time to time, until at length he had the pleasure of seeing his hated rival pass hastily and alone from the door of the hotel.

"Wouldn't I like to see him further?" the young actor thought, with an ugly grin.

"Beast!" commented Randolph at the same instant, as his eyes fell upon and recognised the figure slouching along a dozen yards ahead. "That she should have to speak to him—a *thing* like that!"

If he had known that, during the very rehearsal for which "she" was hastily preparing, professional duty would compel her to be kissed by Mr. James Crawford, his feelings might entirely have refused to be kept within bounds. But, happily, no thought of such profanation visited his mind, and he walked on, smiling, with that odd little humorous twist of the mouth that Monica had once observed.

"Poor child!" he said to himself. "I felt a brute to deceive her; but then it was for her own good as much or more than it was for mine. Need the money! I'll bet she did, though she wouldn't have owned it. And, after all, I didn't tell a lie. Of course I wouldn't have opened her satchel or her little portmanteau, not I! Lucky I thought of a way out of the woods. How poor old puss yelled when I made the same use of her paw the monkey made in the fable!"

As this picture from his past rose before his mental eyes, the Marquis of Carabas laughed aloud. But even as he laughed he sighed.

CHAPTER XIV.

"'What is he at the gate?'
"'A gentleman.'
"'A gentleman? What gentleman? Let him be the devil an he
will. I care not.'"

"WHAT do you think Mr. Randolph has invited us
to do?" asked Monica, as Della and she hurried along
together, over lumps of ash-sprinkled ice, to the rehearsal. "He would like us to dine with him in his
private car this evening, and would have dinner very
early, as he knows we should be at the theatre by
seven o'clock. I told him we must have a chaperone,
of course, and he agreed, saying I might ask any one
of the married women in the company I chose. What
do you say? Would you like to go?"

"Oh, wouldn't I!" ejaculated the pianist. "It
would be *grand*. I never was on board a private car
in my whole life."

Even in the dazzled instant of acceptance, the fore-
most thought in the girl's mind was that Nick would
know, and that so magnificent an invitation must
increase her importance in his eyes. She could not
tell that to the sensitive and unhappy young man, it
would seem only to increase the distance that had
separated them.

"Whom shall I ask, then, to be our chaperone?"
reflected Monica. "It is only a choice between evils,

isn't it? Mrs. Montgomery is by far the nicest, but—her hair is *so* yellow, and her dresses—besides, who ever heard of having a Human Flower for one's chaperone?"

"Mrs. Patton would tell Mr. Randolph all about her husband's spangled tights," Della suggested.

"'Darn those tights!' as Mr. Montgomery would say," laughed Monica. "But then, I daresay she did before she spangled them. There's only Mrs. Ambler left, and she's so ill-natured."

"That's just the reason I would have her," said prudent Della; "because, if she's along with us, she can't make any nasty remarks, which she's sure to do if she isn't. My mother used to say to father, 'Stop your enemy's mouth with molasses if you can.'"

Acting upon her friend's advice, the invitation was passed on to Mrs. Ambler, who, not being a stickler for etiquette, received it at second hand without demurring, and even showed herself far more gracious to the juvenile lead, during the progress of the rehearsal, than she had formerly deigned to be.

The Ambler Comedy Company had often played the melodrama called "The Danites," which was actually the property of a manager in New York, and for which they paid no royalties.

The rehearsal was for Monica's scenes alone, and was the hardest she had yet experienced. Fat Miss Marguerite Neland was "starred" as Nancy, the unfortunate young woman hunted into the disguise of boy's clothes, a few sizes too small for her, by the "Danites," or "Destroying Angels." Upon Monica thus descended the *rôle* of Hulda, the pretty schoolmistress, while the Human Flower sang, and danced, and showed her cheap laced petticoats between top-boots and a ragged calico frock, as Captain Tommy.

Mr. Montgomery, the leading man, should have appeared as the generous-hearted hero, Sandy; but unfortunately for his aspirations, a sudden attack of erysipelas or some other equally unpleasant ailment had temporarily lent to his complexion all the rich effects of Lincrusta Walton. Handsome Jim Crawford, the heavy man, who was supposed to be the stage manager's under-study, was therefore called upon to undertake the part for the second or third time that season, and he had been greatly rejoicing in the fact that he should have the opportunity of becoming. Hulda's lover.

Never had he thought fit to put so much earnestness into his acting (such as it was) at a rehearsal, as he chose to do that day. He had seen, or thought he had seen, that the new member of the company scorned the dramatic qualifications of her fellows, large as loomed their experience compared to hers, and he meant as Sandy to do all in his power to impress her.

At last came the moment to which he had looked forward, actually lying awake in the anticipation of it half the night before.

Never yet, since the old decorous days as an amateur, when love-making was left entirely to *the night*, and then portrayed with a tremulous sketchiness of outlining, had Monica been obliged to face the ordeal of a love scene. She had studied the part, and realised something of what it must entail, though she had dreamed of no practical demonstration during the rehearsal.

She quivered a little, involuntarily, as Crawford's arm went boldly round her waist, and then, when it had lain there as long as she deemed necessary to em-phasise the action which accompanied the words, she quietly moved away. But Crawford moved with her. He had felt the slight shiver which ran through her body at his touch ; but the momentary physical con-tact with so fair and refined a thing had thrilled him to the core of his coarse being.

He knew well enough that save for the exigencies of the scene which brought them together he would not have dared to approach her. As he stood with his hand on her slim waist, the image of *that other man* rose luridly before him, the man whom he se-cretly and resentfully recognised as his own superior and her equal. A savage sense of future loss and present power swept over him, and instead of indi-cating the kiss which the scene demanded by a mere peck in the air, as was customary at rehearsals, he bent down, and holding the girl tightly to him, pressed his full, red lips passionately to hers.

She started from him as though he had struck her, pushing him away, and looking up at him with flash-ing indignation in her eyes.

" How *dare* you ? " she ejaculated, furiously.

Everybody laughed aloud, except Della, and Nick-son, who was at heart a gentleman.

" Murder's out ! " cried the Human Flower. " I guess we all know *now* that Miss Nairne's an ama-teur. The idea of an old ' pro ' getting mad at a little thing like that ! "

" Excuse me, Miss Nairne," protested Crawford, anxious to reinstate himself in Monica's good graces, now that he had made his point and nothing could rob him of the triumphant memory, "I assure you I didn't mean no harm. It's in the part, you know, and I was kinder actin' right on, and not noticin' what I was doing. You can ask Mr. Montgomery if I wasn't in my right."

"Certainly he was," pronounced the stage manager, without waiting for the question, and internally chuckling in high glee at the silly squeamishness of the amateur. "What's that *French* thing they say, Miss Nairne? I reckon you're up in it. 'Honey swah, quee mally pants,' eh? You'll have to take a good many kisses like that before you've been on the stage a year, I guess, and the better actress you are, the better you'll get to like it—see?"

Monica felt strangely sick. She trembled all over, and her hands were cold. Protesting no longer, she went on with the rehearsal of her scene, outwardly as though nothing had happened; but the hot, moist touch of those full, red lips seemed continually to be upon hers. She repented her hasty exclamation, only because of the lecture and the general ridicule it had brought upon her. Though she unwillingly accepted Crawford's apologetic explanation, and Mr. Montgomery's testimony that the proper thing, and only the proper thing, had been done, she could not rid herself of the feeling that her flesh had suffered pollution, and that Crawford had had no real right, as a stage lover, to kiss her in the way he had—a way in which she had never been kissed before. She was glad that he was aware of her disapprobation, even though self-consciousness made her regret that she had voiced it aloud.

When she had reached her room at the hotel, she went straight to the washstand, and dipping a corner of her one flimsy towel into water, she thoroughly soaped it, and scrubbed her mouth and chin till the skin tingled. Even the unpleasant prickling sensation seemed to afford a certain relief, as though she were purified through penance. But, at the dinner-table, Crawford's eyes on her face brought back the sick faintness from which she had suffered before, and again she could feel the hateful melting of those thick lips as they had closed down upon hers.

She wondered, shudderingly, when the hateful recollection would pass away. Though she had previously been delighted with the part of the young school-mistress, all joy in it had now faded, and she looked forward with dread and repugnance to the inevitable performance at night.

Meanwhile, there was the dinner in the Marquis of Carabas's private car. A note was despatched by one of the little coloured boys, who haunted the hotel for odd jobs, to inform Mr. John Randolph that he was to have his three guests. And though Mr. Ambler had forestalled the complaints of any members of his company who might have wished to drive from the station, by saying that no conveyances could be procured, a commodious vehicle now mysteriously appeared at the Hotel Mars for the accommodation of the ladies.

The car was *en fête*, from the drawing-room, so well remembered by Monica, to that portion devoted to the art of dining. How the Marquis of Carabas—as the girl still called him in her thoughts—had managed, despite the season, and the poverty of Poddiwiski's resources, to procure hot-house flowers for the table, was a second mystery only explainable through the guess that he had brought them with him from the purple East. At all events, the flowers were there, and there were fairy-like electric lights gleaming from jewelled glass and satin menu cards, and so many courses of marvellously prepared viands, that Mrs. Ambler was deeply impressed, and poor Della wished that she had asked her companions to address her in the presence of the princely Mr. Randolph as De Audrey.

Even Monica, brought up between a convent and a provincial English town, had never seen anything so grand; but she, at least, experienced none of the anguish which for once united Della and Mrs. Ambler in the common dread of using the wrong knife and fork, or eating some strange dainty in improper fashion. The lack-lustre blue eyes of Miss Marguerite Neland, and the deep-set brown ones of Miss Thomas, were fixed with the same desperate anxiety upon Monica's hands, or Mr. Randolph's, whenever a new course made its appearance on the table. Should one or the other seem in no hurry about taking the initiative, the unhappy watchers sipped their wine, or crumbled their bread, until optical demonstration had safely assured them what would be the right thing to do. Della was too humbly absorbed in her own distresses to take note of those endured by others; but Mrs. Ambler saw all the poor pianist's embarrassments, battened meanly upon them, and felt contempt for that in Della which she glossed over in herself.

The carriage was to return for them at seven, as they could drive to the theatre in five or ten minutes, and by the quarter before the hour they were eating such luscious forced fruits as Della had never expected to see, save in the stories through which the haughty Lady de Audrey and her kindred swept or floated.

"I've got my box at the theatre again for to-night," Randolph remarked to Mrs. Ambler, with a dubious glance at Monica. "I shall have to go away to-morrow, I'm afraid, so I wanted to give myself the pleasure of seeing the play this evening."

"Oh, please don't!" were the words which sprang to Monica's lips; but the complacent look on the leading lady's face restrained her. Miss Marguerite Neland was particularly pleased with herself as Nancy in "The Danites," and was delighted that her host should see her at what she thought her best. If Monica should protest against his going, the manager's wife would be as angry as surprised, and, out of sheer spite, would very likely describe, by way of a good joke, the incident of that morning's rehearsal. The girl forced herself to be silent, therefore, though her face burned. When they should leave the dinner-table she might be able to steal a moment with him alone, and would then put her request in such a way that it could not be refused.

Even as she so decided, comforting herself with the renewal of hope, there came a sudden sound of voices in the passage-way which led from the drawing-room to the dining-room.

"Bettah let me 'nounce yo' name, sah, or take in yo' keard. Mistah Randolph's mighty particula', sah," the coloured factotum was insisting, only to be interrupted and boisterously laughed down.

"Nonsense, go along, Tom! You mind your business, and I'll mind mine. I guess I know Randolph well enough by this time to take the liberty of giving him a little surprise."

If Monica's eyes had been on Randolph's face she would have seen a slight accession of colour there, and a contraction of the straight, dark brows. But naturally, her gaze was turned towards the portière which covered the doorway, and which was almost immediately pushed aside, to admit a tall, stout figure, with black Tom's expressive features and responsibility-disclaiming gestures for a background.

"Hello, Jack!" exclaimed the newcomer, having gained his own way at last. He was apparently older than Randolph by half a decade at least, but was a remarkably handsome man, with considerable freshness of colouring and outline for his years, which might have numbered forty-two or three. At first glance, had it not been for his girth and maturity of form, Monica would have thought him almost boyish in appearance; but with the next, her eyes had noted the falling away of the light curly hair from the round forehead, and a certain looseness of the muscles under the heavy chin. Yet the smile which accompanied his first words showed a great many square white teeth, and was altogether useful in the extreme.

"Hello, Jack," he said. "Excuse me for running in on you and your friends like this; but I've come a good many miles to see you, and we're too old friends to stand on ceremony at this time of day, I hope."

Randolph had risen, and now took a step or two forward to shake hands with the unexpected addition to his party. There was, however, no great cordiality

in his manner, and one who knew him well would
have seen that he was annoyed.

"How are you?" he responded, rather shortly.
"This is something of a surprise."

"That's what I wanted it to be, old man. I guess
you'd like to hear where I've sprung from, and how
the—how I ran you to earth in this queer hole. But
it's a long story. Perhaps, as I'm here, you'll introduce me to your friends, and let me have a cup of
coffee with you, by and by."

"If the ladies will allow it," corrected Randolph,
his lips narrowing into a thinner line than their wont.

Mrs. Ambler, who felt herself now a brilliant lu-
minary in the midst of gay society, smiled amicably
at the stranger, with great play of painted eyelash.

"Of *course* we'll allow it," she said, bridling be-
comingly.

Randolph did not appear as grateful for the per-
mission as he ought to have done.

"Then let me present my—Mr. Silas Jewett," he
mumbled, frowning over the duty.

Mr. Silas Jewett, having bowed engagingly, helped
himself to a chair, and drew it up to the table near
Monica's place, though the black waiter, at a sign
from his master, had sprung to set one in another
quarter.

"I didn't quite catch your name," he observed,
looking very intently into the fair English face, letting
his large yellowish grey eyes travel over her delicate
features, from the wide brown arch of brow, down the
straight-bridged little nose, to the mouth, with its
haughty, short curve of upper lip, such as Nature's
chisel never cuts on the American side of the Atlantic.

" I don't think Mr. Randolph mentioned it," she replied, smiling, " or the others. But those are Mrs. Ambler, and Miss Thomas, and my name is Nairne."

" Thank you. Now, let me guess. You're English, aren't you ? I knew that even before you spoke. And a curious thing, now, Jack—your friend Miss Nairne (it *is* ' Miss,' I'm sure ?) reminds me a little of a lady I—er—once knew in England. She "—turning to Monica with an exaggerated gallantry—" was one of the very most beautiful women I ever saw in my life."

The girl flushed uncomfortably at the barefaced compliment; and yet, something in the man's face fascinated her oddly. It was not that she felt drawn toward him with sudden liking, but that, though she was almost certain she had never seen him before, his personality had instantly connected itself in her mind with some haunting, yet elusive memory of the past.

" What was the lady's name, if I may ask ? " she questioned.

Mr. Silas Jewett's eyes fell away from hers. He appeared to search through space for something he had mislaid.

" Well, it's the queerest thing, I can't recall the name at the moment," he returned, " though—er—I ought to know it as well as my own. But it wasn't Nairne, so the likeness, or the expression, rather—for it's hardly more than that, must be a mere coincidence —a delusion and a snare. Besides, it was a long time ago when I was quite—quite a boy. It makes me feel an old fogey when I think how long ago, but I daresay it was before you were born."

Monica had not yet reached that period in life's

journey when a woman begins to alter the markings
on the milestones, and she would have gone on with
the gratuitous information that she was not as youthful as she was often taken to be, when Randolph broke
into the conversation. He seemed suddenly to have
become anxious that his latest guest should have a
course or two brought back to the table for his benefit,
and insisted, at all events, upon fruit, as well as the
coffee, which would presently appear.

" You haven't told me yet how you happened to
find me out here," he hastily remarked, when Jewett
had consented to play with some grapes.

" Why, I heard it at Ardabula, where I was stopping
over an hour or two for a chat with Crane, the general
manager of this road, you know. He knew your car
had gone down the line, and mentioned that it had
been switched off at a little fly-speck on the map,
called Poddiwiski. We were wondering what the—
what you were up to here, and, after a little chaff, I
said I'd run along down, and drop in on you. So
here I am, and "—with a comprehensive glance at the
ladies—" in great luck, I think."

Turkish coffee, in egg-shell cups, with standards of
filigree, gold, had now come in, and the three actresses, whose departure must follow in a few moments, took it at the table.

In the midst, Tom, who had been deputed to look
out for the carriage, returned to report its arrival at
the railway station, which was as near to Randolph's
house on wheels as it could be brought.

There was a certain lifting of the gloom from the
face of the host on this announcement, which scarcely
accorded with his previous delight in hospitality ; but

it passed unobserved in the general movement from
the table. It would almost have seemed that Randolph was anxious to speed the departing, with as
much alacrity as he had welcomed the coming, guests ;
but, notwithstanding, Mrs. Ambler found time to
turn and coquettishly inform Mr. Jewett that she
"hoped they might have the pleasure of seeing him
at the hall."

"My hushand's company's playing a week's engagement here, though it's a *much* smaller town than we
are accustomed to do," she announced, with the *aplomb*
of the distinguished actress. "You should take the
box opposite your friend's," she continued, not forgetful of the four dollars and the "sharing terms" of
the local management. "Then we shall have somebody to clap us on each side of the stage."

"Jove, I will! I didn't know that I had the honour
of talking with professional ladies," exclaimed Jewett.
"The other box by all means."

Monica bit her lip, the candid blood mounting to
her cheeks, as it had an unfortunate habit of doing
when she was the prey to any species of emotion.
Jewett, who had missed noting but few of the changing expressions upon her face during the half hour
which had elapsed since first he had looked upon it,
wondered at and was interested by the sudden increase of colour. If there had been any doubt of his
readiness to accept Mrs. Ambler's suggestion, there
was none remaining now. Monica's eyes waked
strange memories within him, and he wanted to know
the reason of that blush. As her glance had travelled
in a troubled way, at the moment of its deepest tint,
to Randolph's preoccupied face, Jewett was quick to

put two and two together, and by the time he had
thoroughly scrutinised both countenances, he had
reached the opinion that the biting of Monica's lip,
and the bloom on her cheek, had some connection
with his beloved friend Randolph.

As for dear old Jack, it was easy enough to see *his*
little game. There was only one possible member of
the feminine trio in whose honour this dinner-party
on board the private car could have been given, and it
was natural that Jack should have been put out at the
appearance of another man—especially a man rather
famous for his successes among women. If only Jack
had chosen to behave himself, and not show his vexa-
tion in so open and boyish a manner, he might have
been rewarded by being let alone. But, as it was, it
would be very good fun to hang on a bit, and cut Jack
Randolph out. Good old Jack had done him out of
one or two good things in the matter of silver mines,
and tit for tat was the rule of the game. At all
events, Jewett reflected comfortably, he would "lie
low" and see what cards turned up.

The ladies were escorted to their conveyance by
both men, and seen to drive away. Then the two
went back to the car.

"Pretty girl that," said Jewett, as they sat down in
the smoking-room, with Randolph's best cigars.

"Which girl?" questioned the younger man tersely.

"Why, *the* girl, of course," was the lazy reply.

CHAPTER XV.

"It is possible that on a little acquaintance you should like her?
That but seeing you should love her? And loving, woo?"

MONICA had had a bewildering amount of study
during the few days that she had been with the
Ambler Company. Though she had as yet only
rehearsed and played three parts, she was already up
in as many more, and would act in a new one every
night that week, to say nothing of the matinee.

She had sat up late and studied, she had risen early
and studied, and a confusion of lines in a kaleidoscopic
variety of *rôles* danced through her throbbing head,
in dreams and waking.

There had been so much, also, to think of outside;
so many curious new experiences to live through.
She had read authorities who gave it as their opinion
that life was only valuable for the number of separate
and distinct sensations which it might afford; and
according to this theory, her brief career as a professional actress had so far, if only so far, been a remarkable success. She had got her first sensation when
Mr. Ambler tapped her on the shoulder in the railway
station at Bagra, and scarcely an hour had been without a new one, up to the moment when Hulda, the
Californian schoolmistress, had felt her lover's realistic
kiss.

With Mr. Silas Jewett's appearance on the scene,

and Mrs. Ambler's hospitable mention of the box at
the theatre, all hope of preventing Randolph from
witnessing her crowning humiliation had left her.
Curiously enough, though she would greatly have preferred that the second man should be absent, it was not
of him she thought, as she clenched her cold hands and
swallowed an ever-rising lump in her throat, when the
time for the love-scene drew near. She thought only
of Randolph, and the disgust he would feel when he
saw her submit to being pawed about, and kissed by
one of the men whom he had most angrily classed
together as " cattle."

The excitement of the novice in acting a new and
somewhat exacting part was overwhelmed by this
new terror. The ringing up of the curtain on the fatal
act sounded like the knell of hope in her ears. It's
coming! *it's coming!* " she warned herself, with a
quickly beating heart, getting through the lines which
brought *it* nearer she scarce knew how.

At another time, in other surroundings, she would
have been nervously anxious as to what impression
her acting might make upon the Marquis of Carabas ;
but now, if the thought occurred to her at all, she
dismissed it hopelessly. What could he think of the
"acting" in a company and a theatre like this, save
one thing—that it was beneath contempt ? He would
be too kind of heart to laugh at her and her tawdry
associates ; at least, he would be too kind to let her
see him do so ; and, at worst, he might have pitied
her for the accident which had brought her to such a
pass. But—there was this kiss, which must banish
from his heart all other feelings save sheer disgust.

" He shall not—he *shall* not kiss my mouth again ! "

Monica resolved desperately, when the last moment came.

She felt Crawford's arm wind itself round her, she felt the hot breath, faintly reminiscent of whiskey, and then she spasmodically turned her face aside. But her chin was taken between a strong thumb and finger, her unwilling lips turned up, and for an instant everything swam before her eyes.

When she was released, her gaze involuntarily turned to the tawdrily curtained little box, from which, but a few minutes before, she had been uncomfortably conscious that Randolph was looking at her. The coarse Nottingham lace curtains were shaking perceptibly, but the box was empty. Randolph had gone.

No comment which he might have made could have been more cutting to Monica. Her little ears burned under their light *soupçon* of stage rouge as though they had been smartly boxed.

She hated Crawford. She hated every one in the company, not excepting herself. And she hated Randolph, too. Indeed, she was of the opinion that she hated Randolph most of all.

"Della," she whispered eagerly, at the end of the performance, when the pianist had come round from the front to put on her hat and cloak, "I beg that you'll go to Mr. Crawford's door and tell him that he is not to wait for us this evening. Speak kindly, but —but let him understand that *I won't have it.* If he wants to ask me why, I will talk to him about it to-morrow, but not to-night."

Della's eyes grew large. "I—I don't think I can, Angel. You know I'd do—most *anything* for you;

but Nick and Jim Crawford dress together. I don't feel I can go to their door."

Monica, knowing nothing of the old love duet, whose melody had been so rudely broken by her advent, looked a little hurt.

"Oh, very well," she said, in a changed voice. "It must wait till I am dressed then. I can speak to him myself."

This was more than Della could bear from her beloved. She flew to the door, on which Mr. Montgomery or Mr. Todd had scrawled in red grease paint, "Crawford and Nick."

As it happened, it was Nick who opened to her—Nick in his shirt sleeves—and his dog-like eyes brightened wistfully when he saw who was standing there. A wild hope was in his heart that she wished to "make up," and ask him to come back to her, as in the old days—to tell him that these fine new people with whom she was associating were but as shadows compared with what he had been, and yet might be. But, with downcast eyes, she soon made him aware of his mistake. Crawford was summoned, in the midst of removing his grease paint—a much more elaborate and cleansing process since Miss Nairne's coming—and made bitterly despondent by the message.

There were at least four very miserable people in the Poddiwiski theatre that night.

Monica was, as usual, longer than any one else in preparing to go home, and as she dressed and folded away her things for the night, she heard Della softly improvising a plaintive little melody on the cracked old piano in the auditorium. Suddenly the music ceased. All was still, so far as Monica could hear, for five or ten minutes, and then the playing began again. Very shortly after, Monica came out, looking tired and wan.

"Let's make haste home now, dear," she said, linking her arm within Della's rusty black sleeve, with a homesick longing for comfort and sympathy.

"Mr. Randolph and that Mr. Jewett were here a little while ago," the pianist said, as they tripped down the stairs, with no gallant Crawford in their wake.

Della had a habit of inserting an expressive "that" before the name of any one who had not, in any complete degree, won her esteem.

"What made them come?" inquired Monica, her heart giving an uncomfortable throb, all out of time with its ordinary beating.

"They weren't together. Mr. Randolph went out of his box in the midst of an act. I saw him go, and slam the door. The instant the play was over, Mr. Jewett darted out of his; and *he* went behind scenes, I know, for I saw him run up the steps to the stage; and afterwards, when I was—was speaking to Nick, he passed the door, walking with Mr. Ambler. They seemed to have quite made friends. But while I was playing on the piano, Mr. Randolph came hurrying in from outside, and asked me if you had gone. I said no; we always went together; and I was waiting for you. He seemed pleased at that, and cried out: 'That's good! That's as it should be! That's just what I came up to ask you about!' I was going to answer, when in popped Mr. Jewett, from downstairs this time. He'd come back for us, he said—Mrs.

Ambler sent him ; but Mr. Randolph only laughed, took him by the arm, and, calling out good-night to me, walked Mr. Jewett away."

"Oh," said Monica, shortly. She was sure now that Randolph had felt too utterly disgusted to wish even to speak with her again, and suddenly a realisation of the bitter chill in the night air made her shiver.

"Oh, do, *do* hurry," she exclaimed. "I'm so cold, and I want to be at home."

Next morning she awoke with a dull sense that something had happened—something which must darken this day, and other days to come. Rain was beating against the windows, and torrents had apparently fallen during the night, for where snow and ice had lain in patches, now remained only seas of chocolate-coloured mud.

"Perhaps he's gone away rather that see me after *that*," thought Monica, as she dressed.

She and Della were late at breakfast. Every one else had gone, and they hurried through the unappetising meal, as Decildia and a sullen darky noisily cleared away all traces of the others' repast, preparatory to re-setting the table for dinner.

As they came out into the hall, Crawford stood waiting for them by the foot of the stairs.

"I'd like to speak to you a minute, please, Miss Nairne," he said, without taking the slightest notice of Della.

Monica stopped rather impatiently. Already she had seen reason to repent her rash resolution to "improve" Mr. Crawford.

"Very well; you may speak to me now," she returned.

"But I want to see you alone," he pleaded.

"Miss Thomas," said Monica, with dignity, "may hear anything which you can have to say to me."

His face grew scarlet, and the florid skin glittered disagreeably.

"My God! Miss Nairne," he tragically exclaimed, "I want to know how I've offended you. You ain't goin' to refuse me an explanation about last night? You promised it; you *know* you promised it."

"Please be kind enough not to use strong language," Monica answered. "I can't see any occasion for getting excited, Mr. Crawford. This is too insignificant a matter."

"Insignificant! Good Lord! it ain't insignificant to me. Yes, I *will* speak out. I'm a man. I've a right. If you will have Della here listening, I can't help it. Everybody saw how you let me go home with you at first, and now everybody saw how you turned me off, like a dog; and they're all laughin' at me, and sayin' I've got the sack. I know I ain't so grand as some of your friends, but I guess I've got just as much heart, and as many feelin's to hurt, as they have. I want to know right now what I've done; and I ain't goin' to let you pass me till you've told me. Say, was it the kiss?"

"Oh!" cried Monica, "this is too ridiculous—too humiliating! Because I let you walk home with Della and me once or twice, you presume—please let us pass."

While the last word still quivered on her lips, the front door opened, and Randolph came in. Impulsively she took a quick step forward, as though to seek his protection from Crawford, then drew back as hastily, only anxious to keep him from all knowledge of the sordid squabble.

Randolph's eyes flashed from her to the shabbily dressed young boor, who had retreated with the sulky cowardice of the bully who sees that his game is up.

Scarcely could sharper lines of contrast have been drawn between two men. Randolph, with his clear gaze, his fresh morning face, immaculate linen and faultless clothes; Crawford, shabby, unwashed, his hair hanging over sullen brows and bloodshot eyes, collar dishevelled, and gaudy necktie on one side. Both, as it happened, had been up all night; but one had thrown off the effects of sleepless hours in the cold depths of his bath ; the other's whole personality was crumpled and sodden with lack of fresh air, lack of water, and lack of most things except whiskey, in which generous liquid breath and complexion seemed to have been steeped.

As Randolph entered, Crawford, breathing audibly, fell back—like night before the day—and stood holding hard by the rickety balusters, which creaked within his vicious grasp.

"Has anything happened, Miss Nairne? What can I do for you ?" Randolph questioned.

Though he had heard nothing of what had passed, instinct and Crawford's face told him that all was not as it should be, and he would have given much for the chance of administering a wholesome thrashing to the cad who had dared press his vile lips to Monica's.

"Nothing—nothing at all, thank you," the girl protested, hurriedly. "But I am glad you have come. And now, Mr. Crawford"—anxious for the sake of peace to pass over what had occurred—"we won't need to trouble you any longer."

With an exclamation that was coarse as the grunting of a hog, Crawford turned on his heel and marched off, continuing to mutter beneath his breath something of a retributory character. As he disappeared into the office to soak his injuries in more whiskey, Monica hastened to cover his departure.

"We had only just come out from breakfast, Della and I," she said, "and met Mr. Crawford, who had to stop us and talk about—about the rehearsal and so on. Now, shall we go upstairs?"

Della ran before them, escaping to her own room, but the two who were left behind were not destined easily to enjoy the *tête-à-tête* which she had thus endeavoured to secure for them.

Clouds of dust puffed out with the draught from an open window as Randolph threw wide the parlour door. The wife of the landlord had yielded to a fortnightly recurring conviction that it was her duty and privilege to sweep away all débris, and with it the bodily comfort of everybody who had helped to collect it.

Monica and her early caller started back, coughing.

"Just my luck!" ejaculated Randolph. "I wonder how long she means to be at it!"

"She means to be at it till this room and all the other rooms are cleaned out and dusted and plumb redd up again!" pronounced a singularly shrill falsetto from over the open "transom." "And I guess that won't be much short of an hour, if you want ter know."

"Thank you," returned Randolph, agreeably.

"And I suppose, Miss Nairne, you've got one of those confounded—I beg your pardon—you've got a rehearsal coming on?"

"At ten o'clock this time."

He looked at his watch. "And now it's nine. I wonder if any man ever had as much to say as I have, and as little time to do it in? In fact, I don't see that I'm going to get to say it at all. This is another instance of inconvenience because there's 'no room at the inn!' I suppose you couldn't go out and take a walk? I wouldn't ask you; and I wouldn't have come at this unearthly hour, but the chances are I've got to be off this afternoon. I've had a wire, and there's about a hundred thousand dollars hanging on it. There's just one thing, though, would make me stay."

"What is that?" Monica questioned, innocently.

"That's what I want to talk to you about. And, I tell you, I want it *badly*."

"Then "—and she smiled—" I'll take that walk."

"You will? You're an angel."

"So Della says. But I'm afraid I shall come back with feet of clay."

"That's so. The mud's something awful. And it's raining cats and dogs. I'm a brute to ask you to go."

"My curiosity is aroused now," laughed Monica, "and I couldn't be persuaded to stay at home."

"I don't mean to try. I could get that old Noah's ark you had last night, you know, Miss Nairne. 'Twould be just the thing for a flood like this, but— but perhaps——"

Monica shook her head. "Actresses mustn't go

out in arks with agreeable Noah's, even in floods, I'm afraid," she said. "That is, in country villages where the majority of the inhabitants have been preserved from the waters. Luckily, there was no gossiping on Ararat. We'll trust to our feet, and if they fail us, we can take refuge in the theatre."

In five minutes she had returned with a very English-looking little umbrella, and a still more British mackintosh.

The wind struck in their faces with the opening of the front door, and set Monica's curling hair in frantic commotion under her Tam. Had she been dependent upon hot irons for the little brown rings and waves which added so bewitching a feature to her personality, it is very probable that she would not so readily have offered to walk with Mr. Randolph in the rain. But Monica knew that her hair and complexion were at their best in stress of weather.

As they left the house behind them (one umbrella, and that Randolph's, making a barrier between them and the storm) the big gold chronometer was once more in requisition.

"Ten past nine," he remarked, in a voice which would have been pregnant with excitement if he had let it, but because he didn't, only sounded intensely business-like. "Ten past nine. That means that I've got exactly fifty minutes to ask you to marry me, and show you all the nine hundred and ninety-nine reasons why I'm dead sure you ought to do it."

Monica was so blown against the bulwark of her companion's shoulder by the match-making wind, that he could feel the start of surprise which quivered through her body. Yet she laughed lightly.

"We poor English girls are too slow-witted, I'm afraid," she said, "to keep up with you nimble Americans. You spring your jokes upon us so unawares."

"Jokes!" he echoed, almost fiercely. "I never was further from joking in my life. Now, there's three good minutes wasted already. I shall have to begin all over again. See here, Miss Nairne, will you do me one favour? Will you just promise to let me talk on like a house afire, and not once interrupt me till I'm through?"

Monica could not help smiling, though the action of her heart was perhaps rather more rapid than physical motion alone could account for.

"I must be guided by circumstances," she replied.

"Then, for the Lord's sake, look on me as circumstances for fifteen minutes. See here, Miss Nairne, just now I told you I wanted to get you to marry me, and that there were nine hundred and ninety-nine reasons why you ought to say 'yes.' Well, there are really a lot more than that, you know, but it would take up too much of your valuable time to listen to them all, even if you were willing; but I'll just begin with a few of the most important ones—from my own point of view, you understand. Now, wait! It isn't fair to interrupt me yet. I haven't got a start."

He stopped merely to take breath and hold the umbrella lower. He would now be enabled to steer away from imminent collisions, only by a timely vision of would-be passers' legs.

"The first reason," he went on, "is because I'm head over ears, and fathoms deep beside, in love— though you may say that's nothing to you. That's half my reasons, you see, all in one. Then the five hundred and first is that I'd give myself, and my life, and all I've got, to make you happy. The seven hundred and fiftieth is, that I believe I could *do* it, too, if you'd just give me half a chance. The nine hundred and ninety-eighth is because you must not and shall not stay where you are a day longer. And the nine hundred and ninety-ninth is a woman's reason— just *because.* I'm not sure but that's the best of any. Women say it is."

Monica's breath was taken away, and not by the wild February wind that flung itself against her face with its flurry of rain.

" Is it possible you mean it all ? " she questioned.

" All? A great deal more. You know I told you I had considerable to say inside of fifty minutes. I had to begin at once, without any working up, or I should only have got to the point by the time you were ready to bid me good-bye."

" But "—she was half merry still, half serious—" I thought we were *brother* and *sister ?* "

" So we were. But that was yesterday. This is to-day. Lots of things have happened since. Besides, the brother and sister part was only to be a beginning. One must begin somewhere, you know."

" And stop somewhere as well," hinted Monica.

" Not till you force me to. See here, Miss Nairne, we Americans are different from your men over on the other side of the herring-pond. We rush things a lot faster than they do, but we hold on just as tight in the end. It takes us about ten minutes to make up our minds that we want a thing, and would go through fire and water to get it, where it takes them a month. The minute I set eyes on you, standing up to pull a book off the shelves in my car, I thought you were the sweetest, prettiest creature I'd ever seen, or was ever likely to see again. That was about as far as I got until after we'd said farewell to each other, and I'd begun to realise perhaps we might drift apart—you in your life, I in mine—and never meet each other any more. I tell you, I couldn't stand that, and the feelings that I hadn't even warned you about all you might have to put up with seeing the night side of the theatrical profession, as I knew you were bound to do.

"As true as you're alive, and I love you, I meant every word I said to you yesterday. I wanted you for myself by that time, but I didn't mean to spring things on you like this. I just hoped you'd let me be your friend, and, some day, perhaps, I might get you to care for me a little more. But—do you know where I spent last night?"

The question was as abrupt as it appeared irrelevant.

"In your car, I suppose," ventured Monica. "Sleeping, I trust."

"Well, you'll have to guess again. Or, rather, I'll save you the trouble. I spent last night prowling around the streets, and the hills outside the village——"

"In the pouring rain?—oh, how miserable!"

"I guess it did rain a little, perhaps; but I vow I never knew it till I got back to my car about six o'clock this morning for a tub and a cup of hot coffee, and found that I was pretty wet. I wasn't cold, though. I felt as if I had a sort of furnace inside me that didn't need much of any stoking. I was worrying about you, dropped down in the midst of these people, like a pearl among swine, and I swear, Miss Nairne, it nearly drove me mad. To think that you—

a girl like you—should be subjected to—well, there's no use talking, you've got to be taken away."

"I know what you mean," murmured Monica, humbly. "I—I didn't know there would be that sort of thing to put up with till yesterday. I wonder that—you can care for me at all after—what you saw."

"Care for you? Well, you wouldn't understand, but I cared so much that I could have done *murder*, that's all. Now, look here, Miss Nairne, I don't expect you to do anything but like me a little, and think me an honest, decent sort of fellow, I hope, though perhaps, after a long time, I might get you to care for me enough to keep you from being sorry. But I do ask you to marry me; and, if you could bring your mind to it, I want it to be at once. I got a cable this morning, which ought to take me to Europe right away; but I'd wait till you said 'go,' if you could give me any hope you'd start with me.

"I never cared much for money before, but now I thank God I'm a rich man, and could give my wife anything on earth she wanted, except the Kohinoor, and, by Jove, if she'd set her heart on it, I'd make a pretty good bid for that. There, now! I've said my say, and I've left you fifteen minutes to talk back to me."

Monica squandered at least sixty seconds of this valuable time before she began to answer. At last she said :

"I think, Mr. Randolph, that you are the kindest and most generous man it was ever my good fortune to meet."

"By George! You don't say so? It never struck me that I was either; but it's to my advantage not to contradict."

He spoke lightly, with a certain humorous dry-
ness, such as he had used from the beginning, to conceal his real depth of feeling—as a boy covers fire
with dead leaves.

"You know nothing of me," Monica went on earnestly; "not even whether I have given you my real
name, and yet——"

"There are some people, women especially, you can
afford to take for granted," he interpolated.

"And yet, the fourth time you have ever seen me,
you ask me to be your wife. You are sorry enough
for me to offer me your whole life to save me from
what you look upon as a degradation. Well, I thank
you from the bottom of my heart——"

"You needn't," said Randolph, rather unsteadily.
"You know well enough that it isn't because I'm
sorry for you. I'm reserving all my pity for myself
if you say 'no.'"

"But that is just what I must say."

"Do you mean that? Can't you give me a shadow
of hope?"

Monica shook her head, and all the little shining
curls shook too, as though, if only it could have been
heard, they might have rung out a chime of fairy bells.

"Don't you believe I could make you happy?"

"You could, if—*if there wasn't some one else*—if
there hadn't always been some one else. But there
has, and there always will be, I'm afraid, even though
I don't suppose I shall ever see him again." The
girl's voice broke a little, and Randolph drew in his
breath sharply between his teeth. "I thought I'd
better tell you this," she added, "so that you would
—understand."

For many minutes they had been wandering on, without thought of where they were going, in a reckless way that never would have done for crowded city streets. They had passed beyond the confines of the little straggling village, and instead of sidewalks, hardened with a liberal sprinkling of ashes, they had come out into an open road. Suddenly Monica's foot went down into a slough of soft mud, which oozed over her shoe top, and, as she struggled to draw it forth, out slipped the small foot in all the extravagant bravery of a black silk stocking.

It was a terrible anti-climax to her self-renunciating speech. Never since offers of marriage first came into fashion, it seemed to her, could a girl have been obliged to hop about in the mud on one stockinged foot, in the midst of a proposal, with her hand wildly clutching at the arm of the man whom she had just refused.

Scarcely had she had time to realise the situation, however, when she felt herself bodily lifted off the ground, and carefully deposited on a higher and drier spot, with a man's handkerchief laid between the mud and the black silk stocking.

" Stand there a minute," said Randolph, " I'll have your shoe out in a jiffy."

There was nothing for it but to obey, and watch him exhume the lost article, caked with chocolate clay. With another handkerchief the worst of the mud was tenderly wiped away from patent leather and silken ankle, and Monica meekly supported herself with a reluctant finger or two on the back of her *preux chevalier*, as he bent on one knee to put on and carefully tie her shoe again.

"You are very good in emergencies," she pronounced at last.

"I'm glad I'm good for something. And, see here, Miss Nairne, I want you to look on this little thing that's just happened as a sort of *omen*. I was lucky enough to get you out of the mud and set you on higher ground, where you could feel more at home. Well, I'm going to do that figuratively speaking, too. You can't let me manage it in the way that would have made me happiest; and I sha'n't bother you about it again—you may trust me for that. But we'll go straight back to yesterday and begin all over at being brother and sister. I've told you my plan, and it's no good. Now, you just confide in me, like a kind sister, and we'll fix up some other plan."

"There aren't any plans for me," said Monica, feeling inexpressibly sad, as the rain wept cold tears upon her face. "I must go on, and 'dree my own weird,' that's all."

"Till that other one—that happy fellow—comes and fetches you home."

"He never will. Oh, Mr. Randolph, you've been so good to me, would you care to have me *really* confide in you, and tell you something of my story?"

"Rather than anything else except *one* thing, and that I can't have."

"Well, then, in the first place, Nairne is not my name at all."

CHAPTER XVI.

*"'And what's her history?'
"'A blank, my lord.'"*

SHE waited, as if for a question, but none came, and she continued slowly :

"It isn't as though I had taken the name like a cloak to hide under, I always believed it to be mine until a few months ago ; and then I heard the truth, told me with so many other truths, that it was like a hailstorm pelting on my defenceless head. Isn't it strange, Mr. Randolph, that when people remark that they are going to tell you the truth, it inevitably turns out to be something disagreeable ? "

" So you've discovered that already ! " he said.

" I've been discovering so many things lately. All the first part of my life I spent in not finding out anything at all—I mean, in learning how to be a blameless English maiden. Perhaps, though, they ought to have labelled me under my front hair or somewhere, 'Made in France,' for I was there from the time I was seven until I was nearly nineteen, growing up in a convent like a little starved plant without room to spread my roots.

" I can remember so well the night I was taken from home ! Mamma had gone away on a visit, and then one day a tall, gaunt woman, with a long nose and an upper lip like an over-mantel, appeared at the house, and said I had no mother any more. My father, who was a soldier, came home suddenly, and when I had run to him, crying, he turned from me and said, 'Oh, take her away.'

"It was soon after that that the gaunt woman carried me off to France, and I felt as though we must have sailed in the night over the edge of the world.

"When two or three years had passed, one of the Sisters at the convent—the one who was kindest to me—took me on her lap, and told me that there had been fighting away off in another country, and that some wicked black men had killed my father. Before that, at Christmas time I had had presents, though never any letters. But no presents ever came any more.

"When I was older, and began to ask questions, which had to be answered, they told me that the woman with the lip and the nose was my aunt—that she was the only blood relation I had in the world —so now you know why I hate the words 'blood relation.' When I was eighteen, she was to send, or come, and fetch me away to live in England, and so she did. I had never seen her since the dark night when we sailed over the edge of the world; but she was just the same, except that her face looked as though it had gone farther back into the perspective of her nose.

"I was to live with her until I should find a place as a governess, she said. Her house was in Leeds. There were antimacassars on all the chairs, and clocks and Japanese vases on most of the mantelpieces. I had not been with her more than a week, when her son—my cousin, though I hadn't known of his exist-

ence before—came home from Cambridge. He had
been hurt playing football, and he was laid up for
nearly half a year. There was no talk of a situation
being found for me while he was ill. My aunt was
glad to have me with her, to run up and down stairs
and read aloud; but she wouldn't have been so glad if
she had known how glad *I* was—how glad we both
were. When he grew better, but not yet well enough
to be as active as before, he wanted to be amused, and
he and his friends got up theatricals. I was given a
part in them, and I could act rather better than some
of the other girls.

"One night we played 'The Lady of Lyons.' He
was Claude and I was Pauline. That was the night
that we found out we cared for each other. He
thought it better not to let any one know, and I trusted
to him. We were engaged secretly for more than a
year, when his mother accidentally discovered everything. By that time I was going out as a daily governess, and had saved up a little money of my own—not
much, but it was all I had, except my father's pension,
which had kept me at the convent.

"Well, my aunt was bitterly angry when she
learned the truth, and accused me of ingratitude, and
most of the other sins set down in the calendar. She
said that I was a penniless beggar, and should never
marry her son. She told me then how she was only
my mother's *half* sister, and impressed it upon me
that it had been very good of her to bring me into
her pious home. I am afraid I answered back in a
bitter way, for I'm not really an angel, you know, despite what poor Della thinks. And then—then the
truth came out. My mother had not died, as I had

been taught to believe. She had run away with some one, and left my father and me, bringing disgrace upon the family, and breaking my father's heart.

"I was not fit to be the wife of an honest man—I was my mother over again—vain, deceitful, trying to attract the notice of men. My aunt had given me the name of another branch of our family—Nairne—that no one need know whose daughter I was. This was for her own sake, not for mine, as otherwise she would not have cared to have me in her house.

"She had seen my mother coming out in me, she said, ever since I showed such a wild desire to act. My mother had been an actress, and, for all my aunt could tell, was an actress still, in America, where she had gone so long ago. 'Then,' said I, 'I will go to her. I will go and be an actress in America, too.' So I came; and that is the end of my story. You see, it only runs up against a blind wall, for *this* is as far as I am likely to go towards being an actress, and—I am no nearer to finding my poor mother than I was when I first arrived."

"It was her photograph, then, that you showed me that first day?" asked Randolph, thoughtfully.

"Yes, I found it among some old things that had been saved for me. Oh, I do so long to find her! No matter what her mistakes have been, she is my mother, and, if she is tired and lonely and weary of the world by this time, perhaps she would be glad to know that she had a daughter ready to forget and—care for her."

Randolph's brows were drawn together, and Monica, looking up into his face, misunderstood what she saw there.

"You are glad, now, that I said 'no'!" she exclaimed. "But, if things had been different, I must have told you this about—my mother—before I gave you any answer at all."

"I am just about as glad that you said 'no' as a man is when he hears that he's going to be hanged," returned Randolph. "I was thinking about something, my little—sister. Would you trust me enough to answer me a question or two?"

"Yes," Monica said, looking up at him with a light in her eyes—that fatal light of kindliness and gratitude of which he must now beware.

"Then see here. What did the cousin—lover say when his mother had talked to you like that?"

"He—why, he was given so little chance to say anything. He was very sad, and thought she had been hard and cruel, I know."

"But he let you come away?"

"Yes. He couldn't help that, you see. He hoped some day to be a barrister, but he had no money of his own, except the allowance his mother made him; so it would have been hopeless to go against her will."

"I see. Just for a little while. But by and by, in a year or two, perhaps, he meant to get money somehow, and come after you, and make up to you for the past?"

Monica's long lashes lay upon her cheeks, and her words came falteringly.

"It would have been no use for us to build such plans," she explained, hastening as well as she could to the defence of her lover. "He would never earn money enough in a year, or many years, to risk going against his mother. Before we knew what reason she had for disliking me, we thought that she might come to consent in the end ; but when she had told all of that wretched story of the past to us both, we ceased hoping that she would ever change. And so, when I came away, it was good-bye for ever, between Eric and me."

" He gave you up ? "

" We gave each other up ; but I think we both cared too much to forget very soon."

" I can't imagine any one ever forgetting you," said Randolph, quickly. " But now just one question more. Do you suppose, if you had been a rich girl, with, say, three or four hundred thousand dollars or so of your own, that hard-hearted old skinflint—I mean, your respected half-aunt—would have felt just the same ? or would she have been willing to shut her eyes to all that—*other nonsense* she wanted to bring up between your cousin and you ? "

Monica laughed rather bitterly. " I think she would have shut her eyes so tightly that only a larger fortune belonging to some other girl could ever have opened them again."

" Thank you for answering me," Randolph said. "That's all I wanted to ask. And now, here we are, you see, at the theatre. I hope you don't mind, but I've brought you back exactly five minutes late."

" I don't mind," she reassured him, trying to smile. " We have fifteen minutes' grace. That is the rule of the profession, it seems, and is maintained even in Poddiwiski. When shall we—I mean, when shall I see you again ? "

He looked at her for an instant without speaking,

and as his eyes held hers, she realised, as she had
scarcely done before, what a brave, dependable face
his was, not handsome, or buoyant with youth, like
the original of that photograph which, while Della
was saying her prayers, Monica slipped secretly under
her pillow every night; but honest as well as clever,
true as well as keen, with generosity in the dark eyes,
and firmness in the square, smooth-shaven chin.

She had to repeat her question before he answered
it, and then he gave a perceptible start, as though she
had roused him from a brown study.

"I told you, didn't I," he said, "that there was
only one thing that would keep me here after the
telegram that was forwarded me to-day? Well, that
thing hasn't come off, so the sooner I get away
about my business the better—though, by Jove! I'll
stay yet, if you'll let me help you to something which
will make it easy for you to leave this show."

"I can't do that. I must stay for a time, at all
events," interrupted Monica.

"Very good; then, this may as well be good-bye.
I'm running over to Germany and England for a few
weeks. Is there any message you would like taken to
—Leeds?"

"No, thank you. No message at all. Why, you
don't even know—their name, or mine; the one
which really belongs to me, I mean. Shall I tell you
—that?"

"Monica Nairne is enough for me," he laconically
responded.

"Think of me as Monica Drayton. It is the name
I shall keep only for my friends. As for the others
their names can't interest you."

"No, since there is no message." But there was that in his mind which made him say to himself that it would be easy enough to find out, if occasion arose, in Leeds. "I shall leave here by the first train that will let me hitch on behind," he continued. "There'll be a little telegraphing back and forth first, but it won't take long. I shall be off, I dare say, in a couple of hours or so. There'll be just time for you to do me a big favour before I go. I'd rather have it than a cheque for a thousand dollars; but it's more than likely you'll say 'no,' as you did to a still bigger one just now."

"I promise you to say 'yes'!"

Monica's soft remorse inspired her to rashness.

"It's to give me that little shoe that I picked out of the mud for you. I reckon you've got plenty more?"

Patent leather shoes did not grow on blackberry bushes with Monica, but—there was the thirty pounds; and she did not withdraw her promise. The shoe should be wrapped up in paper, and his servant might call for it at the theatre, she said. In a box in her dressing-room there was a pair of boots that might be made to answer.

"What'll you do with the other one?" Randolph eagerly inquired.

"Throw it away, I suppose," was the indifferent reply.

"No, don't do that. Hang on to it, and if ever you're in any sort of trouble or bother, you just send it on to me. John Randolph, Denver, Colorado— that'll reach me, sooner or later, even if I'm not there. And, by Jove! it doesn't matter *where* I am, once I get that message, I won't be there *long*. One shoe's only to remember you by ; a pair will bring me to you from the other end of the world. Now, I mustn't detain you from that rehearsal of yours. Keep up a brave heart, little girl. 'Dark's the hour 'ere the dawn.' Good-bye, good-bye."

He wrung her hand and was gone, intent now, since other schemes had failed, on "collecting" Silas Jewett with the rest of his impedimenta, and removing him from Poddiwiski and Monica Nairne.

As he disappeared at a swinging pace round the corner, a curious pain stole into the heart of the girl. She had never felt anything quite like it in all her life before.

CHAPTER XVII.

"It is the stars,
The stars above us, govern our conditions."

"Do you know," said Della, "I never liked that Jim Crawford much, but I'm awful sorry for him now."

She stood at the bureau taking off her shabby hat, and the exquisitely-mended gloves with which she preserved economy, and at the same time paid the respect due to her pretty hands. Della had been out with Mrs. Ambler, helping to choose for that masterfully-inclined lady a simple girlish frock, which her skilled fingers were hurriedly to fashion into shape.

Monica looked up from the MS. in which she was endeavouring to perfect herself as Miss Ashford, the elderly and spiritually-minded spinster in "The Private Secretary."

"What has happened to Mr. Crawford?" she inquired, without much show of interest in face or voice.

"Perhaps you'll be mad with me if I tell you? It's got something to do with you. I know he's common, and not fit to wipe dust off your shoes, Angel, but he's so dead in love with you that he's 'most sick.'"

Was ever any daughter of Eve *genuinely* angry at being told that a man—even as low down in the social scale as a purveyor of garbage—had fallen ill with hopeless love of her?

Monica was therefore not angry, but she naturally wished to appear so. She turned down the corners of her charming mouth with an elaborate sneer, and breathed aloud the one potent word, "Disgusting!" Then, however, she found that her conscientious effort had been too successful. Della, shocked at having caused annoyance to her beloved, and fearing that her broken confidence, on so mean a subject, had been in poor taste, closed her lips upon the remainder of her revelation. She put away her hat and gloves (she had never been used to putting things away until fired by her friend's example) in shamed silence.

Monica retired within herself, as embodied by Miss Ashford; but, having turned a page or two of the part, she looked carelessly up.

"Who told you that nonsense?" she sharply questioned.

Della was obtuse. Already her thoughts had flown to something else, or, rather, led by the contemplation of Crawford's sufferings of heart, she had returned to meditation upon her own.

"*What* nonsense?" she repeated.

It was very aggravating to be required to explain. However, Monica's curiosity could not otherwise be appeased.

"That nonsense about Mr. Crawford," she vouchsafed.

"Oh, don't you really mind if I talk to you about it, Angel?"

"Well, perhaps, if there's anything in it, I might better hear it and have *done* with it," Monica sighed.

Della was nothing loth. Her own love troubles had softened her heart, and inclined her to sympathy with those of another—even poor Crawford, whom as she confessed, she had never either trusted or liked.

"Every one in the company knows," Della made answer. "But it was Mrs. Ambler was talking to me about it to-day. We met the poor wretch in the street, and, honestly, you'd hardly know him for what he was only three or four days ago. Of course, since you've turned him off, and wouldn't speak to him, he's kept away from you, and you've only seen him in the theatre, so you couldn't really tell how he looked. And I—I've been around with you always; and I haven't come across him anywhere outside since last Wednesday morning, when you scolded him in the front hall."

"Well, it's only Friday afternoon now," Monica reminded her. "Surely he can't have altered much in that time."

"Oh, but he has! He used to take so much pains, oiling his hair down in a curl on his forehead, and fixing himself up with pretty neckties, and making his old shoes shine. But to-day—you just ought to have seen him! You'd have felt sorry for him, too, Angel. His hair was all dry and rumpled up anyhow, as though it hadn't been brushed for a week; his eyes had red rims around them; his skin looked kind of blotchy and yellow, like wax; and, honestly, he's got thin; his cheeks were quite sunken. As for his shoes —why, there ain't a man in the company wouldn't have been ashamed of 'em, and *that's* saying a good deal. He was walking so queer, slouching from one end of the sidewalk to the other, with his head down, and his battered old hat over his nose, and a sort of glazed, dull look in his eyes."

"I suppose," suggested Monica, from an airy height of disdain, "that the person had eaten something, or, still more likely, drunk something which had disagreed with him. I can't see that these unpleasant symptoms point in any way to me."

"He *was* half tipsy, poor beast," hesitated Della, fearful of further shocking her Angel. "That's why I'm so sorry, for, however common and horrid he may have been in other ways, he never was the kind that drank very much. A little, perhaps, in the hotel office, with the other boys,—they all did that, even— even Nick,—but never to get drunk. Only now he's so miserable about you that he don't care what he does, or how he looks, or what happens anyhow."

"I'm sure you must be mistaken," Monica protested, half-heartedly. "A little more than a week ago, and he had never even seen me."

"Ah, but you know it's different with show people," said Della, remembering, with a pang, how Nick had begun to "keep steady company" with her the second day after their first meeting. "They get acquainted so soon; and then, you know, we're all together so much, unless we keep away on purpose, that a week's more than knowing any one at home for a month. Just look at *us* now. What friends we've got to be, and *haven't* I begun to improve a little already, trying to be like you? I speak better, I'm almost sure, for I do want so bad to please you—and—why, I feel as if there *never* could have been a time when I wasn't loving you as hard as ever I could."

Della was down on her knees, with her arms round her adored one's waist; and even the miserable Crawford was incidentally allowed to share the warmth of Monica's softening heart.

"Mrs Ambler says that she and Mr. Ambler are

awful worried for fear, if the thing goes on like this,"
Della continued, "Crawford'll have to leave the company, and won't be fit to act. He went all to pieces
in his big scene last night in the 'Two Orphans,' and
it would be hard to get anybody to fill his place. I
know you don't think he or any of 'em, except Nick,
can really act much; but the people in these towns
ain't any wiser than to like him. They believe he's
great, and then he's what they call a 'good looker,' and
the girls are always wild about him. He used to be
always out mashin' till you came in the company, and
that was one thing I thought was so horrid about him.
He don't think of any one but you now (just like me)
and they all say he don't eat or sleep since you threw
him over, or do anything but drink, drink, drink!"

"I *threw* him over!" Monica echoed, in disgust.

"Well, Angel, you know what I mean. *He*
thought, poor wretch, you would let him go with you.
Of course you couldn't do *that*, for you're so far
above him, and *I* understand just why you ever let
him come near you, if the others don't. But couldn't
you—couldn't you do something kind, just so he
won't drink himself to death?"

Monica was silent, but her brain was busy. If this
unfortunate young man had been tempted by a sin-
cere though sudden passion for her into the commission of the offence which had nipped all her good intentions toward him in the bud, the offence itself
might be made to appear less black in her eyes. Of
course, she deeply regretted the growth of this foolish predilection; but it would be wrong, perhaps, to
feel hardly toward him for cherishing it. No man's
love, if it were the best he had to give, could insult a

woman, no matter how far she might be above him. And, possibly, for that very reason he should seem the more forgivable. It showed there was *something* in the man, that he should turn his thoughts toward that which was intrinsically desirable.

"I don't quite see what I could do," she said, at last, with signs of willingness to be made to see in her soft tone and softer eyes.

"You know you wouldn't even let him speak to you the other day," Della gently reminded her; "but when Mr. Randolph came in you just sent him right away."

"That was far more for his own sake than mine. If Mr. Randolph had dreamed how he had vexed me, he would have done something which Mr. Crawford would never have forgotten, I am sure."

Monica spoke with a certain thrill of pride in the courage and prowess of the man whose love she had refused.

"Still, if he asked to speak with me again, and would promise never to—to take the liberty he took on Tuesday, both at the rehearsal and in the play itself, why, I might—rather than he should be really *unhappy*, you know—I might try to forgive him."

"That's like you!" exclaimed Della, adoringly. "I'll tell him myself, to-night, that he may speak to you to-morrow, and that you'll be kind." Then she began to cut out the short-waisted, white "cheese cloth" gown which, with a blue sash, would do its best at to-morrow's matinee to turn a woman of forty-five into a girl of sixteen.

As a matter of fact, Monica did not at all fancy having to play the part of Miss Ashford. She had not been engaged as a "character actress," she had ventured to inform Mr. Montgomery, when the stage managerial fiat had gone forth ; but, according to the voice of that authoritative oracle, the post of leading juvenile in some respects resembled Charity. If it did not exactly "cover a multitude of sins," it could, at least, be made the cloak for a number of incongruous duties.

It was ridiculous, Monica considered, that while she, a slender girl of twenty-one, mopped and mowed as an ugly old woman, a mountain of flesh, *ætat* five-and-forty, should tie a ribbon about that portion of the body where the waist was rendered conspicuous by its absence, and try to impose upon the audience as a skittish maiden. There was no help for it, however, save possibly in a violent quarrel, which must end in indignant retirement from the company ; and therefore Monica had wickedly resolved outwardly to perform her task, inwardly to console herself by an ingenious revenge.

"You must part your hair in the middle and put flour on it, you know," directed Mrs. Ambler, before the matinee performance on the eventful Saturday. "I've brought some over with me from the hotel for you, for fear you'd forgotten it."

The leading lady was kind enough to interest herself in many details of the new juvenile's stage toilet, therefore Monica was scarcely surprised at this delicate attention. She accepted the flour with thanks, and having laid the newspaper cornucopia containing it contemptuously in a corner of her dressing-room shelf, she proceeded to the execution of her vengeance.

Yes, she would obey her rival's instructions to the letter. There should be nothing neglected of which

the lady could complain. Her hair should be parted
in the middle, and brought down over her ears.
There should be plenty of violet powder on it, too.
But—well, there *might* be a "but" in the case!

As she carefully made her toilet, a great trampling
could be heard in the front of the house, noisy feet
of crowding children, shrill juvenile cries. Scarcely
could the Pied Piper himself have attracted a larger
following of little men and women than had been
caught by the gaudy wax doll and the baseball displayed since Monday in the show window of Poddiwiski's most pretentious "dry goods store."

Della had dressed the doll, Mr. Ambler's boldest
penmanship had ticketed it and the ball which was
to buy the patronage of boys : "To be given away to
the holders of the lucky number at the Ambler Comedy Company's Matinee of 'The Private Secretary,' a
Pure Play which Children love. Opera House, Saturday, 2 o'clock, February 7th."

Monica stood unobtrusively in the wings, before
the moment for her entrance came, watching Miss
Fanny Free and Miss Marguerite Neland, who were
the two beauteous maidens of the piece. The Human
Flower was pretty, if somewhat meretricious ; but the
leading lady's opulent charms, enhanced by a tangled
golden wig (greatly resembling in texture that of the
prize doll), were calculated to strike terror into the
innocent hearts of children.

"Oh, what a fat girl ! See, ma, she looks older'n
you do !" babbled a guileless infant in the front row
of chairs, and at that inauspicious moment Monica
made her entrance. She was dressed in a plain black
gown, with a white frilled fichu, and with her lovely

young face, rouged cheeks, brilliant eyes, and frame of curling snowy hair, she looked as though she had stepped from an old-fashioned picture.

The children cried out in naïve admiration, and Monica's revenge was complete. Mrs. Ambler's glare, and the Human Flower's dimpled, giggling amusement, were as balm to her sorely injured soul. She played the scene joyously. Nobody looked at the two girls while she was on the stage; but pride—as has often happened in the history of successes—was to come before a fall.

Old Mr. Wilts, known as "pa" among his compeers, intercepted her on the way back to her dressing-room.

"I'm kind of disappointed in you, Miss Na-i-rne," he drawled, unconsciously counting the warts with which his poor grey wisps of hair were apparently buttoned on, as was his habit when excited. "I thought you were different from the other women in this set of mummers misfortune and increasing age have placed me among. I fondly fancied that in you, young and untried as you are, I saw the makings of an artist; but this afternoon has taught me my mistake."

"I don't understand what you mean, Mr. Wilts," stammered the confused girl, for even the praise of poor old superannuated "pa" would have been sweet.

"Say *do not*, not don't, if you please, Miss Na-i-rne. If words are worth speaking at all, they are worthy their full value, as I have many times tried to impress upon each individual in this combination. The very fact that you cannot understand is an argument in my favour. You have to-day satisfied your vanity by appearing as an attractive young girl, instead of the eccentric middle-aged woman required by the part. But what of the audience? What of your own self-respect? As I remarked, I am disappointed in you, Miss Na-i-rne."

Having thus delivered himself, the pedantic survivor of an elder school dragged his lame foot away, and Monica was left, shamed, and stricken with remorse.

Before the next scene, Miss Ashford had unaccountably attained a ripe old age, though but a few hours were supposed to have passed over her powdery head. She had all the lines and hollows of sixty, while a pair of Della's spectacles, and a palsied top-knot of hair, gave the required touch of eccentricity.

But these tardy sacrifices on the altar of art were not to be made with impunity. Virtue is its own reward, no doubt, but Miss Ashford was to have no other. In the exaltation of mind attending the pious alterations of her make-up, the one thing which above all others should not have been forgotten was incontinently lost sight of.

Miss Ashford (looking like " She " after her second bath of fire) was sauntering coolly toward her centre entrance, approving her own conduct, forgiving her enemies, and smiling for the first time upon the sullen but wistful Crawford, when that culprit started suddenly into frenzied eagerness.

"Your night-gown!" he cried, hoarsely. "Lord! you've forgotten it!"

For an instant, but an instant only, Monica was inclined to resent the apparently gratuitous mention by these lips of so esoteric a garment. Then, like a flash, she recalled the stage manager's directions for the coming scene. Night was supposed to have fallen over stageland. The private secretary, concealed under a table, was inadvertently to rouse the house, and Miss Ashford's appearance in an old-fashioned night-gown and ruffled cap, with a candle in her hand and maidenly terror in her face, was to bring down the curtain.

Instead of conscientiously adding a score of years to her age, Miss Ashford should have occupied her short wait in hustling the property night-gown on over her dress, and tying the cap-strings under her chin. She had done neither, and the huge unbleached cotton garment, supplied by Mrs. Ambler, was reposing in her distant dressing-room.

In this dreadful extremity, her late feud with Mr. Crawford was blotted from her memory.

"Oh, what *shall* I do?" she appealed to him, as deeply distressed as though the fate of a nation depended upon the night-railed entrance of Miss Ashford.

Crawford's eyes sparkled. New life flowed through his whiskey-tainted veins, for he saw a chance of reinstating himself in Miss Nairne's lost favour.

"You shall have it! You shall be in time yet!" he ejaculated. "I can get there and back three times as quick as you!" With a bound he had disappeared in the direction of the dressing-rooms.

Monica stood waiting with loudly thumping heart, hearing those on the stage coming every instant nearer and nearer to the fatal cue. There would be a row, she knew, if she were not prompt in responding to it, for being at the end of an act, where all must close with a wild *mêlée* of bustle and excitement, a wait would be fatal to the effect. This, coming after the deliberate defiance of Miss Ashford's make-up, would cap the climax of her misdoings ; and Monica hated being scolded when no defence could be forthcoming.

Would the man ever get back? Three speeches more, and she must run on, night-gown or no night-gown. Yes, he was flying along the narrow passage between unused sets of scenery at last. He was waving something yellowish-white in either hand. Perhaps she could do it yet !

" Miss Ashford ! " groaned the property man, tearing up from the prompt box, with his book of the play. "Good Heavens! aren't you ready? They're waitin' for you on the stage."

" Light her candle for her, man ! " panted Crawford, battling among voluminous folds of the night-gown ; and, with the good will if not the deftness of a *femme de chambre*, flinging it over Monica's shoulders.

Dizzily she struggled in the enveloping mass, which covered her like an extinguisher. Head and face were hopelessly muffled. She could not find her way out, though Crawford fought valiantly to release her. In the midst came the expected cue. She must go on, or ruin the end of the act, and with it, the united tempers of Mr. and Mrs. Ambler and the stage manager. Into one groping, desperate hand, Todd thrust the lighted candle, into the other Crawford had mechanically put the night-cap. Headless, to all appearances, and preternaturally tall, the frantic Miss Ashford rushed upon the stage.

The effect was instantaneous, and the uncontrollable merriment of the barn stormers fed that of the audience. Even the solemn stage manager so far forgot himself as not to give the signal for the descent of the curtain. Poor Monica was helpless to release herself, both hands fulfilling important and simultaneous engagements.

Butting forward her little powdered head, she at length forced the nodding top-knot through the twisted opening of her shroud, and then, with a lifting of the chin, brought the night-gown round her shoulders, just as the curtain hid her from the anxious audience.

"Oh, I'm so sorry!" she had begun, between laughter and tears, when she felt herself suddenly caught by the shoulders.

"Stand still, for God's sake!" said Crawford.

She stood still, stricken dumb with her surprise. Something—it must have been the lighted candle—was snatched from the heedless hand which had held it. The big night-gown was seized, and rent from top to bottom with a shrill sound of tearing cotton, while every one cried out in astonishment or terror.

"Oh, what is it—what is it?" Monica exclaimed.

She need not have asked, for as the torn night-gown fell, and Crawford sprang forward to stamp upon the crumpled heap, a small tongue of flame curled up around his feet.

"Lucky they didn't see that from the front, or there'd have been a stampede among those brats out there," calmly commented Mr. Montgomery, when only smoke and a strong smell of burning was left to tell the tale of Monica's escape. "You silly girl, you, didn't you know you were settin' fire to yourself?"

"If she had a-know'd it, I guess she wouldn't have done it!" flung out Crawford, radiant in the championship of his fair lady. " Jinks! how I've burnt my hands ! "

In reality, his injury was slight, so slight that a child would scarcely have curled down a lip for crying. But it was an opportunity not to be lost for snatching at the sympathy of her whose saviour he had been, and he had not that delicate instinct which would have kept a man of Nickson's type from confessing to pain far less endurable.

Some of the others grinned and exchanged a wink or two. It was easy to guess now how the wind would blow. The fire, at least, had saved Monica from a further scolding ; and, without another word from the stage manager, she was allowed to follow the retreating Crawford impulsively from the stage.

"If you'll come to my dressing-room," she said, rather timidly, " I will bind up your hand in a handkerchief with some vaseline. If it hadn't been for you, I might have had a very serious accident."

" Don't mention it! " gallantly responded Crawford, though he would have been deeply chagrined if she had not.

He did not wait for a second invitation to the dressing-room whose cleanliness and comfort she owed to him. Holding out his hands, which he was charmed to see were actually reddened in two or three places, he basked in the delight of having them laved by her little fingers, and smeared with a wholly superfluous supply of vaseline. Never once during the entrancing process did he remove his eyes from the lined mask which hid the beauty of her young face. He drew long, ecstatic breaths as she rolled her handkerchief, torn in two parts, round his awkwardly extended digits. Her lashes had been downcast throughout, but as she fastened the last of the safety-pins which were to hold the impromptu bandages in place, she lifted them, as by an effort, toward which she had been forcing herself for some anxious moments.

"There!" she exclaimed. "I am sure that will keep the hands from blistering. Thank you, again, very much, for what you have done. I want to tell you that I think the more of your kindness after what has passed."

"Are we go'n' to be friends again?" he asked.

"Yes. We'll forgive and forget, won't we? I took offence where none was meant, maybe, and you—you'll be more careful of my feelings after this, I'm sure."

"I'll do anything—before the Lord I will, Miss Nairne. You don't know what I've gone through on your account this week. I've been half crazy—you bet I have."

"You take things too hard," she answered, uneasily. "We are only slight acquaintances, you know. But if you want to please me, really, and win my friendship, you'll turn over a new leaf, and make yourself worthy of a woman's respect."

"I *can* do it," he said, "if you'll help me; but not without. Are you go'n' to let me come round after you and Della again evenin's after this, like you did before?"

The injured hands appealed conspicuously and consciously to her mercy.

"Oh, dear! I suppose so!" exclaimed Monica, desperately. "Now you must go away and let me dress for the next act."

It was another slip down a perilous path if only she had known it.

When the curtain had descended on the last act of "The Private Secretary," and Mr. Ambler had stepped out to inspect the numbers of all tickets, and award the prizes to the brave and fair, there came presently a great roar of laughter to the barn stormers in their dressing-rooms.

"What's up?" they elegantly asked each other over the conveniently low partitions. Nobody could answer at first, and then Mr. Montgomery sauntered, chuckling, through the passage.

"Fan, guess who's got the doll?" he jovially shouted to his wife.

"Any kid I know?" followed the question, rendered slightly incoherent by the savage adhesiveness of caramel or butter-scotch.

"Pretty big kid. 'Bout as big as Mr. Silas Jewett, Miss Neland's swell mash!"

A protesting shriek from the lady involved in this statement.

"*Get* out, you big booby, you! As if we didn't all know Mr. Jewett went off with his friend three days ago!"

"Well, he's back. Guess this show kinder suits him. Anyhow, there he was as large as life, walkin' up to draw the doll. *Gosh!* Didn't everybody yell!"

Poor Randolph, standing at that moment beside the captain on the bridge of a certain big Cunarder, watching the stormy sea, and thinking of a little mud-stained shoe down below in his steamer trunk, might not perhaps have joined with much heartiness in Miss Marguerite Neland's exultation on the return of her prodigal mash.

CHAPTER XVIII.

"And your experience makes you sad. I had rather have a fool to make me merry, than experience to make me sad ; and to travel for it, too ! "

" GUESS the ghost ain't go'n' to walk this Saturday neither."

The gloomy prognostication was uttered in a low and ominous whisper by Mr. James Crawford, standing outside the door of the dressing-room shared by Monica Nairne and Della Thomas, in the alleged Opera House at Moonsville, Arkansas, popularly known as " Arkinsaw."

Monica had been, at the time, two months a member of the Ambler Comedy Company, and she had the best of reasons for understanding the esoteric meaning of Mr. Crawford's speech.

Unfortunately for her, and for all whom it concerned, the apparition referred to had not appeared to those who waited with any (not even a spectral) degree of regularity during the past five or six weeks.

Since Poddiwiski, the show business had been almost unvaryingly bad. The advance man, whose province it was to inflame the minds of the country folk with eager anxiety for the advent of Mr. Ambler's talented comedians, had had to contend against benighted indifference. Even the charms which he freely sang, of the Brilliant Emotional Star, Miss

Marguerite Neland ; the English Professional Beauty, Lady Monica Nairne ; and Miss Fanny Free, the Little Human Flower, failed adequately to impress the inhabitants of Missouri and Arkansas. Indeed, this was scarcely to be wondered at, perhaps, considering the extreme repulsiveness of the lithographs popularly supposed to portray the features of the misrepresented ladies. But then, the paper was cheap and highly coloured, and Mr. Ambler obstinately saw no reason why it should fail to please.

"No salary again!" echoed Monica, dolefully. "That makes four weeks without!"

She drew her pretty brows together with a worried look. Once relieved of the uncomfortable impression that she had been made the involuntary recipient of Randolph's charity, she had been generous with the remainder of her thirty pounds during the reckless days when the ghost had faithfully, if grudgingly, kept his tryst with the company each Saturday night.

She had bought Della a new dress and a spring hat, to say nothing of the same indulgence for herself. She had lent money to poor old Pa Wilts to pay for his divorced wife's funeral. She had helped Miss Fanny Free with a long existing debt to a second-hand clothes woman, who had been threatening to have the law of her. She had advanced a considerable sum to Mr. Crawford to purchase a new suit; and she had bribed Mr. Todd, the property man, for several little extra conveniences in the matter of trunks at hotel and theatre.

When the weekly wraith ceased to stalk, Monica had seen reason to repent her general free-handedness ; but, like most earthly repentances, hers came too late. The money was spent, the exchequer empty, and no fresh supply was pouring into the void that ached. Even had she wished it, she could not have separated herself from the company, where, thus far, the common expenses of her daily life had been met by Mr. Ambler. She had but three dollars remaining in the purse which had once been so objectionably plump; unless the fortunes of the comedians improved suddenly and remarkably, there seemed no chance of adding to her store, and yet the name of her wants was legion. It was, therefore, not surprising that her eyebrows should have united their forces in an anxious frown.

"I suppose, then," said Della, resignedly, "there's no use in waiting here any longer. We might as well go home."

"Every one else has cut sticks," Crawford returned, stealthily looking round the door-post. "There goes Mr. and Montgomery now."

"That means they've *all* "given up the ghost'!" Monica exclaimed, with a dismal attempt at mirth. But nobody saw the joke.

"'Tisn't as though Ambler *couldn't* pay," grumbled Crawford, as they marched in Indian file along the narrow strips of board, raised above the Arkansas mud that formed an integral part of the side-walk. "He's a rich man, Ambler is, has saved up a pile; but he'd sooner see us folks all starve an' rot than shell out a red cent that wasn't profits. Oftentimes I kinder think that he's got some little game, though I'm blamed if I kin see what it is. Perhaps he wants to get money to run the show out o' that Jewett feller, that's always popping up along our route every other week or so,—and I shouldn't wonder if he did it, too."

Monica scarcely listened. She did not attach any importance to these suspicions of Mr. Jewett, of whom, during their travels, she had lately seen a good deal in a friendly, desultory way. She was very tired of Crawford, very tired of the mission which had been undertaken in the vain hope of effecting his mental and moral reformation. She was still languidly sorry for him, because of his hopeless defects and his equally hopeless affection for her; but she had come to the pass of impatiently exaggerating the former and depreciating the latter. In some moods, the young man's coarse personality was absolutely nauseating to her, and she repented in bitterness that she had ever bound herself with the habit of his companionship.

It *had* become a habit, at last, which it seemed to her almost impossible to break. So gradual had been the growth of her mistake, added to at first through sheer softness of heart and girlish vanity, which would not let her hurt the feelings of a poor wretch who was sick for love of her, that she had not realised how each day some new link was welded in the chain.

At the beginning, there had only been the escort home from the theatre at night. Then Crawford had begged to walk with her and Della to "the hall," carrying such parcels as needed to be taken to and fro. Later, it had become a matter of course that he should saunter beside the two friends between the railway-station and the hotel. If they went out for a breath of fresh air and a "constitutional," Crawford appeared almost invariably to be wistfully standing by

the door; and, when so much had already been permitted, it would have seemed hard to send him about
his business. Sometimes, too, it must be confessed,
Monica found it not inconvenient to have an able-
bodied man at her beck and call. Crawford was ever
ready to run out on an errand in the rain. Crawford
could be counted upon to fetch something in the way
of supper to their bedroom door, if the girls were hungry. Crawford would bring up coals or wood, if hotel
servants were recalcitrant, and build a fire. Crawford
would joyously clean boots, brush mud-covered skirts,
or run up with a breakfast tray, if Monica were ill or
tired. Like adversity, he had certainly had his uses;
and every little kindness which he was allowed to do
for "the Princess," as he had begun to call her, made
the way of Monica's retreat more difficult, the way of
his advance more sure.

Gradually, continual association with her fellow barn
stormers had dulled the English girl's sense of their
general deficiencies. She still realised that they were
common; she never failed to be more or less shocked
by their vulgarities, or disgusted by their facility for
finding *doubles entendres* in her most innocent speeches.
But she had accustomed herself to their ways, and
inevitably identified her interests with theirs. Even
their claims to acting were gravely considered by her,
and she no longer experienced the keen pang of self-
conscious shame which once had stabbed her whenever she appeared among them on the stage. But
this leniency of habit was extended to the *company*,
not to each individual composing it. The constant
and almost enforced companionship of Crawford had
got upon her nerves, and sickened her. She could

scarcely tolerate the slang and the dull jokes or efforts at love-making (invariably nipped in the bud) which constituted his ideas of conversation. Any excuse to break with him would have been eagerly welcomed; but none offered, and the straits into which the poverty of "business" had brought them all only seemed, by necessity, to draw them closer together. There were confidences and mutual distresses, and altogether, on this night of early April, a climax in Monica's feelings seemed to have been reached.

"What shall I do with him? How *shall* I rid myself of him?" she irritably asked herself, as Crawford poured into her inattentive ears his hopes, his fears, and his suspicions.

No longer did she mentally class him as a rough diamond. Slowly she had been finding out all his pettinesses, all his silly conceits and deceits; yet never since the early days in Poddiwiski had he attempted any liberty in act or speech which might afford her the desired opportunity for absolute dismissal.

The air was full of the soft, lazy sweetness of the southern springtime. An indescribable suggestion, rather than an actual fragrance, of growing, budding things came from the earth and trees, and the young shrubs and sprouting grass. A profile moon, honey-yellow, hung in the western sky, and the tall cotton-wood and butternut trees stood out black and gaunt against a hazy radiance. From their branches, on which by sunlight baby leaves stretched and unfurled their golden-green crinkles, trailed a sombre drapery of Florida moss, waving in the slow breezes like the long hair of a woman who bends and weeps above a grave.

Not a gleam of lamp or candle came from behind the curtains that seemed to have shut the eyes of all the low-built houses which lined one side of the long, straight road. Neither was the street artificially illuminated, and all would have been dark save for that voluptuous young moon, that looked down between the trees, throwing up here and there an ominous gleam from the waters of swampy land not yet "reclaimed" by the town.

There was a poem in the night for those who had hearts to understand, and Monica thrilled with it in vague longings that had more of pain than conscious pleasure. She was sad for the present, and anxious for the future, and Crawford's presence more than ever jarred upon her mood. She thought of a spring, only a year ago, when she and her cousin, Eric Stannard, had walked together; and she cherished the soft pang which answered to the recollection. She could have wished that it had been keener, and by conjuring up all possible details of those dead delights, she endeavoured to twist the knife with which she probed the wound.

When she reached home she decided, looking yearningly up at the languorous moon, she would take her poor, precious Eric's photograph from her trunk, and, after kissing it in the moonlight at the window, she would slip it under her pillow as of old. *"As of old!"* ah, there lay the sting! Somehow the exigencies of travel had interfered with the regularity of that sacred rite, once as much a matter of course as the use of soap and water, or the hair-brush. On two or three occasions such unpleasant little accidents had happened, too! By some inexplicable temporary

aberration of mind, she had neglected to remove the
treasure, after conscientiously putting it in place, and
the coldly curious eye of Mary Ann had gleamed
bleakly upon it when dragging off the sheets in the
morning.   Once also (horrible to recall) she had very
nearly gone away from an hotel and left the picture
of her lost love behind, it having been only retrieved
at the last moment by the thoughtfulness of careful
Della, who was not supposed even to wot of its existence.

But to-night (ah, this soft night when dreams of
the past came crowding!), she would begin all over
again.   Of course, though her love was hopeless, and
she had been *very* wise to banish it below the surface
and into the depths of mind and heart, she cared no
less for Eric than she had cared in the beginning.
She was only oppressed by other sordid matters.
That was the explanation of an apparent neglect, for
which there was really no need that she should accuse
herself.   What it would be to see that moon with
Eric by her side—*her* Eric, as she had once hoped
that he might be for ever!

With this yearning desire, pumped up by considerable effort from the core of her being, Monica's foot
slipped off the board that lay between the wary pedes-
trian and the material from which man is popularly
supposed to have been created.   There followed a
suggestively oozy sound, accompanied by a slight
exclamation of annoyance, and Crawford sprang forward from his place in the procession, to extricate the
sufferer with a ready arm about her waist.

"Oh, *don't!*" cried Monica sharply, shaking herself free from his support.   He had meant well, and

she ought to have been grateful. But a sudden flash of recollection had shown her Randolph rescuing her from a somewhat similar though more serious predicament, and kneeling down in the driving rain to wipe the mud from her black silk ankle. She could see the back of his neck as he bent over, showing a narrow rim of white between the close-cropped dark hair and the high collar. She could see the look in his eyes, as he had lifted his head from the self-appointed task to glance up at her and ask if she was " all right." It was strange how clearly the trivial scene came back to her, with all its details painted in far more vivid colours than she had seen them at the time.

She shut her eyes on the picture, venting her disapproval of it and of herself on Crawford, who would persist in asking what was the matter, and what he had done that was wrong.

What a nice smile Randolph had had! For an ugly man, almost middle-aged, he had been very attractive in some ways. His eyes, for instance—or was it, perhaps, his mouth?

Darling Eric, how difficult it was to wait until she could reach home before refreshing herself with a long look at his dear portrait!

"Have you got a headache, Angel?" questioned Della from behind.

" I ? " she echoed, introspectively. " Oh, I'm only a little worried about money and—and things."

"Everything's horrid, isn't it, love?" said Della, linking her arm in Monica's, as soon as they had passed beyond the unsociable boards, and attained the more civilised side-walk of brick, which informed the initiated that the hotel was close at hand.

"*Horrid!*" repeated the adored one, with an emphasis comprehending much that to the mind of her less complex friend was dark.

Crawford, in injured silence, opened the gate, and the two girls passed into the extensive yard which surrounded the old-fashioned Southern hotel. It was a two-storied frame building, which, if it had ever been painted, regretted the vanities of its past, and did its best to cover them from notice. All round ran a double verandah (or "piazza," as it was called in the vernacular), with thin pine supports undraped by vine or creeper.

Monica had here a bed-chamber to herself, as there were plenty of unoccupied rooms in the rambling old Jefferson Davis House. Her quarters were situated at the back, in an addition known as the "L," on the ground floor, while Della's were directly above, and communication could be quickly had between the two, by means of an exterior stairway, which led up from one floor of the piazza to the other.

A boarded path wandered from the front to the rear of the hotel, and by way of this Monica and her companions usually went at once to her own private door, which opened upon the verandah. To-night, however, there was a certain air of bustle and disturbance about the place, which attracted them to the main entrance.

The Ambler Company had been inmates of the Jefferson Davis House since the preceding Monday, and had grown accustomed to finding all quiet and dark on their return from the theatre. If a stealthy light burned for the benefit of late and thirsty ones in the office, it was decorously shrouded behind heavy green shutters, which saw no shame in keeping out the dewy balm of April air.

But on this Saturday night things were different. The front door was wide open, and a stream of yellow light revealed several figures grouped about it both outside and in.

The office shutters had not been closed, and a crowd was visible collected round the bar.

" Hullo, something's go'n' on," exclaimed Crawford, and by common consent the three, instead of taking the circuitous path to the " L," marched up the steps of the front verandah.

CHAPTER XIX.

"Alarums and excursions."

MISS FANNY FREE was having hysterics in the dining-room. Scarcely did the late-comers need to be told of this, because her cries were loud, and her voice was unmistakable.

A black-bearded, yellow-faced landlord expounded matters in a loud, drawling harangue to casual customers at the bar, also, without exception, bilious of visage; for marshy Moonsville and the vicinity were malarial in their influences.

Outside the office, in the hall, stood the landlord's wife and daughter, with several of their female acquaintances, and the male appendages of such acquaintances. A snort was the only greeting vouchsafed to the "show people" by the ladies most intimately connected with the hotel; but one of their friends condescended so far as to say, with an indicating nod of the head, "She's in there."

Monica pushed open the door of the dining-room, and went in, followed by Della. The Human Flower sat in a chair near the table, supported by her husband, while Mr. Todd, with ardent solicitude, "spatted" her hands.

A glass of spirits and water had been tipped over, and its contents spilled upon the dirty tablecloth,

which would deck to-morrow's breakfast. A strong
smell of brandy polluted the air, and Monica was oppressed by a presentiment of imminent disaster.

"What is the matter with Mrs. Montgomery?"
she asked.

"Just the same thing that's the matter with the lot
of us, I guess," growled Mr. Todd. "That snide
Ambler has hooked it, and left the crowd here in the
lurch, without a dime among the lot of us—unless
you've got it, Miss Nairne?"

"I have got exactly three dollars in the world,"
she answered very slowly ; and Miss Free's hysterics,
which had abated in violence for an instant, alarm-
ingly increased.

Monica's generosity had won her the reputation
of possessing mysterious, but undoubted, pecuniary
resources, apart from her known professional income
of eight dollars a week. Involuntarily, the hopes of
the stricken comedians had, in this crisis, pinned
themselves to her. She had constituted herself their
banker on so many less trying occasions that it had
seemed tolerably sure that she might be counted
upon to do so again. But her tragic disclaimer carried with it so stern a ring of truth, that those who
heard it could not doubt her complete sincerity.

Not one of them, perhaps, but had been through
much the same experience before, and, somehow, had
come out of it with impunity, if not with honour.
Still, that fact did not take the sting from the present
moment of abandonment, or remove the difficulties
from the situation. It was their *métier* to display an
even greater degree of distress and anxiety than they
actually felt, that the sympathies of the landlord

(who was temporarily the arbiter of their fate) might, if possible, be enlisted.

The sensation prevailing from cellar to garret of the Jefferson Davis House was due not only to Miss Free's very creditable hysterics, but to the manner of Mr. and Mrs. Ambler's flitting. The leading lady had returned with her husband from the theatre, entered the hotel in an unostentatious, not to say stealthy, manner, had pluckily assisted her spouse to bring down their mutual trunk, and the pair had all but got off again without being detected.

At the last moment, however, just as they were stepping from the piazza to the path with their booty, the daughter of the house, returning from a stroll with her "young man," had entered the gate, and been deeply puzzled by the strange proceedings. Drawn up in the road before the hotel stood a wagon —an unusual apparition at that hour of the night— and Miss Silsbee and her lover could not help associating its presence with the inexplicable actions of the show folks.

The pair had walked rapidly up the path, after passing the two figures who struggled under the weight of their burden, had mentioned the phenomenon in the office, and been commended for their presence of mind.

Mr. Silsbee, the landlord, being a man of the world, was not long in solving the mystery.

"Carryin' out their trunk, be they?" he echoed; and, with a couple of strides which would have done credit to the owner of the seven-league-boots, was at the front door. The Amblers' luggage was just being lifted into the wagon, and Mrs. Ambler's form, black in the moonlight, was intrepidly scrambling up behind.

"Here, you dog-goned sneaks! Hi, hi, there!" yelled Mr. Silsbee, making his long legs fly down the boarded path.

But Mr. Ambler had leaped over the mud-caked wheel—no time to stop for trifles—the driver had whipped up his horse, and with incredible celerity the steed had bounded away.

Naturally, Mr. Silsbee followed to the gate and beyond, running along the side-walk, shouting to the culprits to stop, warning the conductor of the vehicle that he knew him, and would hold him up to public scorn, pouring forth strange oaths, and generally exciting the population of his native village.

Mr. Silsbee knew—no one better—that the northern express left Decaturville, a town of superior importance some four miles distant, in half an hour. He had no doubt that the eloping manager was also well aware of this fact, and meant to avail himself of it. Pursuit, save on horseback or by bicycle, would be of no avail, and Mr. Silsbee had neither horse nor bicycle. By the time he had run a quarter of a mile, to the nearest neighbour who could afford him the proper facilities, it would be too late to follow. He was " done," as he himself graphically expressed it, and it had been his retributory observations, flung at the heads of the entire company on the appearance of several of its members, which had promptly sent the Human Flower into hysterics.

Others of the comedians who had returned earlier than Monica and her companions had hastily retired to their apartments, either to assure themselves that

the Amblers had made no predatory visits, or to dis-
arm any intentions of immediate expulsion on the
landlord's part by undressing and getting into bed.

The affair was horrible to inexperienced Monica.
She was cold to the heart with the disgrace and shame
of it. Silently she stood regarding the writhing form
of the Little Human Flower—withering apparently
upon her fresh young stem—and listening with preternaturally sharp ears to the warlike threats in the
adjacent passage.

"A passel o' damned play-actors! Wal, I reckon
they'll find themselves up a tree, ef they think *I'm*
the feller to let 'em sponge on me!" The landlord
was holding forth, many of his hearers having been
among the sparse, but enthusiastic, audience lately
assembled in the hall. "Out they go, the hull dirty
pack on 'em. Damned fool I was to take a lot o'
pore white trash like them inside my house, damn
their eyes!"

"Will you turn 'em out to-night?" Monica could
hear a woman asking, in a lower voice.

"You bet your life I will. I've bin an' lost a
week's board on 'em now; an' that's the end. Out
they goes."

"You've got their baggage, anyhow," the woman's
voice suggested.

"Baggage, be damned! What good's their rotten,
stinkin' rags to me, I wanter know? What do you
think they'd fetch, ef I was to try an' sell 'em? Not
but w'at I'll *keep* 'em, though, ef just to show 'em I
ain't the kind of feller to be done, and say nothin'
about it. Lemme go, Suke; there's that Nickson
in the office spittin' out some o' his impertinent rub-
bage. I'll mighty soon shut him up!"

Heavy footsteps shuffled away, and Monica, oppressed with a clammy sensation akin to sea-sickness, supported her trembling body with a hand on the dining-table.

"What are we to do?" she asked of Mr. Montgomery, with pale lips. In the absence of the manager, it seemed that it must devolve upon him to take the lead in affairs. "Is it true what the landlord says? Can he really turn us out of the hotel?"

"Of course he can," Mr. Montgomery responded.

The Human Flower cast herself incontinently into Mr. Todd's arms and wept. Her husband watched her gloomily.

"But—but where can we go?" stammered Monica. "We have no money to go on with—we——"

"We can go to the poorhouse, I guess," said Mr. Montgomery.

"*The poorhouse!*"

Monica fell into a chair, her knees suddenly giving away from under her. Della, equally pale, and equally inexperienced in such crises as these, moved towards her beloved one tremblingly. She took her friend's hands and pressed them in silence; but the touch of the sensitive, cold fingers roused such spirit as was left in Monica.

"We mustn't—we won't submit to anything of the kind!" she exclaimed, with simulated courage. "Something must be done. Surely among us all there is money enough to pay for a few days' lodging. Mr. Montgomery can't leave his wife; but you, Mr. Crawford—you can go out and speak to the landlord. You can tell him that—that—oh, you can tell him *anything!*"

"I can't tell him nothin' that will do no good," asseverated Crawford, endeavouring to increase the chances of convincing his hearers by piling up the negatives. "I'll bet there ain't a dollar between us, except what you've got. I don't know what you want me to say."

"Oh!" Monica exclaimed, hotly. "Then I will go myself."

"Nickson's talkin' to him by now," Mr. Todd suggested; but the girl was beyond reach of further argument.

She threw open the door and passed out into the hall, followed by Della, and more slowly by Crawford.

The noise of battle proceeded from the office now, and thither she bravely took her way.

"You can kick us fellows out if you like," Nick could be heard proclaiming; "but it'll be a durned shame, crying out black agenst you as long as God lets you live, if you don't keep the women. I tell you I'll git money to pay their way sumhow, if it takes my blood."

"Pooh! Your blood ain't no kind o' use to me," returned Mr. Silsbee, almost at a loss to express his contempt. "Not so much as a hog's blood. You kin *do* sumthin' with *that*."

"By the Lord, I'll do sumthin' with yours!" yelled Nick, losing his self-control. But at that moment Monica opened the door.

"I want to speak to the landlord," she announced, lifting her voice above the disturbance. "I've got an offer to make."

They all turned toward her, for her manner commanded attention. At sight of Della, who had been loyally unwilling to let her friend venture into the lion's den alone, Nick's face flushed, and he shrank out of reach of her eyes.

"Wal, what hev ye got to say?" gruffly enquired Silsbee, in no wise retreating from the moral or physical attitude he had taken up.

"Only this. I have heard what you are threatening to do, and——"

"Wal, ain't I got a right to do it?" the man interpolated.

"Perhaps you have, in the sight of the law, and—and I haven't come to ask any favours of you, sir. But I have a few little bits of jewelry, and if they are of sufficient value, I would hold myself responsible for every one's expenses in your hotel, so long as the money lasts. By that time, no doubt, their friends will have sent them something which will help them to get away."

"Oh, you'll hold yourself responsible, will you?" echoed the landlord, reflectively. "Fur 'em all?"

"Yes," Monica said (and perhaps she might even have said the same could she have been granted a vision of the future). "Yes, for them all, while the money holds out."

"Ef the things are in her trunk, Jawge," counselled Mrs. Silsbee, "I doan't see but they're all yourn a'ready, to pay fur this last week's board. They've et an' drunk of our best, an' 'tain't half an hour ago, I give one 'o the men a good go o' brandy for his wife, who was carryin' on like a crazy woman there in the dinin'-room. I reckon thet ort ter go onto the bill."

"The things are *not* in my trunk, as it happens," Monica made indignant answer. "I have them here with me. A little black pearl watch—it cost thirty shil—seven dollars I mean ; and a pearl ring, and this gold brooch I am wearing."

" Let me look at 'em," said the landlord.

Monica tore off the ring which Eric Stannard had begged her to keep in memory of their love for each other, unfastened the plain brooch which had been her erring mother's ; and having thus shed the blood of her ewe lamb, thought little, indeed, of adding to the sacrificial pyre the watch which she had purchased in extravagant days.

Nick started forward from his place of partial concealment as she laid her little offering in the landlord's expectant hand.

" See here, Miss Nairne," he exclaimed, " you can do what you like fur the rest o' the folks; but I fur one ain't goin' to live on you, nor let you sell your bits of things to keep me. I've been in bad fixes before this, an' got out of 'em, too. This feller can keep my trunk, an' be durned. I shall live somehow, but not on *your* money—thankin' you fur my part, all the same. And if there's a man in the company with the spirit of a flea, he'll back me up, you bet."

One man of the company—Crawford—stood close at hand ; and Todd and Montgomery were listening with all their ears at the crack of the dining-room door, Miss Free having finally abandoned her hysterics. The only other male member left was poor old Pa Wilts, who had, with an eye to future emergencies, double-locked the door of his chamber and retired to bed in his most cherished clothes. But from the three to whom Nick indirectly appealed, no answering protest came. Crawford had done a good deal for

Monica Nairne during the two months of their association, and he considered that he had fully earned such
compensation as she was able to make. To be sure,
she had lent him money which it was improbable that
he would ever return—indeed, he had no intention
of making an effort to do so; but he had had no
more than he felt himself entitled to receive at her
hands.

As for the other two, they were frankly ready to
advocate the rights of women; and it was Monica's
right and privilege to minister to their comfort, since
it appeared that she possessed the wherewithal.

Nick looked at Crawford, but Crawford did not look
at Nick. Then the former shrugged his shoulders,
and, with head erect, passed Della and Monica. His
old soft felt hat had been conveniently crushed into
his pocket, but now he drew it forth with an air of de-
termination, if not of defiance, and clapped it well
over his forehead.

"Oh, Nick, where are you going?" Della impulsively cried.

Probably he did not hear the gently-breathed words,
or, if he did, he felt that Della had long ago forfeited
all right of enquiry into or control of his movements.

"*I'm* off, anyhow," he casually remarked to the
assembled multitude, without singling one out for de-
tailed explanation.

He passed out of the room. Once Della made a
slight movement, as though she would have followed,
or tried to hold him back; but her hand dropped.
Turning her face into the shadow, where the light
from the kerosene lamp with the tin reflector could
not pry into its secrets, slow tears fell from her eyes.

She had never quite lost hope that some day she and Nick might come to understand each other again. But now he was gone. He would tramp to his Pennsylvania home, perhaps. At all events, he had passed out of her life forever.

The hardships of pennilessness and contumely had seemed as nothing to her only a moment ago, because Nick had stood up for them all so nobly, in such a characteristic way, and because what had to be borne might be borne together, standing side by side. As his insignificant figure disappeared through the doorway, however, it seemed to poor Della Thomas that all the light and all the warmth had gone out of the world.

Her Angel was left to her, and that was much; but never had she realised how indispensable Nick had actually become to her happiness until she knew that he was irrevocably lost.

"Is this all you've got?" grumbled Mr. Silsbee, viewing with disparagement the ornaments displayed upon the capacious cushion of his palm.

"Yes, that is all," Monica answered. "Surely those things could be sold for enough to keep us here for a week. After that——"

"Sho!" the man interrupted. "There's eight of you left, ain't there? Wal, at four dollars a week each, which is what I was chargin' Ambler (an' dirt cheap, it was, too), that tots up to thurty-two dollars in seven days fur the lot. In the devil's name, how much do yer suppose these yere bits o' trumpery is wuth?"

Monica grew pale. She saw her beloved souvenirs sacrificed, and no practical object attained.

"I had thought they might bring thirty or forty dollars," she said, sadly. "The ring alone must have cost nearly that."

The landlord snorted ostentatiously.

"I put it to anybody in the room," he proposed. "Say, Mr. Cochrane, you'd orter know. You travelled fur Smith of Decaturville once. How much should you say was the markit valoo of these yere things—heh?"

Mr. Cochrane, an individual shrunken with malaria and clouded with quinine, advanced and inspected the articles gingerly.

"Twelve dollars fur the lot would be about the price, I reckon," he pronounced.

"H'm!" ejaculated Mr. Silsbee, relapsing into mental calculation. "You hear what the gentleman says? I guess there ain't no doubtin' *his* word, whether yer'd be inclined to take mine or not. My prices is more by the day than they is by the week. That's so at all first-class hotels. At seventy-five cents a day apiece, twelve dollars would last you eight folks two days, Sunday and Monday. You kin deposit these yere ornerments with me, or you kin try an' sell 'em yourself, when the chances are ye woan't git even as much as that fur 'em. Anyhow, there's where it stands. You seem to kinder want to do the squar' thing by me, so I'll take yer trunks fur this last week's board, up to ter-night—no matter ef I *do* lose on it, an' I'll keep you folks till Tuesday mornin'. I reckon 'tain't many men you'd git to do as much as that."

Monica turned to Crawford in despair. The instinct of the female to appeal to the superior business qualfications of the male was inherent in her, and

Crawford was the only one of whom she could ask advice.

"What shall I do?" she implored.

"I guess we'll have to take up with what we can git," he replied, at once putting himself into partnership with her.

"Very well," she resumed, desperately. "Keep the things, then, and let us all stay here until Tuesday."

She would have wished to sell the jewelry herself, or commission Crawford to do so, but she feared that the landlord might be right, that a local dealer would offer less than the price suggested by Mr. Cochrane, who had travelled for Smith of Decaturville. She must not miss the insignificant substance for an illusive, if tempting, shadow; and so she shut her eyes upon the objects which had been so dear to her.

Having seen them pocketed by Mr. Silsbee— shortly after to be annexed by wife and daughter— she clasped Della's sympathetic arm, and, scarcely knowing whether she might deem herself successful or a failure, she wended her way dolefully back to the dining-room.

The Montgomerys and Mr. Todd were still there, having been torn between conflicting desires. One bade them flee to their respective bedrooms, and conceal such articles as they needed most among their personal belongings. The other, even more potent, prevailed upon them to remain and listen to what passed between Monica and her dragon. After all, there was little in their hotel trunks which was absolutely essential to their comfort. They had lived before and could live again without night-gear, or brushes and combs; and old habits of precaution had accustomed them to trusting such things as they valued most to the protection of their theatre trunks.

A gloomy group of five collected about Monica in the dining-room, Mr. Wilts and Mrs. Patton alone being missed among the remnant of the shattered company.

"What are we to do?" questioned the preserver of the common fortunes. "The evil day is only put off. Have any of you friends at home to whom you can write and borrow money?"

There was a general shaking of heads. Mr. and Mrs. Montgomery had no home; Mr. Todd had been disowned by his relatives for reasons; and Mr. Crawford's pecuniary necessities had long ago drawn from a doting aunty all possible financial aid.

As for Della, when she had had money, she had sent away all that she could spare. Nothing was to be hoped for from the bugbear step-mother or the henpecked father.

"Couldn't we go on playing at the theatre," suggested Monica, "and make a little something for ourselves?"

"No good," responded Mr. Montgomery. "Crowe's Minstrels have got the hall fur the first three nights o' next week. If they was a decent set o' folks they might help us, bein' brother professionals; but they're a low lot, with a reg'lar skunk for a manager. They won't do more'n enough business, either, to get out o' town themselves."

"Then what's to become of us all after Tuesday?" Monica asked, with no hope of what the answer might be.

"The Lord alone knows," said Mr. Montgomery,

with unusual devoutness, "unless—unless—now, *you* could see your way to writin' to some of your rich friends."

"I have no rich friends," the girl returned hastily ; but a look went round the room, and she knew what it meant. They were all thinking of the wealthy admirer who had actually paid eight dollars for two nights in a stage-box, and who had given a dinner in his private car, described by Mrs. Ambler as having surpassed the wildest dreams of magnificence. They were wondering why she did not summon him by electricity to her aid and their aid in this dilemma ; but she would not do it. She had refused his love —she could not ask for his money. Whatever happened to them all, that course would be impossible.

She was silent, though four pairs of eyes were fixed upon her downcast face.

Upstairs uncouth sounds of bumping and dragging heavy articles along uncarpeted floors told that the trunks were being taken over by the landlord for their owners' debts.

CHAPTER XX.

*"Why lamb, why lady! fie, you slug-a-bed! Madame, sweet-
heart! What, not a word?"*

NEXT morning Della was ill. She was subject to
terrible headaches, which prostrated her for twenty-
four hours at a stretch, during which time she lay
silent, with closed eyes and swollen, purple lids. But
to-day, when Monica stole like a hunted thing up the
stairway on the verandah to her friend's bedroom on
the floor above, strange murmurings and fitful bursts
of laughter answered her knock upon the door. She
opened it fearfully at last, wondering if Mrs. Montgomery had for once overcome her predilection for
late hours, and come forth for an early chat with the
pianist.

To her amazement, Della was alone, tossing on the
bed, uncovered, but in the clothes she had worn the
night before. Her hair hung in brilliant disordered
masses about her flushed face, the hairpins, which
had not been removed, tangled in its meshes here
and there. Both arms were flung above her head, and
her beautiful hands, of which she was so innocently
vain, played a fantasia upon the brightly-painted bed-
stead.

"Why, Della!" Monica exclaimed miserably, struck
with a sense of desolation in the midst of her sorrow
for her friend, at finding herself bereft of the conso-

lation and sympathy for which she had yearned.
" Della, dearest girl, what's the matter? Don't you
know me?"

"I can't play it any faster," muttered Della. "It's
in the wrong time, and the wrong key, too!"

The wrong key! Yes, everything in life seemed to
be in the wrong key now. Tears rose to Monica's
eyes, and lay on the surface without falling, like little
shining lakes. She went quickly to the bed, and took
in her own one of the hands that drummed upon the
head-board. The touch of it fairly scorched her, and,
when she laid soft cool fingers on the upturned forehead, it too was burning hot, and moved restlessly
from side to side under the light pressure. Monica
felt suddenly alone in the world. There was no Della
to comfort her. All her strength and all her resources
would be taxed to help this poor, wild, delirious, dishevelled creature on the bed.

The sick girl had stopped playing with the hand
that Monica had felt, and seemed feeling with it for
something which she expected to find among the
tumbled bed clothes.

" I haven't got any photograph of you, Nick, like
Angel has of her sweetheart," she went on piteously;
"but you never asked for this back again, so I kep'
it. I guess you've forgotten long ago, but *I* ain't—I
sha'n't forget, ever, ever, ever."

Her voice rose to a wail at the end. She had found
what she sought, and seemed aimlessly to be convey-
ing it toward her dry, parted lips. It was only a grey
woollen sock, carefully darned, which in old days Nick
had given her to mend for him.

Monica looked on, astonished. Despite their many

girlish confidences, each had guarded the secret nearest her own heart, and Orestes had never dreamed that
Pylades had a carking sorrow to conceal.

Down on her knees she went beside the bed, and
the lake of tears overflowed the banks of her sad eyes.

" Poor Della! poor, dear old Della!" she sooth-
ingly said; but Della's ears for once were closed to
her, and Della's dim eyes, though staring into hers,
saw only one who was far away.

"You're so kind to come back to me, Nick," the
sick girl babbled on. " I thought you would some
day, maybe. You didn't understand. I couldn't
have you in the room. Angel wouldn't have liked it,
and I owe her even more than you, Nick, so I just
had to wait; but now it's all right, ain't it ? "

"Yes, dear, it's all right," Monica echoed, with a
sob in her throat. " It's all—right."

She got up from her knees and walked to the window, looking out on the pink and white radiance of
the apple trees in the orchard behind the hotel. It
was so very far from right really, and it was so hard
to know what to do. Nick was gone—where, she
could not tell; and she was afraid that Della was going to be really ill.

Monica had never seen any one who was delirious
before. It seemed to her a terrible thing, and she
was sorely frightened in her loneliness with this new
responsibility laid upon her shoulders.

If only this could have happened at some other
time, it would have been comparatively simple; but
now, when there was no money for a doctor or for
medicines, the misfortune of sudden illness seemed
little less than appalling. Things had been bad

enough before, but this was the last straw. Perhaps there was *always* a last straw! And to think that all this time she should have been selfish enough, blind enough, to have been keeping a pair of lovers apart— to have found it out only when it was too late!

The girl had had no experience of illness, and knew not what to do; but a gentle feminine instinct bade her smooth out Della's tangled hair, pluck away the sharp hairpins (it would not do to *throw* them away— no one knew when more might be forthcoming), open the tight collar of the dress, and turn the pillows that were so hot and tumbled.

As she did so, her brain also was busy searching ways and means,—how to have Della cared for as she must be cared for; how to soften the landlord's heart, and keep him from putting the sufferer out into the street when the time of indulgence should be up. Suddenly and joyously she remembered that she had still three dollars in her purse. With that sum she could call in a doctor, buy such medicines as he should prescribe, and perhaps have enough remaining to keep Della for an extra day at the hotel; for the others, hardships did not seem so much to matter now.

She had no longer a watch, but she guessed the hour to be about half-past seven. Some of the people must be up by this time. Mrs. Montgomery never rose early, and invariably had her breakfast carried to her in her bedroom by her melancholy and well-trained husband. Mrs. Patton, however, was generally the first one to make her appearance at the table, and to her Monica would go now. She was reluctant to leave Della alone, even for a moment; but there was nothing else to be done, as she herself must either run for a doctor, or find some one else who would be ready to go in her place.

There was Crawford, for instance. She had decided last night that she must break with him at once and completely. His attitude when adjured by the spirited Nick had increased the disgust she had already begun to feel for him, and she shrank from the man with a stronger aversion than before. But this was not a time to let her personal feelings interfere with Della's welfare, and she told herself that Crawford's services must be utilised again.

She ran to Mrs. Patton's door, and, regardless of the fact that that lady's teeth reposed in a tumbler of water on the bureau, insisted upon her proceeding without delay to Della's room. With or without teeth, it did not signify, if only she kept her wits, would hold her tongue, and use her hands.

Then on Monica sped to find Crawford, who had shared a bed-chamber with Nick, adjoining one recently occupied by Mr. and Mrs. Ambler. To her surprise the door was open. She called, without venturing to look in.

" Mr. Crawford ! Oh, Mr. Crawford ! "

No answer came, but some one was stumbling heavily upstairs. Out of doors, Sabbath bells were ringing, and it was morning, grey and green, with softly falling mists of earthy-smelling rain. But here in the passage-way night appeared still to linger. The very shadows seemed sodden with the odours of stale beer, and liquors kept in casks, that rose pungently from the office immediately below. The feet that shufflingly mounted, step by step, the plungings of some solid body against the protesting balusters, the

rubbing of a groping hand along the wall, all struck
Monica as belonging to the dank spell of darkness
that enveloped the whole place.

She called Crawford's name for the third time, hoping that he might yet come forth from his room, or
perhaps from another near by ; and, though no door
opened, she heard his voice answering thickly close at
hand.

"Hullo! comin'!" he said ; and then, from the top
of the stairs, he lurched towards her.

It was plain to see that he had not troubled his
bed during the night lately past, and wherever the
money to get drunk upon had come from, it was evident that liquor had not been spared.

His eyes, under heavy lids, dwelt vacantly upon
her. His lower lip hung stupidly down and the smile
which he tried to give did not not lift it. He
dragged himself along, with a hand scraping against
the wall.

"Heard you a-callin'," he mumbled. "'Ud allays
hear you, Princess, no matter—no matter what—but
never—hic!—never mind. Can't shay all—should like
to. Been—been talkin' things over with—fellers
downstairs—makin'—hic!—makin' a night of it. Wha'
—what can do for you, swee—sweetest?"

Monica shrank from him with a shudder that ran
coldly through her veins. He reached towards her
shoulder, with a large red hand, over which the shining skin seemed tightly stretched ; but she started
away in time to escape it.

"You can do *nothing* for me," she said, icily.
"Nothing now, or in future ; please remember that."

As he called after her, and followed, staggering,

she ran from him along the passage through which she had come, and which led to the "L" in which her own room and Della's were situated. She could hear his heavy boots clattering uncertainly in pursuit, and suddenly she turned and faced him.

"Not another step!" she commanded, in a tone she would have used to some disobedient mongrel cur. "Do not dare to come after me!"

Many things can a woman forgive in the man she loves; but one thing which, in the man she does *not* love, can never be either forgotten or forgiven is permitting her to see him soaked in the vileness of intoxication.

Her look, her gesture, and her words, went far towards sobering him; but the barrier of her repulsion kept him from her. Supporting himself by some one else's door-knob, and swaying as he stood, he watched her turn again and go from him; then, slouching back in the direction from which he had come, he slunk into his bedroom like a whipped hound.

After all, it was her fault, he dully told himself. How she had spoken to him the night before, when he tried to help her out of the mud! How she had looked at him, when Nick had called upon all the men of the company to do as he did! All that, on top of the general misfortune that had overtaken the company —was it any wonder if he took a little something to drown thought? She ought to be sorry for him, and beg his forgiveness, that she ought; but her heart —why, there wasn't anything on earth hard enough to liken it to! She had better look out for herself. She'd find he wasn't the sort of man who would stand being treated like a d—d dog, she would.

But, thus encouraging himself with loud mutterings against Monica and Fate, he lay down on his hard bed, and was soon snoring with stertorous regularity.

The girl took her hat and went out into the street. The gently falling rain revived her, as it softly sprayed against her upturned face.

In the direction of the theatre she recalled having seen a painted signboard advertising the residence of a doctor, and she was glad to be relieved of the necessity for questioning any one in the hotel.

As she hurried along, it occurred to her to recount the money on which she was depending. There ought to be three dollars in her purse, she knew ; but it was possible that beside the pair of greenbacks, the silver fifty-cent piece, and the two quarter dollars with which she had for long been on friendly terms, there might be an extra dime or so, which would prove particularly acceptable in this crisis.

She opened the shabby little pocket-book with eager fingers and with anxious eyes. The two bills were there, safely rolled together ; but her throat contracted with a sudden spasm of dismay at the emptiness of the next compartment. A small, round, solitary dime (value ten cents) had strayed into a corner. In the other was a larger, though less intrinsically precious "nickel." She had been robbed of eighty-five cents, almost a third of her possessions, and more than enough to have bought Della an entire day at the hotel.

How it could have happened she was for a few moments at a loss to imagine, and in her perplexity she passed the doctor's house without seeing it. What had she spent yesterday? Only a few pennies for a reel of cotton, which she and Della had bought together. Crawford had been with them. They had wandered out of the village, plucking violets. He had offered to keep her purse for her, as she had no pocket, and her hands had been fully occupied with flowers. She had given it to him, and then forgotten all about it. Hours had passed before he had come to her door and tossed the purse on to an adjacent table.

The girl sickened as she recalled each bit of evidence which pointed toward Crawford as the petty thief. She would so gladly have given or lent him the money if he had asked, but that he should *take* it from her—the girl he was supposed to worship as a star set in high heaven—was too much. Once she had heard a whisper of gossip which surreptitiously accused the young man as a "picker up of unconsidered trifles"; but he had been high in her favour in those days, and she had disregarded it as slander. Now, however, the words came back to her, and with bitter scorn and loathing she told herself that it was on *her* money that Crawford had, in his own words, been "making a night of it."

CHAPTER XXI.

MONICA did not like the doctor. He had not the soft, slow ways of the Southerner, but had come from the North avowedly to coin money by his own brains and his neighbours' lack of them. He was, however, the only practitioner in Moonsville, the kindly old physician, whose face had been known in the village since the first pine shanties began to go up, having died but a few weeks before. Dr. Henry Hart could scarcely have borne a less appropriate appellation; but he was a man who knew his business, and meant, as soon as he could screw enough money out of Moonsville's malaria to do so, to carry his accomplishments to a more congenial sphere.

He had not been at Della's bedside five minutes before he pronounced her to be suffering from acute congestion of the brain, complicated by malarial symptoms. Her system was evidently run down, and though she had not complained, doubtless she had been suffering for days. Now she must have good care, the best of nursing day and night, well-cooked nourishing food, with certain luxuries, such as ice—which could easily be obtained from Decaturville—or her illness might assume a serious if not perilous form.

"Could she be moved without danger on Tuesday?" Monica inquired, in a strained voice.

Dr. Hart, who was of an age and type not easily impressed by a woman's fascinations, looked at her as though she were a new and peculiar form of excrescence.

"Nonsense!" he said, sharply. "You may begin to talk of moving her perhaps, if all goes well, by Tuesday week—very likely not even then."

Monica was silent. When the doctor was ready to go, she handed him one of her two remaining dollars, which he accepted with a short "thank you." She must send out for the medicines at once, he warned her. And he would call again in the evening.

In these country districts, and with strangers, physicians claimed their fees "on the nail," unless they were of lenient dispositions and generously saw reason to do otherwise. But Dr. Henry Hart never did see reason to do otherwise.

When the medicines had been purchased at the drug store round the corner (which was open for one hour out of twelve on Sunday), the surplus fund would not suffice to pay the doctor for another visit.

Fear, deadly cold and heavy as the putrid burden which hung round the neck of the Ancient Mariner, weighed on Monica's heart. Through the long hours as she sat by Della's bedside, listening to the sick girl's murmurings, she thought and thought, until the wheels of her mental machinery refused to turn.

What was to become of them all, especially of poor Della? What could they do? Surely there must be some way out of the dilemma, if she could only find it! There was *one* way out, indeed, which kept constantly recurring to her, though she would as often put it from her mind; but, at last, as the time drew near for the doctor to make his appearance, and Mrs. Patton had come up from the supper-table to sit with the invalid, she dragged herself wearily downstairs.

In the office, doing Sunday penance over a newspaper, sat the landlord alone, his chair tilted back against the wall, under the light of the reflector lamp.

Monica hesitated in the doorway for a moment, and was almost resolved to go away again, leaving her errand undone, when Mr. Silsbee raised his eyes and fastened them upon her.

"I should be much obliged to you," she said desperately, "if you would let me get something out of my trunk. Nothing of any value, I assure you. You may come with me if you wish and see exactly what I take."

"I doan't know about thet," he pronounced, with a not unpleasant sense of his own authority. "There wasn't no such agreement made. You can tell me, though, what it is you want to hev, and then I reckon I'll think it over."

"It's only an old shoe that has no mate," she answered, suppressing her indignation. "I—I have promised to send it away."

An hour later, a small, oddly-shaped brown paper parcel, stamped with five dearly bought stamps, and addressed to John Randolph, Esq., Denver, Colorado, was ready to go out with the early letters from the hotel to the post office.

"It is for Della," Monica reminded herself, as she had done before when the first five pounds had been reft from the sacred thirty. And when the doctor

called and grumbled because his fee was not forthcoming, he was earnestly assured that his bill would
be paid in the course of a few days.

The landlord's further indulgence was also purchased
on similar terms. A message had gone, he was informed, to Colorado, which, with absolute certainty,
would result in the most satisfactory manner at the
very earliest moment when an answer might be received. Two days must be allowed for the message
to reach its destination, and two days more, or even
three, might elapse before a reply could come. But
at the end of that time there would be money in
plenty to discharge all past and present indebtedness,
and, therefore, it would be greatly to Mr. Silsbee's
advantage to let the company remain under his inhos-
pitable roof.

So decided was Monica's manner in making this
statement, and so practical had been her former efforts
towards the salvation of her companions, that the
landlord was inclined to accept her proposition.
Things might remain as they were until the Monday
following the date previously set for the show folks'
exodus, but not a day longer. If by that morning
relief had not arrived, the company must go, leaving
their theatre trunks as well as their hotel luggage behind them.

Firmly as Monica had spoken, there had been
doubts in her heart, which she had not dared to
betray.

When Randolph had left her in February he had
said that he was going abroad for a few weeks.
Possibly he had not yet returned; or, if he had, he
might not necessarily be at home in Denver. The

poor shoe might have to tramp half across America before it found him, and accomplished that errand which brooked no delay. When Randolph opened the parcel he would lose no time in obeying its dumb summons she was sure, even though he had ceased to care for her as once he had professed to do. He was true and dependable, and he would come, whatever change might have taken place in his feelings; but her fear was that he would come too late.

Still, she had sent the shoe to perform its mission, and she had not hesitated to deal with her hopes as though they had been certainties. At worst, there would be a respite of nearly a week, and even if the deluge came after, meanwhile Della's life might have been saved.

Monica's action was known and approved by the company. To whom she had written they were not sure, but they were profoundly impressed by the conviction that Miss Nairne's supply of rich friends was unfailing, and that she had but to ask and receive.

So the days crawled on. When the week was half over, Della's delirium had subsided, but the pain in her head remained; she could not sleep, and sometimes her teeth chattered in a malarial chill that quickly gave place to fever.

Monica seldom left the sick-room, and had seen nothing of any members of the company save Mrs. Patton and Fanny Free, who were both ready to do their clumsy best in the way of nursing.

By Wednesday, she had carefully calculated, it was barely possible that she might receive a telegram from Randolph. She had not enclosed a line in her parcel, but she knew that the postmark would tell

him where she might be found. The day passed,
however, and nothing came. On Thursday he might
actually arrive. Each footstep creaking by the door
made her start, always expecting that it would stop,
and that she should hear the news which now, despite
her shamed reluctance in sending for him, she had
come to long for beyond all other things.

But the steps went on, and there was no news for
her. By Friday night the face of Mr. Silsbee became
ominously overcast. During meal times on Saturday
and Sunday he stood in the dining-room door, and
watched each mouthful of his food as it was carried
to the self-conscious lips of the unfortunate barn
stormers.

Monica could eat nothing; and through the endless
hours of the night she sat, never sleeping, by Della's
side. *She* was the guilty one. She had undertaken
the burden of responsibility for all, and she had failed
them. To-morrow they must go. No further grace
could be obtained, and, as there was no hospital
within many miles, she could see nothing for it but
that Della should be taken to the poorhouse. She,
Monica, would go with her, of course; but perhaps
she might not even be allowed to nurse her sick friend
in that place whose very name was like some evil,
preposterous dream.

The grey light of dawn crept in through the staring, uncurtained window, and touched the sharpened
outlines of Della's face. The closed eyelids shone
white as the drifted petals of flowers in the dark hollows of their sockets, and all the pretty dimples had
gone from the hand which lay helplessly curved upon
the blue calico coverlet.

Monica laid her own hand beside it. It, too, was thin and eager-looking, she thought, like that of a miser. At all events, she and poor Della had done but little execution among these provisions which the landlord grudged!

The girl felt very weary and old. It seemed a strange thing to her that there should be thousands of other girls in the world waking up to this morning with joyous anticipations of one more pleasure about to come into their happy, inconsequent lives. She and Della were going to the poorhouse. It was very difficult to make it seem true—such a queer, irrelevant sort of thing, such as one read about over a comfortable breakfast-table of one's own, saying, " How sad! " and taking another sip of coffee, the sort of thing that happened only to the people one didn't know, or ever could know—the *other people* whose troubled lives were necessary to fill up newspapers for the public's reading.

And yet it was now going to happen to her. The light of morning, growing even brighter, and even suggesting possibilities of crude, yellow sunshine, seemed a cruel reminder that the hour had come. Perhaps people who were going to be hanged felt rather more uncomfortable than she did ; but she was inclined to doubt it, and class the sensations in much the same category.

Randolph would be sorry when he knew—but perhaps he would never know. At all events, in an hour or two more the house would be stirring, and it would be too late. Poor Della would be carried away without any breakfast, perhaps, for all her broth was gone. Monica wondered, dimly, what sort of breakfasts they gave you in the poorhouse, and how, when unfortunate wretches had once got in there, they managed to get out again.

Della stirred in her sleep, which had lasted for several hours now, murmuring a name that Monica knew without hearing. The tired watcher laid her dark head down on the pillow beside the auburn one, just for a moment she meant it to be; but the miserable waking fancies transformed themselves into dreams; and the light grew brighter, and still Monica lay motionless.

She was brought back to consciousness again by a tapping as of long finger-nails, or a bird's beak, on the door, and, half dazed with sleep, flew to open it, lest the continued noise should rouse Della. It was Mrs. Patton who stood on the verandah, unkempt and incongruous in the morning sunshine. By the look on her withered face, and the drop of moisture that hung neglected on the end of her nose, like the thawing of a pointed icicle, Monica knew that there was bad news in store for her.

"Well?" she questioned anxiously, stepping out on the verandah and closing the door. "Well?"

"That's just what it *ain't*," mourned Mrs. Patton. "It's nine o'clock, and Todd's been to the post office. There ain't no letters fur you, nor none of us; and the train's in from the west. There won't be no other till night, and before *that*——"

"Yes," Monica broke in, with a certain impatience. "I know what is likely to happen before that. Here comes Mrs. Silsbee to tell us all about it now, I fancy."

It was indeed the small black walnut of hair at the back of that lady's head which shone in a sudden glint of riotous southern sunlight, as she advanced up the stairs.

A curious frozen resignation settled bleakly down upon Monica. She criticised the pattern of the landlady's calico wrapper, and noticed that there was a hole in her stocking, which permitted a glimpse of dry, yellow skin, where the flapping slipper was down at the heel.

"Good-morning, Mrs. Silsbee," she heard herself coolly saying.

"*Good*-mornin'!" snapped the dame. "My husbin' told me to come up yere, and ask what you thought of doin'?"

Monica smiled a chilly smile, which felt as though it might have fitted some one else's face better than her own.

"Thank him for us, please, will you?" she responded. "And kindly ask him what would be *his* advice in the matter."

Mrs. Silsbee's countenance grew sullen. It was really very odd, Monica thought, that she had never noticed before how much it resembled that of a rocking-horse, quite a cheap rocking-horse, with spots of red paint for nostrils, and hasty flourishes of dark paint over the eyes.

"There ain't no advice about it," drawled the disagreeable voice. "We can't keep you folks no longer, and there ain't no kinder use to talk."

"Very well, then," returned Monica, "we won't talk. Though I *should* have liked Mr. Silsbee's advice as to how this poor sick girl is to be——"

"Suke! Say, Suke, be you up thair?" shouted the landlord from below stairs.

Mrs. Silsbee doubled herself over the rough balustrade.

"Ya-as, I be."

—"Wa'al, then, tell the folks there's a gent down yere callin' for Miss Neerne."

All the ice of cold resignation to the inevitable which had hardened Monica's heart, and seemed to stiffen her very muscles, suddenly melted, and left her trembling and half fainting. She could hear the blood singing in her ears, feel it pulsing through the full veins in her temples. *He had come.*

She leaned against the door-post, and closed her eyes for an instant or two.

"Tell him—tell Mr. Silsbee to say I—I will see him at once," she managed to say.

Mrs. Silsbee roared the information as requested, and Monica mechanically started toward the stairs.

"Mrs. Patton, you will—sit by Della, won't you?" she stammered, a strange little fluttering in the throat interfering with the even tenor of her words.

"That's what I come for," said Mrs. Patton. "But say, child, ain't you a-goin' to fix yourself up a bit before you go into the parlour? I guess I would if I was you."

For the first time in her life, perhaps, Monica had been absolutely oblivious of her own appearance.

The little grey cloth frock had reached the extreme of shabbiness at last. It had been crumpled by its wearer at Della's bedside night after night; for the dainty dressing-gown, together with many other luxuries (once fondly thought to be necessities) reposed in the trunk confiscated a week ago by Mr Silsbee for the unpaid board.

Vaguely, hardly conscious of what she was doing, the girl splashed cold water over face and hands, brushed back the wandering hair from her heavy eyes, and then, vexed at finding she had aimlessly repeated the same process over again, she hurried along the verandah to a door that opened into the main building of the hotel.

The parlour was at the back. He would be there —he who had come to save her, and save them all— he whom she—to whom she was so deeply grateful. In just one moment more she should see him again. She fumbled with the knob, but her hand trembled so that she could not turn it. Some one inside had impatiently pushed back a chair, and was walking briskly across the floor to her assistance. The door opened inward, and Monica, clinging to it, lost her balance, and pitched dizzily into somebody's outstretched arms.

For a second she lay there, realising her own utter weakness.

"Let me go," she said softly. "Oh, Mr. Randolph —it was good, oh, *how* good of you to come!"

"Great heavens! my dear girl, whom do you take me for?" queried an astonished voice.

Monica, quivering from head to foot, looked up into Mr. Silas Jewett's handsome, middle-aged countenance.

CHAPTER XXII.

"It may be you have mistaken him, my lord!"

"And shall do so, even though I took him at's prayers. . . The soul of this man is in his clothes. Trust him not in matters of heavy consequence."

"JACK RANDOLPH'S gallivanting around on the other side of the ocean," he announced, cheerily. "I'm sorry, though, if you'd rather have him than me."

"I was expecting him," she said, simply. She was erect enough now, and the dizziness had gone—but hope had gone with it. Had not she just heard that Randolph was "gallivanting around on the farther side of the ocean"?

"Oh, if that's all!" ejaculated Mr. Jewett, with a brilliant smile. "Unexpected things are just as welcome sometimes as the other kind, I hope. Do sit down, Miss Nairne. You're as white as a little ghost, and you look ready to drop. If this old duffer of a landlord here has been treating you badly, why, I'll make things hot for him, that's all."

"You've heard, then?" faltered Monica.

"Heard everything, I guess. Had a letter from Ambler in Chicago, telling me what was up, and asking me to lend him some money; but I knew a dodge worth two of that. I just came right down here instead to see what I could do for you. I was ready to

kick myself because I hadn't had the sense to give
you my address, in case of anything, knowing you're
a stranger on this side of the water, and might be in
need of a friend. But I hope you thought I'd come
the moment I heard what was going on, didn't you?"

"No, I didn't," Monica confessed. "I didn't think
of it at all. You see, you were Mrs. Ambler's friend,
and——"

Jewett laughed aloud, wrinkling up his well-shaped
nose in a rather disagreeable fashion he had.

"Say, did I really fool you as much as that?" he
exclaimed.

The girl looked at him in a puzzled way.

"I don't think I quite understand you."

His large, yellow-grey eyes fell aside from hers.

"I couldn't have hung around this company as
much as I did without making talk," he said, "unless
everybody had thought I was spoons on the manager's
wife. But it wasn't that fat old woman that I was
dangling after. I—" (with a quick look he searched
her face, which was grave and preoccupied), "well, it
doesn't matter. There was always—er—something
about theatrical people that kind of fascinated me;
and then, I was sorry for you. You see, I'm old
enough to be sorry for a pretty girl. And now I've
come down here, post haste, to do anything for you I
can—*anything*. I guess I'll begin by paying the hotel
bills; but mind, Miss Nairne, whatever I do, I do out
of friendship for *you*."

Monica sat very still in her corner of the sofa. He
had moved from his chair, and seated himself on the
same article of furniture, and she knew that his eyes
were upon her; but she would not look up.

"I can't bear to have you put it that way," she said, in a low, distressful voice.

"But it *is* for you. It's for you and your eyes, that are like those of another woman I used to know ever so long ago. Wouldn't you rather take it from me than leave everybody in trouble and misery, when you could save them just as well as not?"

This was hardly the method that the Marquis of Carabas would have chosen, and Monica felt it though she might not have been able to express the subtle difference in words.

"I've been making enquiries," he went on, "and I know something of what you've had to go through. I know how sick your friend's been, and all. Why, it might make her go off like that" (he snapped his finger and thumb together) "if she had to be moved to—to some uncomfortable place, where she couldn't be properly looked after even now. I'll tell you what I'll do if you like, Miss Nairne. I'll pay the bills, first of all, and get you back the luggage you've been doing without. Then Miss Thomas shall have everything on earth her soul can wish for. She'll be up and about in three days on some of the tonics we'll get in for her from Decaturville. Everybody'll be so happy and grateful to you that they'll be ready to fall down and kiss the dust off your pretty little shoes; for it will be *you* that's done it, and nobody else.

"Well, then, when all's as jolly as can be, we'll organise a new company, get a new advance man, and have some splendid paper down from Chicago, with you billed as the star. And we'll go to big towns, too—none of your little tenth-rate mud-pie villages like this and the rest you have seen. Why, you'd be looked on as a regular angel! Not only would you get the crowd out of their scrape, but start them off with a new engagement, which, at this time of the year, they might starve before they'd find otherwise. How do you like the idea?"

Monica was utterly taken by surprise. She was grateful, yet doubting. The man was so voluble, so plausible, the way out of the slough of despond seemed made so easy, and yet—and yet—!

"I wish you would leave me out of the matter entirely, or at least as much as possible," she said. "You know how much I would thank you for any-thing you did for the people. I—I have suffered so dreadfully this last week, and I haven't slept or eaten much. My brain doesn't seem quite so clear or quick to think as usual, but——"

"Let me think for you," he pleaded. And then he took one small cold hand between his two large warm ones. It struggled a little in a vain effort to free itself, but at last lay still. After all, Mr. Jewett was quite an old man, as he had said—old enough to be her father.

"I'm sufficiently frank to confess," he continued, "that I don't care a hang about the company. They can starve, for me. But I should like to do some-thing for you, and I've just tried to tell you what I stand ready to undertake. There, now, don't look so worried! You can pay me back, you know. Every-thing shall be managed in the most ship-shape way. You shall sign a paper, which I will give you, and then, when your show begins bringing in money—as it's sure to do with you for the ' star '—you can wipe off all the indebtedness, if you like to call it so."

Monica brightened visibly. She was the most un-business-like young woman in the world, and to her Mr. Silas Jewett's exposition of his plans began to sound both disinterested and attractive.

"Oh, if you will let me do *that*," she exclaimed. "And you really think money might be made, by re-organising the company?"

"Of course I think so. Then you give me *carte blanche* to make myself happy, and everybody else happy, in your name?"

"That is what you Americans would call a large order, isn't it?" she said, trying to be merry and at ease. But she had gone through too much. Her lips trembled, and tears filled her eyes. She turned away her head to hide them. It was very ungrateful, no doubt, but she grudged owing her thanks to this man, instead of to Randolph—Randolph, who had forgotten her perhaps, in his 'gallivantings on the other side of the ocean!' "You are very good," she added, with a sigh. "You must do what you think best. I believe I am too tired out even to think."

"That's a dear girl, to trust me!" Jewett ejaculated. And Monica, wishing he would not call her a "dear girl," felt at the same time that after all that had passed, it might be ungrateful to resent it.

"You'll be surprised," he continued, trying to stroke a small evasive hand, which apologetically yet decidedly slipped away from him, "how soon things will be set going. Bills paid in twenty minutes; confidence restored. Comforts of all sorts, and a trained nurse got down from Decaturville for Miss Thomas—*your* present to her; one hour more. Meanwhile, telegrams sent to Chicago to an agent I know there for a good advance man, and as many new people as you want, all to report here, in three day's time. As soon as paper comes, letters written (by me) to managers of theatres in good-sized towns, for immediate dates. Rehearsals begin—advance man goes off—Miss Thomas gets well—everything ready to start, with a boom, a week from to-day. We might open with a couple of new plays here, just to see how things work—principle of trying on a dog, you know. I suppose you'd want all the present people to stay on, wouldn't you, Star?"

She was beginning to be fired by his enthusiasm; or, at least, she felt that she ought to be, and would be after she had had one good cry, and perhaps an hour's sleep.

"Oh, of course we must have them all, poor things!" she began; and then she stopped, with an abrupt drawing in of the breath. "Except—there is *one* man I do not feel that I can have anything more to do with," she hesitatingly went on. "If we could pay him something—give him enough to get home with, and live upon until he found another engagement, our consciences would be clear; and—it would be *such* a relief to have seen the last of him. I could never, never act with Mr. Crawford again."

"Then, you sha'n't. I remember him—bold-looking fellow. It'll be pleasure to take the responsibility of sending him off, if only because of the charming little way you had of associating me with yourself, saying 'we' and 'our.'"

Monica flushed vividly. It would have been much pleasanter if Mr. Jewett had not persisted in making remarks of this nature, and if he would have sat a little farther away ; but beggars could not be choosers, and he meant to be so kind. Some people could not speak without flattering—but it was only a trifling fault of manner, after all.

"You will tell him, then?" she asked, rising. "I don't want to be unkind; but—something happened a few days ago which has made me feel I can hardly bear even to see him again. Whatever you do will be right—about that, and all the other things, I know. And now, I must go—back to Della."

"I must go, too," he briskly replied, "and begin to get matters in train. Give me your hand for good-bye, or rather *au revoir*, as I shall be constantly obliged to consult my new star."

She gave him her hand, and he kissed it gallantly. As he did so, and she drew it softly away, the old feeling of having seen him before, or having passed through some such experience as this, with which he had had an intimate connection, darted through her brain, with a faintly distasteful pang. She seemed to see herself, as a little child, standing beside a woman, and clutching the skirt of her gown, as she looked wonderingly up, to see a man bend and touch his lips to beautiful, white, jewelled fingers. The picture was gone, like a flashing scheme of colour in a kaleido-scope, almost before she had fixed it upon her mental retina, and she would have felt at a loss even to de-scribe what it had been. But the oddly disagreeable impression remained.

Slowly, still discussing the lightening future, they went to the door together, and Monica paused for an instant to watch Mr. Jewett walking with a determined air toward the office, where he would find the landlord, and proceed to wipe the debts of the company off the slate.

He looked back once over his shoulder to nod encouragingly to the girl as she stood gazing after him; and then, stepping across the threshold, was lost to sight.

Monica, too, would have turned, but, hardly had the door of the office closed upon Jewett's soldierly form when it opened for the exit of a familiarly insignificant one.

"Why, Mr. Nickson!" Monica cried out, excitedly.

They had never had very much to say to each other, these two representatives of widely-severed classes, but she felt at this moment wondrously overjoyed to see him. They had never touched each other's fingers, even in the exigencies of stage life—the juvenile lead and the shy comedian—but now Monica held out both hands to him.

He took them as though they had been remote and dreaded contingencies; and having shaken them up and down two or three times in a conscientious manner, which might have been effective with a pump handle of unyielding disposition, he replaced them at her sides.

"Thank you, Miss Nairne," he said, devoutly. "Say, could I have a few words with you, or are you too busy just now?"

"Too busy?" she echoed, more lightly than she had spoken for many a day. "Why, you don't know how glad I am to see you! We all thought that you had gone—that you were very far away from us by this time."

"Only as far as Decaturville," he said, flushing, and

appearing to be absorbed in the movement of his foot, which chased a ball of dust along a crack in the floor. " I never meant to stir no further, if I could help it, till I seen how things was goin' with you all. I—I hadn't the heart to clear right out, with—with some of you sick, an' all. I just thought if I could earn a few dollars, why, there might be a use found for 'em ; so I got a week's job as a waiter in an eatin'-house I know'd when I was this way with another show a couple o' years back. And I kinder speculated with a little of the money playin' cards. I had pretty good luck—I most generally do—and one way or another I got near thirty dollars put together. That was las' night, an' I was for tryin' again, when who should come along but Clinkaberry, the advance man Ambler had. He'd caught on to Crowe's Minstrels party, an' was makin' fur the South. We had a bite o' supper together at the place where I was workin', an' a talk. He'd had a letter from Ambler, and when I'd hearn what he'd gotter say, I jest started out an' tramped it over here to Moonsville, double quick."

"I think," said Monica, gently, "that if you had heard what *Della Thomas* had had to say, you would have tramped here long, long ago."

" I don't know what you mean," he retorted, seeming to retire within himself, after the obstinate fashion of a hermit crab.

" May I tell you what I mean ? "

" I guess there ain't no hurry," Nick said, sheepishly. " Better hear what I've got to say first. Mine's business."

"Ah, but mine's far more important than mere business. Oh, don't turn away, Mr. Nickson. It's only this "—very hurriedly and confusedly—"I've been hating myself so for my selfishness and blindness this last week, I *must* speak out now you're here, for my own sake, if nothing else. I never knew—I never dreamed that you and Della had been—dear friends, until she lay ill and talking in delirium of things that had been preying on her mind, and helping to turn her poor, weary brain. She had borne it all for my sake, because she thought I had been kind when—when she was to have left the company. Not a word did she speak, in spite of all her suffering; yet, since she has been lying there unconscious, not an hour has passed but she has cried out for you, and begged you to come back to her."

Nick's eyes, like those of a dog that waits for some movement from his master, had fixed themselves on Monica, and there was a curious dilation and contraction of the pupils, as though his breath came and went through them, instead of the tense nostrils or rigidly compressed lips. At the end his clumsy hand, with the square, stubby fingers, came up to his face, and he turned away, shaking all over.

"Gawd!" he said beneath his breath. "Gawd! is it true? You ain't foolin' me?"

"One day she kissed an old mended stocking of yours. It's been under her pillow ever since; and sometimes I've seen her poor little thin fingers feeling for it there. No, I'm not 'fooling' you."

"She's go'n' to get well?" Nick's teeth were set, and he whispered through them.

"Yes. Oh, she is much better already; and when she hears you have come back, it will do more for her than all the medicines in the world. She knows me now, though she hasn't been allowed to talk very much as yet. Let me go up and tell her that—Doctor William Nickson has come to prescribe for her."

"Yes, tell her that," he assented, with a pink stain smeared beneath his great brown eyes. "Don't let anybody else hear you, but tell her I—I prescribe *gettin' married.*"

Monica laughed outright, joyously, and took a step from him, in haste to deliver her message; but Nickson strode after her.

"Wait!" he said; "you made me forget. There's somethin' I think you'd oughter know. Don't you put too much trust in that big feller in there, Jewett, I seen him just now, and that set me to thinkin' more'n ever of what Clinkaberry said. He tells me, Clinkaberry does, that Ambler says to him in the letter he'd written, he'd been paid five hundred dollars to clear out the way he did, an' break up the show. It was a put-up job, says Ambler, and he couldn't afford to do without the money he got fur it. He sent Clinkaberry twenty-five dollars to square him; and says Clinkaberry to me, 'I bet it's Jewett's at the bottom o' the whole snap.'"

Like the delicate, almost invisible, strands of a broken cobweb that blows across the face of an unwary passer-by, enmeshing him, Monica felt the filaments of distrust and mystery weaving intangibly about her.

"But what—why should he wish—what object could he have?" she began to stammer. "Oh, surely Mr. Clinkaberry had nothing to go upon; he must have been mistaken."

"I don't want to do no one an injustice," said Nick

sturdily. "Still, I never used to fancy that man Jewett; and you know, Miss Nairne, you don't need to take nothin' from him. I've got thirty dollars, and every cent of it's fur Della an' you. I didn't want it fur myself. I could hev got home all right. I've done it before. But now, things is kinder different. Where Della stays, *I* stay, and I'd like to sorter look after you both."

"Thank you," responded Monica, rather wistfully. "I should be glad if you would. But—but Mr. Jewett couldn't have done that. He has been very kind to us, and is going to be kinder. It *must* be all right. And—and things have got so far that—that I'm afraid it would be too late to go back. Now, we must hope for the best, and—I'm going upstairs to tell Della."

CHAPTER XXIII.

"Oh, God defend me, how am I beset!"

MONICA stood in her dressing-room at the Moonsville theatre—the " star " dressing-room, which, a fortnight ago, had been sacred to the unapparelled charms
of Miss Marguerite Neland. Now it was hers. She
was the star. Crawford's poor efforts for her comfort
in earlier days of barn storming had been outdone.
A white fur rug covered half the floor. A long
Psyche mirror, sent down from Decaturville, with its
luxurious brightness, seemed but to render the darkness and bareness which lurked in the corners more
visible. In a cheap glass vase on the long shelf, was
a bunch of " American Beauty " roses, set in a halo of
strong green leaves, and redolent of a hot-house.

From the front came the strains of a harp and
violin, welded together by the deeper notes of a piano.
Though eight or nine days had passed since the fate-
ful Tuesday when Mr. Silas Jewett had appeared in
the nick of time to save the wrecked fortunes of the
stranded company, and Della was about again, she
was scarcely strong enough to do duty as pianist, and
musicians had been sent for from Decaturville.

Mr. Jewett had announced that the *début* of the
new star was to be made in grand style, and to the
best of his own and Moonsville's resources he was
keeping his word.

Everything had come to pass according to his prophecies. Money, and plenty of it, can oil the wheels of time. Mr. Jewett had money, and was ready to spend it when he had anything to gain ; thus there had been no hitch so far in the prompt execution of his plans. Moonsville was, as the new and pushing advance man expressed it " billed like a circus," with such gorgeous pictorial paper as had never honoured that astonished town. There was a new leading man from Chicago, who actually wore a tall shining hat and a " Prince Albert " coat, and caused every other male member of the company to blush for his shabbiness. Mr. Montgomery had stepped into the background and the unfortunate Crawford's place, to play " heavies " in conjunction with his stage management. Several new actresses had come, several new sets of portable scenery had been painted ; new furniture had been hired, dozens of plays had been sent down from that Sinbad's valley, Chicago ; and to-night the new combination, headed by Miss Nairne as star, inaugurated their future successes in the comedy of " Pygmalion and Galatea."

Monica stood before the Psyche mirror, looking, in her clinging Greek draperies, like Psyche herself, and feeling as though she were about to essay the first and not the least arduous among the famous labours of that much tried maiden.

" A real, live star," Della had affectionately called her, before she went out to sit in front. It was pleasant to feel the self-importance of being a star. It was delightful to be going to play the part of Galatea, even for a Moonsville audience ; and then there was the vista of other more desirable towns stretching into

her future. Still, her heart was heavier than the heart
of a young beauty with so many wishes unexpectedly
gratified should have been.

Strictly speaking, it ought not to have mattered to
her whether Randolph or Jewett was the bountiful
bestower of these many benefits. She had met Randolph first, but she had seen Jewett far oftener.
Jewett should now be considered the older friend;
and, after all, what was Randolph to her but a gracious memory? Why should it matter that he tarried
across the ocean while a message from her waited un-
kenned or disregarded in Denver, Colorado?

Still, she could not deny that she would have been
happier if it had been Randolph to whom she owed
her new honours as a dramatic star. She would have
been happier, too, if the members of the company
had seemed more appreciative of the efforts she was
making so largely on their behalf. She would have
been lighter of heart had there been no heavy recollection there of a morning when Crawford had thundered for admittance at her locked door, fiercely
demanding to know if indeed it was by her wish that
he was sent away, swearing fierce oaths such as she
had never heard from his lips when she had answered
from behind closed panels. She would be glad, too,
and easier in her mind when this first night was over,
and she might be able to tell whether or no she was
destined to be really a successful actress.

It was certainly a lovely face and figure, ringed
round like a portrait painted in delicate water colours,
that was framed there in the Psyche mirror. The
white, uncovered arms and neck; the eyes dark with
excitement that looked out from under Galatea's

snowy, classic curls; the coins on the graceful shoulders; the long, soft draperies that folded about the little pink silk feet in their Greek sandals. And she had to thank Mr. Jewett's thoughtful generosity for it all. She was grateful that he had really given her a paper to sign—a sort of undated I. O. U. he had tried to make clear to her unpractical, preoccupied mind. That seemed to put things on quite a business-like footing between them, and very soon, no doubt —judging from what he and the new advance man said—she would be able to pay back every penny out of the profits of this forthcoming venture.

She was thinking of this as she reddened Galatea's lips, and added a touch of extra whiteness to the statue's already swan-like throat, when a quick, impatient knock that she had learned to know beat out a summons on the thin pine-wood of her dressing-room door.

She was fully arrayed for conquest, and she answered the demand in haste. It was Jewett, in evening dress, looking very handsome, almost young, and somewhat excited.

"Couldn't wait," he said ; "came around to see how you were getting along, and just how irresistible you were making yourself. By Jove, you are pretty— about the prettiest thing I ever saw. A good investment for my money ! "

She looked up, slightly startled or shocked at the expression ; but his face was smiling and pleasant in its undisguised admiration.

"As pretty as the mysterious lady you are always saying I remind you of ? " she asked, lightly.

"Even prettier. Poor thing, she'd have been an old

woman by now if she'd lived, and I can't stand old
women—so it's lucky she didn't. Yes, you're as handsome a Galatea as ever walked the boards, I'll bet.
I'm proud of you. There's a good house—all country
' punkins ' of course, but they'll know a pretty woman
when they see one. Cynisca's walking around on the
stage with Pygmalion, and she looks very well; but
she's not a patch on you. Little Fanny Free's not
bad as Myrine either; but talking of her reminds me
of Montgomery. Look out for him. He's mad, you
know, because he has to play Leucippe instead of
Pygmalion, and he'll break you up in your scene, I
shouldn't wonder, if he can—at least, that's what little
Nickson thinks. He looks awful funny with his bow
legs, dressed up as Chrysos.

"And oh, by the way, I meant to tell you ! Don't
be surprised if you should happen to look out in front
and see Crawford. He's sitting there in the front row
as large as life. Hope he doesn't mean to make a row,
or do anything nasty; but if he does, he'll be hustled
out of the house, by a couple of fellows I shall put on
to the job, before he can say Jack Robinson."

Monica was pale, but, luckily for her reputation with
Jewett as a girl of spirit, her pallor was not visible
under the stage make-up.

"I thought he had left town," she said, anxiously,
"the day after you had him dragged away from my
door at the hotel."

"So he had, to all appearances; but evidently he
was lying low for some reason or other. I guess it'll
turn out to be only for the satisfaction of hissing the
new man—and getting put out for his pains; so
don't you bother about it. But I just thought I'd

better warn you, for fear the sight of him might give you a kind of start."

"Thank you," said Monica, rather dolefully, "for thinking of it, and for everything you've done." Already the road to theatrical fame seemed strewn with divers thorns among the roses!

"They'll be ringing up in a few minutes," went on Jewett. "Hadn't you better go out with me and get posed behind the curtains on your what-you-may-call it?"

"I suppose so."

She moved toward the door, but, as she passed him, Jewett caught her hand.

"Aren't you going to add anything to that 'thank you' of yours, my pretty statue?" he inquired, with a spark leaping up in his yellow-grey eyes.

"What do you want me to add?" she questioned in return, speaking gently, yet with a certain hauteur.

He looked at her intently for a long moment, still holding the hand which she had made a suggestive effort to reclaim.

At last he dropped it with a certain abruptness.

"Never mind just now," he said. "It can wait till the play's over—but, by Jove, little star, it can't wait much longer! Now go; I don't want you to get excited."

He opened the door, which he had all but closed after his entrance, and she slipped past him just in time to escape a kiss which he would have planted upon her bare white arm.

It is not likely that the heart of the statue (waking from marble into life with the prayer of Pygmalion) beat in its first wild pulsings as tumultuously as did that of the poor little Moonsville Galatea when she climbed to the safe sanctuary of her paper-covered pedestal.

The applause which greeted the revelation of the white figure against its red canton-flannel background was like a draught of sparkling champagne. It was only Moonsville applause, but it was all her own, meant in honour of the star and in admiration of her beauty—the very first round of hand-clapping and stamping which had been vouchsafed to her alone in the course of her brief theatrical career. She warmed at the sound of it, forgetting even Crawford and the ominous possibilities called up by his presence. The scene went well, and she knew that she was acting creditably, that, at least, she was not disgracing her exalted position. Every laugh gave her new courage. She thought of dainty little points to make which had not occurred to her during the few hurried, perfunctory rehearsals. Each one scored a hit, and Monica was almost happy. She enjoyed her pretty scenes with Pygmalion and Myrine; but there came a slight sinking of the heart at last when the bold Leucippe's entrance was nearly due, and she remembered Mr. Jewett's warning regarding the ingratitude of the vengefully-minded stage manager.

He was to come in from the right upper entrance, she knew, carrying over his classically draped shoulder the property fawn, transported at some expense from Chicago; and, as the time for his cue approached, she mentally braced herself for any emergency.

"He shall *not* break me up," she said, with inward self-encouragement. "I'll be prepared for *anything.*"

And so she might have been, perhaps, prepared for

anything save the one thing that happened. In
Leucippe sauntered at the appointed moment. The
proper words were on his lips, but in his eye was a
baleful gleam, and over his shoulder, instead of the
property fawn (which he was supposed to have shot),
was flung a lately deceased hen, of singularly large
proportions.

Its yellow claws protruded through the hand that
so nonchalantly held them. Its body flopped solidly
on the floor of the stage as Leucippe dashed it down
close to the footlights, and in full sight of the wondering audience.

"Property fawn was lost. Had to get this or nothing," he deceitfully murmured to the stricken Galatea
behind his hand, and between Leucippe's sonorously
uttered sentences.

There was no help for it. The poor vivified statue,
wishing herself a mere grease spot on the face of the
earth, a pelican of the wilderness, or anything save
what she was, had to go down on her knees, according
to the requirements of the scene, beside the unspeakable fowl, caress its upturned beak, kiss its ill-favoured
wings.

"Poor little thing, I *know not what thou art!*"
murmured the unfortunate star, choking upon floating
particles of chicken down, which wafted themselves
into her nostrils, and produced a stifled sneeze.

The line was hard to say. She *did* know so well
what it was, and so did the audience! And she knew,
also, what must be Mr. Montgomery's triumph in his
ill-gotten revenge.

But no one laughed unduly in the audience, not
even Crawford, whom she had feared might be malig-

nantly capable of catching at this scene for his share of vengeance.

The fact that he was silent encouraged her to proceed. Surely, if he had meant to make any demonstration, he could have chosen no more opportune moment. He had let it pass, and the neglect augured well, in Monica's opinion.

Act after act went by, each one received more enthusiastically than the last; and at length the final curtain had descended on the picture of the statue—Galatea having preferred the coldness of stone to the cruelty of the world.

It was over! Crawford had made no sign, and Monica Nairne, as a star, seemed to have achieved a brilliant initial success.

Every one crowded round to congratulate her as the acknowledged head of the company. Cynisca, the new " heavy woman," Pygmalion (who had already begun endeavouring to win her admiration for his own personal attractions), and even Mr. Montgomery, profuse in his apologies for that " gosh-darned chicken."

"You were heavenly, Angel, simply *heavenly !* " whispered Della, still thin and pale, but radiant with her own new-found happiness and unselfish pride in her beloved friend. I just sat out there and adored you ; and I could hear ever so many people all around me saying nice things."

She squeezed Monica's hand, and then she slipped away, doubtless to breathe a word of congratulation in the ear of some one else. She was the most deliriously happy girl in the world to-night. Everything seemed too good to be true! And she was to be married to Nick the very next night—on the stage, after the performance, among plenty of flowers, and five canary birds in cages, borrowed from the relenting landlady at the hotel. Such a nice minister was to perform the ceremony; and all the company would be there, and the audience, too, if they liked to stay. The people of Moonsville would be talking of the wedding for a year. Then they were to go on as usual, only she and Nick would be man and wife, and the whole world would be different.

She flitted back and forth between her Angel's dressing-room and the stage, gossiping happily in the former, as she had never done in all her grave, self-contained young life; gazing about at the latter, with her head on one side, and an eye to the decorations for to-morrow night. But when Monica was at last ready to depart, Della had disappeared. The stage was empty and dim when the weary star wandered forth to find her satellite; but, as she glanced wistfully round, with a soft call for "Della! Della!" Jewett's robust figure issued from the concealment of the stage-manager's dressing-room close by.

"Della's gone," he announced, with the impersonal air of one who imparted information. "Gone with little Nickson. No doubt they've got a lot to talk about, so I took the liberty of sending them on ahead, and waiting for you. You're such an unselfish little thing, I knew you wouldn't grudge your friend this last unmarried evening alone with her lover."

"Oh, no—it isn't that," faltered Monica.

"Well, then, come on, Star. I've got a lot to say to you, my dear."

He took her by the arm and led her from the theatre, with a noticeable accession of possessorship in voice and manner.

CHAPTER XXIV.

"Oh . . . that I were a man!
I would eat his heart in the market-place!"

THE moon saw a strange thing in the Arkansas
village named in its honour that night. It was a
round, full moon, and shone red as it rose among the
boles of the black pines and butternuts, like a bonfire
blazing at midnight on the horizon. Crimson as was
its huge disc, the light it shed was pale and pensive,
casting dark, fantastic shadows along deserted roads
and roughly built streets, and never touching the
swamp that Moonsville children believed to stretch
away into the wilds of nowhere.

There were two shadows that moved together at
first, and the lamps of the theatre went out suddenly
behind them. At last one separated itself with
abruptness from the other, fleeing swiftly, followed for
a time by the shadow which had been its companion.
Then, it was only the smaller of the two which darted
like a hunted thing past the mean, low houses, where
the moonbeams glinted bleakly on uncovered panes
of glass. It was undignified—even for a shadow—to
give chase, and with none save the moon to see.
After all, sooner or later, the race could end in but
one way.

When Monica Nairne reached her own room at the
hotel, she was quivering in every muscle and nerve,

like one who had been under the lash. With a rush,
as if she feared pursuit, she slammed the door, which
opened inward from the verandah, and flinging her
body against it, thrust the old-fashioned bolt fiercely
home.

"Thank God! thank God!" she panted. "I'm
here at last!—I'm safe from him!"

Having secured herself from intrusion, she proceeded to do what all other normal women in agitation of mind would have done. She let herself fall in
an inert little heap on the bed, burying her hot face
in the pillows. Their cool touch was grateful to her.
She fairly hugged them in the effort to realise more
fully her escape, the sense of being at home, and
alone, and safe.

For a long time she lay there, not crying, but
breathing hard and fast. Occasionally a shudder ran
through her, and she hid her face still deeper, as
though an ugly, obtruding thought had to be pushed
away.

"Horrible—horrible!" she murmured among her
pillows. "That there should be men like that—what
an awful world for a girl to live in—and *he thought I
knew*, all the time! He thought I was leading him
on. Oh, what a miserable fool I've been! It's easy
enough to see it all now, when it's too late. Beast—
beast! I wonder if he *did* think I *knew ?* "

She pushed away the sheltering pillows, and slid
from the high bed to the floor, where she stood still,
looking aimlessly, half wistfully, about the room.

Della had been in and lighted the lamp, which
burned dimly on the mantelpiece. The place was
poor enough and bare enough—just one of the ordi-

nary tenth-rate hotel bedrooms which Monica had learned to know so well in each characterless feature; but to-night it seemed to her like a haven of peace.

On the chest of drawers, under the small cracked mirror with its eye helplessly tilted towards the ceiling, stood a saucer filled with wood violets and their crisp, heart-shaped leaves.

Monica went to them, and laid her lips softly against the little upstanding petals.

"Oh, you are so pure!" she said aloud. "No man has ever breathed the breath of his own vileness upon you, withering and shrivelling you, like the trail of some slimy thing. You can look to-morrow's sunshine in the face, but I——"

She pushed away the disordered rings and waves of hair from her face, and stared at it with an odd eagerness of curiosity in the mirror. It loomed weirdly out of a greenish twilight, and the eyes looked large and unfamiliar. It seemed to her that there was a vague, repulsive change in her appearance, a hateful light of evil gleaming out from under the shadow of the lashes, which well-nigh frightened her.

As her gaze, and the gaze of the eerie, whitefaced thing in the glass remained fixed upon each other, she recalled, with a curious wave of self-pity for the girl she had been then, the day when she had studied her own "points" in the mirror at Mrs. Potter's smart Madison Avenue boarding-house, and laughingly jotted them down in her answer to Mr. Ambler's advertisement.

"Poor wretch, you little knew!" she whispered. Other memories connected with that time came thronging back. She had thought, in those days, that she understood what trouble was. How foolish she had been to fancy so! She had been poor and without prospects, to be sure; but in New York, a young, healthy woman could always make an honest livelihood of some sort, even if it were not the career of which she had ambitiously dreamed.

She ought to have been thankful if she had even had to take a place as housemaid or shop girl. At worst, and friendless as she had been, she had then only herself to think of. Now, she had undertaken the responsibility of providing for a dozen others.

This she had not meant to do, and had not known what she was doing. The papers which Jewett had given her to sign, she had signed gratefully and promptly, only thankful that he had thus placed his kindnesses on what seemed to her a thoroughly business basis. Womanlike (and anxious to flaunt the trust in his integrity she had always tried to feel since the day his help had been so freely offered) she had not even glanced at the few lines already written above her signature. But to-night had been a night of explanations. There had been, it appeared, on both sides a misunderstanding from the first. She had been willing to think too well of him; he had judged her after his kind, and had thought of her too poorly.

But he had been prepared for the consequences of a mistake; she had not. How he must have laughed when she had signed that paper, the nature of which he had so carefully explained to her to-night. In writing down her name, she had engaged to be responsible for all salaries, all expenses of the company, after the opening performance, and she had promised to repay, within a period of a fortnight, all money expended, previous to that date, by Mr. Silas A. Jewett.

She had been a fool to sign the paper without examining it; but it had seemed so unnecessary, so almost insulting to him, to read it in his presence. She had been a fool, too—doubly a fool—to believe that he had been disinterested. But the lesson of worldliness had not been included in her training, and now she saw herself hopelessly walled in on every side to which she turned. Under certain circumstances, Silas Jewett would destroy the paper before her eyes. Under certain other circumstances—and these the only ones tolerable to her—he meant to use the power which he said the law would give him, to hold her to the letter of her bond. She must see the company (re-organized for her, and, in a way, *by* her) disbanded, without salaries, and in difficulties as dark as before. She must bear their condemnations, she must smart under their angry conviction that she had betrayed and failed them after specious and misleading promises. She must herself be destitute, disgraced, and forlorn, knowing not which way to turn in the hope of escape from the menace of the law—the law which was to her an unknown, all-devouring monster.

"Oh, if I were a man!" she muttered, "I think that I would kill him. Being a woman, the best thing would be to kill myself."

The best thing, and, from one point of view, the easiest thing; yet it would be cowardly, and, at the same time, would require a species of pluck which Monica's failing heart told her that she did not possess.

It must take a stern courage to break violently into the house of life. How did young girls like herself bring themselves to cut open the smooth, gracious whiteness of their soft skins, and see the hidden blood spout over it in crimson gushes? If only blood were not red, she thought, as she looked strangely at the slender column of her throat, it would not be so horrible. If it were pale pink, or blue, or green—anything but that bright, awful red, that seemed to shriek at one, the thing might be done more easily.

It would be almost equally hard to swallow poison, too—to look into a glass and see death there, ready to wrench out one's life with terrible, unnatural grindings and ungovernable anguish.

There was the swamp only a short distance away. If she ran forth to it, keeping in the shadows, and out of the white moonlight—searching the night and the hearts of all who chanced to stir abroad—she need not be seen. One plunge, a few moments' awful struggle for breath in the black, oozy depths, and everything would be ended so far as she was concerned. Even if the members of the company (all but Della and Nick) reviled her as a selfish, cowardly woman, she need never know. It would no longer cut into her heart like a knife that, through her mistake and Jewett's villainy, they were all left destitute.

Nobody would care, except Della. She had no friends who would help her living—not even the one she had once confidently dared to count upon—and there would be none to regret her dead. They might fish her out of the water, and bury her in a pauper's grave, if they liked. It signified little what became of the fair white body, of which she had once been light-heartedly vain.

Yes, the swamp would be best. But here was this

quiet, safe little room, with a bed for her to lie down upon, as she had always lain, every night. And here were violets blooming for her ; and she was well and strong, without a single pain or aching anywhere, except for that dull pang in her heart ; and morning was coming with sunshine and free air from God's heaven for her to breathe. How could she—oh ! how *could* she voluntarily shut herself out of it all, into the unfriendly night, to plunge into those unmeasured fathoms of black, loathsome water?

She had always hated anything that was unclean and malodorous. Her face would be covered with the filthy slime. It would be in her staring, wideopen eyes ; and it would fill up her mouth and dilated nostrils. There were toads there, too; and Nick had told her and Della not to walk through the field by the swamp for fear of snakes. What if one should dart across her foot, or bite her, as she stumbled through the rough grass in the darkness? She drew her breath with a shuddering impatience. As though it would matter what happened to her on her deliberate way to die !

But, no, she could not do it. She could not lie there dead and hideous, in the mud, for the oafs of Moonsville to find and gloat over, as the "show actress" who had killed herself.

She remembered how Plato had said that human beings were the prisoners of the gods, and (freely translating) had no right to break their parole. But if only she could be ill unto death, without coming back from the brink as Della had done, and so, unburdened by any dreadful responsibility in the matter, fade out of the world that had used her so harshly !

It was a curious thing, she reflected, in a dim, impersonal way, that she had always kept on expecting happiness, notwithstanding the disappointments which had been milestones along her path. She had half unconsciously felt that it was her birthright, because of her youth and good looks, and her superiority over a great many of the people she knew. Nothing had ever quite discouraged her before. Some day she would be happy. But now—this seemed to be the end. She had come up against a blank wall, and Fate was laughing at her, because she had been an optimist, because she had dreamed of being exempt from the common lot. She was only such a little atom of dust on the face of the world, in itself a mere grain of sand —and she had dared to fancy herself important!

As she so pondered (sometimes for a moment forgetting her own intimate miseries to wander off into wider philosophising, and then to be brought back with a sharp wrench of realisation), there came a soft knocking at the door. Della's voice called to her.

"Angel, have you gone to bed?"

Without answering, Monica drew back the bolt and the other girl entered, wearing the purple wrapper, now fresh and spotless from the tub and flat iron.

"Nick's just gone a little while ago," she said, with a nervous laugh—for Della had hardly yet accustomed herself to speaking of Nick to Monica as a lover.

She sat down on the bed, where Monica had lain shaking and moaning a few minutes before, and took her knees into her embrace.

"Oh, Angel," she sighed, rapturously, "I'm *so* happy, I know I sha'n't be able to sleep one wink to-night!"

Monica might have truthfully echoed the words, merely prefacing the word *happy* with one short but potent syllable. Yet she only smiled, and gave Della's purple calico shoulder a little pat. She could gain nothing, save a coward's comfort, temporary and unsubstantial, by confiding her troubles to the bride-elect.

She reproached herself for having forgotten Della and the fact that this was her marriage eve. If only, in some way, the crash might be staved off for four-and-twenty hours, and the wedding arrangements left undisturbed! Della had suffered so much, and through her, that she owed the poor girl happiness at last. It would be too hard to bring her hopes crashing down in the ruin of her own.

"Nick's been gone about fifteen minutes," Della went on, smiling at her own thoughts. "I heard you come in, so I slipped on my wrapper and ran down. I hated to go to bed without telling you all over again how lovely you were, and how sweetly you acted. I couldn't help crying when poor Galatea was turned back to marble in the end. You see, it seemed as though it was really *you*, and it's so nice to be here talking with you, and know you're alive and happy, and everything's all right. You *are* happy, ain't you, darling, and pleased about Nick and me, and because the first night of the new company's been such a big success?"

"I'm more pleased about you than anything," said Monica, evasively.

"It'll be a pretty wedding, I think," soliloquised Della, with her head on one side, and a consciousness of the new dress Monica had given her in her smile.

"Nick's goin' to be out picking pine branches, and pretty leaves, and wild flowers and things all the morning, to dress the stage. If I feel strong enough, I guess I'll go too. I—suppose you wouldn't care much about it, would you?"

"I should care about it, but—but I'm afraid I shall be too busy to-morrow morning," Monica answered, speaking softly, that Della might not hear the sound of tears in her voice.

What would happen to-morrow morning? Would the fiend go away, and leave the new company stranded as the old one had been, and at once take measures to bring the law about her ears. Poor Della! Poor Nick! The flowers would fade, but not at their wedding, unless she sacrificed more than any woman had a right to sacrifice, for their sakes. A man might lay down his life for his friend, but a woman might not lay down her honour.

"I'm so glad I thought about the canary birds," Della babbled unsuspiciously on. "Nothing like this wedding will *ever* have been seen, and we owe it all to you. If you hadn't spoken to dear old Nick, when I was so sick, he'd never have come back to me, I guess. And if it wasn't for you being the star of a new company with money behind it, why, we shouldn't have dared to get married. I'm sorry now I didn't use to like Mr. Jewett, and I try to get Nick to say so too. He's been so kind, hasn't he? And do you know, Angel, I kind of believe he's in love with you? Dear me! I s'pose I can't think of anything much besides love and weddings just now! but could you marry him if he asked you, do you think?"

"Never—never! And he has not the slightest

intention of asking me, even if I would," Monica answered in bitterness of spirit. "Come, dear, it's getting late, and if you are to look bright and fresh for to-morrow, you must run off to bed."

"I was thinkin' of staying down with you, Angel, for this one night, if you'd like to have me," said Della, with wistful humility.

This was the last thing that Monica would have desired. Even Della's loving companionship, and Della's confidences, would fairly drive her mad to-night.

"No, no!" she cried, trying to laugh; "I ·know how it would be—we should talk till morning. Don't forget that we—that it's arranged we should leave for Boonestown after the wedding to-morrow. We shall have just time to catch the midnight train; and, though it's only ten or fifteen miles, we must do as much packing as though it were a hundred. We shall have a busy day to-morrow, all of us—all of us. So, good-night, bride!"

They kissed each other clingingly, and Della's dark, near-sighted eyes searched the face of her beloved friend. Something that she saw there vaguely frightened her. She opened her lips to ask a question, but closed them again. Dearly as she loved Monica, the exuberance of her affection had always been held in check by a species of awe. She had sat at the English girl's feet and worshipped, never daring even in thought to elevate herself to the same level.

She heard Monica shut and lock the door after her, when she had gone out, and for a moment she stood on the verandah in the broad moonlight, looking back at the window, which was open at the top, and across which a slender shadow moved, silhouetted on the white paper muslin blind.

Away in the distance a dog howled dismally; but apart from his complainings, all was as still as though the whole world were sleeping. Somehow the silence pressed ominously upon Della's heart, and she was fain to break it.

" Good-night again, Angel," she softly called, standing near the window.

" Good-night ! " Monica's voice answered; and then, as Della turned to go upstairs, she started at a slight noise among the flowering almond bushes close to the verandah.

She paused, looking over her shoulder, one hand on the balusters, the moonlight glittering on her eyeglasses. But silence, untroubled and profound, had fallen again ; and, after waiting for a few seconds in the vain expectation of seeing a furtive cat or dog dart out of ambush, she went slowly on to her own room—her own in solitude for the last time.

CHAPTER XXV.

MONICA, left alone, began to undress mechanically. It struck her with a grim sense of humour that, in a mood which inclined her to suicide, she should still lay her hairpins neatly away, plait her long hair as though for a quiet night's rest, brush her teeth—oh, blatant, ludicrous irony!—and carefully bathe the body that she was minded to throw to the toads down in the black mud of the swamp.

Still, she did everything as she was accustomed to doing it, even to folding all her clothes on a chair, with the bodice turned over the back, and the stockings and pathetically smart little blue-bowed garters laid at a precise angle on top.

Last of all she blew out the light, and rolled up the squeaking blind, to look with an anguish of yearning for the help that could not come, and into the white unresponsive beauty of the night.

"Oh, my mother, my poor mother!" she said, half aloud. "If you had stayed with me, and been to me what other mothers are to their daughters, I should never have come to this strait. You would have told me things—you would have sheltered me with your advice and your own knowledge. I wonder if you could see me now, if you would be sorry that you left me and went away?"

She leaned her face against the cool glass of the window-pane, and then lifted it again hastily, at a faint creaking sound on the verandah near by. But it did not come again, and she concluded that it must have been a rattling of the shutters in the wind. For a moment she was tempted to close the window, but she would not let herself yield to the impulse. She had slept with it open, fearlessly and undisturbed, ever since her first night at the Jefferson Davis House, and it would be ridiculous to begin with extra precautions at the very hour when she had ceased to value the safety of her life.

Leaving the blind raised that the vivid southern moonlight might stream into the room, she climbed into the high bed.

But she could not rest. After half an hour's tossing, with burning head and the blood galloping through her veins, she rose, slid her bare feet into slippers, and flung round her the little dressing-gown which had gone with her through so many vicissitudes. Thus clad she paced up and down the room, until she was physically weary, and at last, having soaked the hair round her hot temples with cold water, she lay down on the outside of the bed, clothed as she was.

"I shall not sleep to-night—for very different reasons from Della's," she said to herself. And then, even as for the hundredth time she searched her mind for some desperate device which might prove her own salvation and the company's, consciousness slipped from her as a garment, and she fell on sleep.

How long she lay thus oblivious of her misery she never knew; but she dreamed a sound, and so dreaming, waked to find it a reality. For a dull instant she lay still, her brain too freshly steeped in the poppy juice of slumber to understand why there was any reason that some one should not be opening the lower sash of her window and getting in. But suddenly, with one great throb of the heart, which seemed like the blow of an axe on her chest, she realised what the thing that was noiselessly happening must mean.

The moon's rays made a wide, white path along the rag carpet, and the window gleamed against the night's outer dimness—a pale square of shimmering light. Across its brightness, slowly and with extreme cautiousness, moved a dark solid body. The sash had been pushed up with scarce a sound, and now a foot, followed by a leg, was being carefully lifted over the low sill.

Thoughts travelled through Monica's brain, naked, unclothed in words, swift as the leap of an electric current through her pulses. Her first impression was one of sick disgust. This must be Jewett, come to take some base revenge upon her for the bitter words which she had flung at him before she ran away, leaving him to make the best of his way home alone! She did not feel fear, but only a veritable nausea of repulsion. In a flash, however, she had seen that the man's figure, erect at last, and black against the moonshine, was slimmer and shorter than Jewett's by several inches.

His hand was on the window frame as he drew in the other foot; for a second a dark outline of profile was visible, and something that he held struck out a gleam in the white light that formed his background. It was a knife.

Monica knew now by some subtle instinct who it

was, and why he had come. It was Crawford, and with that knife—the very clasp knife with which he had been used to cutting her initials, deep and white, in the brown trunks of trees—he meant to kill her.

She could hear the rustling of her dressing-gown as it rose and fell over her breast with the hammer-like thuds of her heart. Often she had heard that it is possible in dreaming to live through eons in the space of a few minutes of sleep ; and now, waking with such keenness of perception, hearing, and sight as she had never possessed before, her whole past and present seemed to move before her in a bewildering panorama, while she could have counted "One—two—three—four —five."

She had lain down on the bed with an unspoken prayer for death. Death had seemed the only solution of her problem. Though she had not the courage or the cowardice to cut the cords herself, she had felt that she would go on her knees to thank another who stood ready to do it for her.

Here then was the speedy answer to her petition.

She had whistled this vulgarian down the wind, and like a whipped cur, he was turning to bite her. Della had gently warned her to be careful, but she had not listened ; her only anxiety had been never again to see the man whose low cunning, drunkenness and presumption had filled her with an uncontrollable abhorrence.

He might kill her, and she would be held blameless for any evil that befell the company. Even Jewett might be struck with remorse for what he had done.

The wing, or " L," where she and Della slept, was separated by some distance from all the other bedrooms in the hotel, and such an errand as this of Crawford's might be finished with impunity. But now that the chance of death was hers, Monica shrank from it with a full-blooded, youthful clinging to life that was well-nigh frantic. She did not want to die! She would not die! That cruel, stealthy wretch, creeping along among the shadows, should not bury his knife in her flesh. As she thought of it, and protested against the horror of it with her whole rebellious soul, she could feel the keen pang which would come with the first merciless touch of that sharp blade, through every little tendril in the nerve system of her imagination.

He was drawing closer now. Emboldened by the silence in the room, he stood in the streak of moonlight, half way between the window and the bed, doubtless peering for the outline of her form among the pillows.

If he came nearer! Another throb of the heart that was like a blow, and Monica had sprung from the bed with the rush of a storm that flies whirling among the mountain tops. She heard herself utter a shriek that was nothing less than appalling in its wild agonising shrillness. "Help! murder!" it rang out through the brooding spring silences of the night.

Even as she leaped and screamed, knowing that she was in deadly peril of her life, a strange, irrelevant thought elbowed its way into her brain. "If I could scream like that on the stage, I should make my fortune!" She shrank from it—it seemed so like madness in its triviality—and shrieked again.

Her flying leap had landed her close to the dark figure in the moonlight. Instead of running from it, and being stabbed in the back, as she would at once have been, instinctively she grappled with the enemy. One step had taken her to him, and with both hands she had caught him by the wrist before he had fairly realised that he had a waking, struggling, screaming woman to deal with, instead of an unresisting sleeper.

For dear life—and never had it seemed so dear—she wrestled with him, strong in her desperation as she had never been, and would never be again. They had whirled round now until her face was in darkness, his in the moonlight, and every feature stood out clearly. Monica could see the thick lips parted in a snarl over strong, wolfish teeth, stained yellow with tobacco. She could see the great, bold, pale blue eyes, the balls floating in a network of red, bloodshot veins. He had been handsome, in a vulgar, flaunting way, in his days of pride and swaggering. Now, the constant drinking and degradation of a fortnight had worked havoc with him, and the once sleek coat of the animal was hideous in its soddenness.

Monica heard him panting like a great, weary dog, and his breath on her face reeked rottenly of stale liquor. It was, she vaguely felt, not a fight with a man, but with a wild, fierce, irresponsible creature of a lower kind.

She had caught him by the wrist, and then, with a quick, unexpected movement, she tried with one hand to snatch his knife away. He drew it through her palm till the blade sliced deep into the delicate skin, but she did not let go. Though she could feel her own blood trickling warmly down her arm, there was no more realisation of pain at the moment than if the knife had cut into a glove of kid.

"Curse you! You sha'n't get away!" he grunted
between clenched teeth. "You've spoiled my life,
you have, and I'm goin' to send you to hell for it!"

Through her cries for help, which did not cease, she
could hear his mutterings.

"D—n her, she's made of iron! It's this d—d
brandy I've got on board! I'm weak—weak as a rag!
But I'll do for you, you white devil, you! You'll get
this knife in your heart!"

Would no one ever come? In truth, not two minutes had passed since Monica's first thrilling cry for
help, but to her, in her extremity of peril, hours
seemed to have dragged by.

He was trying to force the knife, still desperately
clasped in her bleeding hand, toward her left side.
Her strength was leaving her at last; she could fight
no more. With a long, shuddering wail she yielded
with a collapse of every shrinking muscle, as he tore
her fingers from the blade.

"Now—*now*—take that!" she heard him hiss; but,
instead of feeling the pang of the expected knife,
something sudden, and white, and swift, whirled her
away from the murderous grasp, and she, with a
weight that was warm and soft, and palpitating on top
of her, fell backward, grovelling to the floor.

A woman's voice cried out, with the choked, convul-
sive sob of one whose breath had been struck from the
lungs by a fierce, quick blow.

Monica tried to struggle to her feet, but was thrust
back again, and there was the thud of another blow,
and another broken moan. She was protected by a
shield of trembling flesh, a writhing form which shrank
and quivered while it covered her. Over her face

rained a hot spray, that trickled into her eyes and mouth, and tasted like ink. Dimly she realised that it was blood—the blood of one who was dying to save her.

Everything grew vague and confused now. It began to seem that always, for years and years, she had been fighting for her life. It was a *mêlée*—a storm of mingling cries and curses, a waving of arms, and at last a sudden flashing of yellow lights, feet running and stamping, exclamations of surprise and dismay. Then, all was quiet for a long moment. Life was slipping away on a gentle tide. All knowledge of identity was going, too. Only voices were left in the world, far off and hollow sounding.

Some one whom Monica seemed to have known at an indistinct, distant period of time, groaned hoarsely, and called on the name of God—only he pronounced the word differently from the way to which she had been accustomed.

"Oh, Gawd—oh, Gawd, my girl!" he was saying. There was a hum of other voices, too, with exclamations flashing out of the dull monotone, like explosions in her ear. But the one who spoke to God was nearest, and a low whisper answered him, soft and brokenly.

"He's killed me, Nick, I think, but—but it was for *her!*"

CHAPTER XXVI.

"Such smiling rogues as these, like rats, oft bite the holy cords atwain."

WHEN the doctor, who had attended Della in her late illness, was brought in, he pronounced that her wounds, though painful, were not dangerous. But though she would not die, she had been ready to give her life for her friend.

The blow which had been intended for Monica had struck her above the collar-bone, and again, in striving to defend her Angel, she had received another in the shoulder.

She was put into Monica's bed, and every one was turned out save the doctor and the girl for whom she had gone so near to death.

Monica, too, had been in need of aid for a few moments, for she had fainted for the first time in her healthy young life. But, when she had been restored by some one whose ministrations were not necessary for Della, or for the arrest of the criminal—caught red-handed—she forgot her own weakness, and the nervous reaction after the well-nigh fatal adventure she had experienced. She had thoughts only for Della and poor distracted Nick, so nearly separated for ever on their wedding eve.

Even Jewett, who was also stopping at the Jefferson

Davis House (Moonsville's one hostelry,) and who,
roused with the others by Monica's cries for help, had
rushed, half-clothed, to the scene of action, had for the
moment no power to dismay or anger her.

She had not regained consciousness by the time
that Crawford, drunkenly sobbing out repentance now,
was taken forcibly from the room, and removed to the
dilapidated village "lock-up."

Jewett and several members of the company were
still present, however, when she opened her eyes ; and
it was he, assisted by Mrs. Patton, who undertook the
task of reviving her.   But the sight of so much blood,
in places where it ought not to be, Mrs. Patton complained, made her that "seek at her *stummick*, she
was most turned wrong side out " ; and, therefore,
when Monica came to herself, it was to find her head
pillowed on Jewett's knees.   Perhaps it was this fact
which helped her so speedily to self-command ; but
without a word or look at him, after the first, she sat
upright, rose straight as a willow wand to her feet,
and fled to the neighbourhood of Nick and the prostrate Della.

If she knew and was glad when the doctor uncere-
moniously ordered Jewett out with the others, who
were only curious or anxious to be helpful, she gave
no sign, and, though he tried, he could not win her
attention.

On his reluctant way to the door, he turned and
bent over her for an instant, as she sat on the floor
with Della's hand in hers.

" See here, little Star," he whispered.   " You and I
must make up our quarrel to-morrow.   This has been
a bad business, and you'll need me to steer you

through it. Let's look over the past, and commence again. Eh?"

She glanced up unseeingly, her brows slightly contracted in a frown, and then turned her face impatiently from him, as though he had been a troublesome, buzzing insect which she would fain have brushed away.

He went off, shrugging his shoulders, well aware that it would be impossible to press the point, with so many eyes looking curiously on. But he was a man who would not give up what he wanted, and what he had paid good money to obtain, without a much harder struggle for sovereignty than he had already made.

He was glad, purely for selfish reasons, that the girl had escaped scars or damage of any kind, but he was also glad that she had had the lesson, following so quickly on her ungrateful conduct to him, and as he yawned and stretched himself in his hard bed once more, he thought he saw a way in which he might be able to turn what had occurred to his own advantage.

The editor of the Moonsville *Spread Eagle* (unhumourously advertised as a weekly journal) was happy next morning. He had not had his breakfast of buckwheat cakes and maple syrup, when his reporter and sole assistant appeared to pique his appetite with the precious tit-bit of sensation. This would be far richer fare for his readers than the "Stage Wedding," on which he had counted as *the* item for his next issue. The wedding must now be abandoned, or at least postponed, owing to the condition of the bride elect, but praise be to the Jumping Jehoshaphat, and other patron saints, Moonsville could now very well afford to do without it.

While the two enterprising journalists were discussing the best method of obtaining an interview with the bride that was to have been, with Miss Nairne—who was relegated to a position of secondary heroine, or walking lady, by the magnificent courage of her friend—and any other member of the company able to relate or even manufacture intelligence of a readable and exciting character, Mr. Nickson was announced by a little girl with freckles and two bran new front teeth that looked like tombstones. "One of them show folks," she hastily elaborated, seeing an expression denoting bewilderment on the unshaven countenance of her parent.

Mr. Nickson was at once ushered from an uneasy position in the passage to the dining-room, where it appeared, in the course of conversation, that he had come in the hope of inducing the editor of the *Spread Eagle* to keep the most valuable bit of news which had come in his way since boyhood, out of the paper.

This, in a manner truly public-spirited and becoming to one who sought high office in his county, he refused to do. He would waive the interviews, however (which he now saw he was unlikely to get), and could promise Mr. Nickson, on the word of a Southerner and gentleman, that nothing should be said of the two beauteous young ladies concerned, which their mothers might not be proud to read.

So it was that Nick was at last obliged to leave the house vanquished, and not without fear that his very protest would be used for " copy."

Della was doing well, the doctor said, but she had

been sleeping when he left the hotel, and could not be seen. Nick did not feel inclined for other society, and, having been drawn by an evil fascination past the tiny wooden building which might have been an exaggerated chicken coop, but was the "lock-up," he strolled along the side of the swamp between the Jefferson Davis House and the railway station—the loneliest walk he could find. With head down, cap pulled over his eyes, and hands in his pockets, he sidled on with the peculiar gait which had earned him, from the fun-loving Human Flower, the sobriquet of "Picture Frame."

"Hello, Nickson!" said some one close upon him; and coming back with a start from a thousand miles away, and an indefinite number of months in his own and Della's future, he found himself face to face with Mr. John Randolph of Denver, Colorado.

"Hello, sur," responded Nick, in the manner of one who has parted from an acquaintance but yesterday; for it was against his principles, when it could possibly be avoided, to show surprise, or, indeed, emotion of any kind.

Randolph, looking very brown as to his face, and extraordinarily bright as to his eyes, joined the little actor without ceremony. And so long were his steps, and so brisk his pace, that it became at once all that Nick could do to keep up with him.

"I've just come in by the eastern train," said Randolph, "and, of course, because I was in a hurry there wasn't a vehicle, not so much as a milk-cart, to be had. Say, Nickson, how are you all? How's Miss Nairne— and Miss Thomas?"

His words were quiet and commonplace enough,

but there was the vibration of a controlled excitement in his voice.

" Miss Thomas and Miss Nairne got nearly murdered last night," responded Nick, with equally artificial calm, and naturally reversing the order of the names.

"Good heavens, man, what do you mean?"

Nick proceeded, in his slow way, to enter into explanations. Randolph listened, with a face that flushed at first, and then gradually paled beneath its coat of seafaring tan.

"We all wondered what Crawford was up to, hanging around after he'd been paid off an' given the sack," Nick went on. " But not one o' us boys guessed he meant anything worse than hootin' at us on the stage, or throwin' worthless vegetables, or B. C. eggs, or some fool's nonsense o' that sort. If we had, he'd of been hustled out of this town so quick he wouldn't never have know'd whether he was goin' to school or comin' home, the durned, ornary, sneakin' cuss!"

"He is all of that," retorted Randolph, with relish of Nickson's crudely-striking appellations. "Gad! I'd like to lead the citizens of this town out on a little lynching expedition."

"There's been some talk a'ready of tar'n feathers," Nick said, quietly. " The lock-up's only a band-box. We might hev a little fun; but I guess in the end 'twould be better fur the ladies if the measly coward was left alone. They say he ain't et nothin', or done nothin', but roar out that he was crazy with drink, or he wouldn't never hev done what he did. One feller says this mornin' he seen him pour down a hull tumbler chock full o' brandy, more 'n half a pint, at one

go, after the show last night. I guess it's true, too;
and it's a blessin' one way, for ef he'd been himself,
an' tried to do the job, he'd have mastered those poor
weak gurls before they could have said Jack Robinson.
He'll git a few months, like enough, fur southern
judges is kinder hard on chaps that tries to do any
harm to wimmen, you know; an' I guess we kin afford
to let him rip!"

"I dare say you're right," Randolph said, thoughtfully. "But you began to tell me something about
the company being re-organised before Crawford was
dismissed. How was that? Had anything in particular happened?"

"That depends on what you call partickerler,"
returned Nick, with a grim smile. "It seemed kinder
that way to us folks at the time. Mr. Ambler—that
was our manager, you know—was called away sort of
sudden like, with his wife, an', bein' absent-minded,
he took all the money with 'im. We played in pretty
hard luck for a while. I went off, an' shifted fur
myself, hopin' to put a little somethin' together; but
the rest kinder lived on Miss Nairne fur a week or
two. She was a reg'lar little brick; but 'twas a
durned shame they should have took advantage of
her, sellin' the very rings off her fingers to put bread
in their big ugly mouths. Mind, I ain't lumpin' Miss
Thomas in with that lot. She was sick, an' out of
her head, and never know'd what was goin' on, until
after Mr. Jewett had come along, squared up everything, and offered to back the new company."

"Silas Jewett?" questioned Randolph, in a queer
voice, and with a still queerer look on his dark face.

"That's the man, sur." Nick glanced up at him

slyly out of the corners of his great brown eyes. He was wondering how far it might be wise to confide his own suspicions to Randolph, whose frank manners he approved.

"The devil!"

"Well, sur, p'r'aps you ain't far wrong."

"What do you mean?"

Randolph looked keenly down into the face which did not come much higher than his shoulder.

"Folks say the devil's black," said Nick, slyly; "but it kinder seems to me sometimes as though there might be a sort of family likeness between him an' Mr. Jewett. Not but what Jewett's acted all fair an' above board so far as I've *seed;* but I heard things, which I made so bold as to tell to Miss Nairne, afore ever this new show got started on its legs. She thought I was in the wrong, an' maybe I was. I hope so. An' I hope she'll have every reason to go on thinkin' so, that's all."

"Look here, Nickson!" Randolph exclaimed, abruptly, "you and I are strangers. We haven't exchanged half a dozen words till this morning, but I know a man when I see him, and I see one now. You may think I haven't got any right to pry into Miss Nairne's affairs, especially behind her back; but there's some things one can't say to a woman. I'm not ashamed to have anybody know that I asked her to marry me, and she said 'no,' but I'm her friend through thick or thin, and I want you to tell me right now all you know of this Jewett business."

Nothing loth, Nick told him, beginning with the day so soon after Randolph's own departure, when Jewett had drawn the doll at the Poddiwiski matinee.

He went on to touch upon that gentleman's various succeeding visits to the company along its route, relating briefly what the late advance man, Clinkaberry, had had to say, and dwelling upon Jewett's prompt subsequent appearance and lavish expenditure.

"Miss Nairne's a gurl that don't think no evil of folks, not even of men, unless she's got to," ended Nick, delicately. "As I was sayin', she may be right, an' I may be wrong; but though I meant to stick to the show as long as she an' Del—Miss Thomas was in it, I ain't never been easy in my mind about Mr. Jewett's way o' doin' things."

Randolph muttered something under his breath, which sounded uncommonly like a wish prejudicial to his old friend's eternal welfare, but it was not an expression of which Nick was called upon to take notice.

"I'm hanged if I wouldn't give five good years out of my life to have been on the spot here from the night Ambler and his wife lit out!" Randolph went on. "I've been in Europe for the past nine or ten weeks, as luck would have it. Only got into New York night before last. Those fools out in Denver, instead of obeying instructions I gave them before I left, kept everything that came for me in the way of —of private correspondence and so on, for the last three weeks, thinking, as I was coming home so soon, I might miss 'em. Everything was in New York city waiting for me, and—er—among them was a—sort of note from Miss Nairne, or I shouldn't have known without a lot of telegraphing around the country, where to look you up. As it was, I expected to have to chase about a bit, thinking you'd have left this place by now, but the ticket agent down at the depôt said you hadn't gone. By Jove! I'm glad I happened to run across you. You've told me exactly the sort of thing I was most wanting to know. Say, Nickson, is Jewett staying at the same hotel with the rest of you?"

"Oh, yes, he's on deck up there, you can bet, sur."

"Well, come along then. Let's not waste any time. I'd like to give him a kind of surprise party."

CHAPTER XXVII.

" 'Tis not so deep as a well,
Nor so wide as a church door,
But 'tis enough—'twill serve."

SILAS JEWETT was walking up and down, like an uneasy lion, in the parlour of the Jefferson Davis House, where Monica Nairne had once fallen, after the fashion of a ripe cherry, into his arms. She had done so inadvertently on that occasion, but he meant that she should deliberately walk into them with her eyes open, before many more hours had gone over his head.

A written line from her was crumpled in his hand. She had scrawled it in pencil, on the back of the note which a few moments before he had sent to her room, asking her to give him a quarter of an hour's conversation on a subject vital to the welfare of the company.

" I hoped and intended not to see you again," the brief communication which had come in answer said. "But for the sake of others, and *only* for their sakes, I will go down to the parlour and speak with you for fifteen minutes, as you suggest."

When he had for the third time examined the blotched engraving of Washington's death-bed, the chromos of " Asleep and Awake," and the coloured lithograph of three prize Arkansas pigs, which adorned the walls, the door opened, and Monica came in. Her face was almost ghastly in its pallor, and there were deep purple circles under her pretty eyes. It was hard to believe that this haggard-looking young woman was the radiant creature whose snowy arm he had nearly succeeded in kissing at the theatre last night. For an instant, Jewett—who was a great connoisseur in woman's charms—was almost put off his bargain. But he remembered what a trying experience had robbed her for the moment of her bloom, and went towards her smiling, holding out his hand. She put both hers behind her, in a childishly aggravating way.

"What did you wish to say to me?" she abruptly asked.

"So many things. Come over here, and let's sit down."

"No," answered Monica. "I would rather stand. Please begin at once. I am anxious to go back to Della."

"You haven't a very nice way of beginning if you wish to get anything out of me," said Jewett.

A wave of colour rushed to her cheeks, as though she had been struck.

"For Della's sake, and—for the others, too, I would ask a favour of you, if I could bring myself to do it," she faltered.

"That's a little better. What would you like to have me do?"

"I would like you not to press for money at once, but to let the company go on, and pay you back as it can, from the profits."

"You know how ready I am to do that, and more,

my Star. But—there's so often a 'but' and an 'if' in this life, you know—and there is one now. By the way, have you thought how this business about Crawford is going to affect you?"

Monica looked surprised. "It is over now, I should think—thank Heaven!"

"Oh, but it's not over. It's very far from being over, as you'll find. Men don't try and kill women for nothing. Where there's smoke, there's always a little fire, people say—and that's what they'll say about you. You'll come in for a good deal of blame, and your name'll be hawked about in every newspaper, little and big, in the country. You'll wake up in a day or two to find yourself notorious. A notorious woman—think of that? You're known to be English, and so the thing will get copied into the British papers too—every rag that loves a good scandal will have it. Even your best friends will think you must have been to blame in the matter, and as for the others, why, there's *nothing* they'll stop at saying.

"'A disappointed lover tries to kill an actress in her bedroom in the middle of the night.' Well, it isn't the sort of thing I should like said about a girl *I* took any interest in."

Jewett watched Monica intently as he spoke, and he could see a curious effect as of the curdling of her flesh under the soft skin on her face. Her lips opened as if to speak, but she closed them again, resolutely, pressing them so tightly together, with a sudden tumultuous heaving of the breast, that the delicate pink colour left them.

"I could stop it all, you know, if you asked me to,"

Jewett went on slowly. " *You* couldn't, no matter how hard you might try, for it takes money to quash these things, and square the newspapers, and so on. But I've got money, and I don't mind how deep I dip my hand into my pockets if I see any chance of getting a proper return. Now, which is better, to be smirched in the eyes of the world, or——"

"Or in my own, I suppose you would say!" Monica burst forth passionately. "Oh, you coward, you coward! How I hate you—how I despise you! If only I had a brother to stand between you and me——"

"So you have. I guess you must have forgotten that," said Randolph.

The two who had stood so near to each other started apart. Randolph had come in through the door behind them, which Monica had carefully left a few inches ajar.

"Say, Miss Nairne," continued the newcomer, whose eyes alone betrayed the slightest agitation, "perhaps you'd kindly excuse me if I took Mr. Jewett out for a little walk? It seems to me that some exercise would do us both a power of good."

With a look at him—a look such as no man could ever forget—Monica flew past him and from the room without a word.

Afterwards, when she had come, panting, to a halt on the verandah outside her own door, it occurred to her that she had been discourteous in the extreme. Randolph had come at last—his face had told her, somehow, that the long delay had been no fault of his—she had not seen him for months, and yet without any greeting, any explanation, she had run away.

At first she was almost inclined to go back and say just one word to him, but she knew in her heart that she must not, and that Randolph would understand.

When Monica had gone the two men stood looking into each other's eyes like a pair of fencers.

"What's the matter with you, and where do you spring from?" Jewett opened the encounter by blustering.

"I don't know that it's your business, if I sprang from down there," returned Randolph, jerking an expressive thumb towards regions underground. "What I want is, for you to take a walk with me. There are some matters I've got to talk over with you."

"We can talk well enough here," Jewett objected. "I'm staying in the house."

"The air of indoors isn't conducive to my kind of conversation," said Randolph. "I guess you'd better come with me. Besides, they say that walls have ears."

"Let 'em!" ejaculated the other, with a nonchalance not wholly genuine. "You and I can't have anything to say we'd mind walls' ears, or any other sort of ears, hearing."

"If you don't come along, and right now, too, I'll kick you out of the house, and it's just on the cards that you wouldn't like that."

Randolph's nostrils were working in an ominous way they had when he was keyed to a high pitch of excitement, and did not wish to betray himself. Jewett knew that way. He had never, personally, experienced any disastrous effects from the culmination of such a mood; but he had once seen another man endeavour to engage in an argument with his dear old friend, Jack, under somewhat similar circumstances, and remembering the consequences, which had been singularly quick in following, he concluded to acquiesce in Randolph's peculiar desire for fresh air.

It struck Jewett at the same moment that the other looked singularly fit and in good physical training, whereas a long course of good dinners and disinclination for unnecessary exercise had rendered him somewhat slack.

"You have mighty abrupt ways with your old friends, Jack," he said, in a slightly conciliating manner, as they got out into the street.

"You and I were never friends," answered Randolph. "That is an ancient superstition of yours, raked up whenever it may be convenient. From this moment we're enemies, to the death, if there were any need of that; but when it comes to deathbeds, I hope we'll be far enough apart."

"Oh, you haven't got any present designs upon my life, then?" Jewett ventured to sneer.

"Men don't kill dogs like you; they thrash them," responded Randolph, coolly.

"D—n you, what do you mean?"

"I mean that I know exactly the game you've been trying to play with the young lady you were talking to in the parlour just now; and I'm here, not only to stop it, but to punish you for insulting her. Why, man, aren't you satisfied with ruining the mother's life, and sending her in shame and sorrow to her grave, but after all these years you must try and gobble up the daughter?"

Jewett's complexion was his strong point, and

formed the connecting link still between him and his
lost youth ; but now the fresh colour faded, leaving a
sickly yellow tinge behind.

" The devil only knows what you're driving at," he
stuttered.

" Well, then, he's willing to share his knowledge
with you. I'm just back from England, and as Miss
Nairne once asked me to try and find out something
for her about the mother she lost, I did my best to
work up the commission on the other side. I had
something to go on. She'd told me her name wasn't
Nairne, but Drayton——"

" Good God—little Monny Drayton ! " Jewett mumbled beneath his breath. " That quaint, round-eyed
brat ! "

" So you see I hadn't much trouble. I went to
Leeds, looked up her people there, and got all the information I needed for her sake. Then I knew why,
when she had shown me that poor woman's photograph, taken a long while ago, I seemed to recognise
the face—though, Heaven knows, it was changed
enough and sad enough when I saw it, the year before
she died. I didn't know her name then, but I knew
how she'd trusted you, and how you'd used her, and
never since that time, if you'll give yourself the
trouble to remember, have I touched your hand."

" Pshaw ! " ejaculated Jewett ; " I took you for a
man of the world."

" Not your world, thank God ! There was one advantage I always had with you. I understood you,
and you didn't understand me. It was because I understood you that I was mad when you came into my
car the night I had those ladies dining with me, a

couple of months or so ago. I didn't know then that one of the women whose lives you've been proud to boast you've spoiled, was anything to Miss Nairne; but I did know that you weren't a fit man to look a good girl in the face, and I did all I could to put you out of the way of this one."

Jewett could not resist smiling. Let come what might, for once he had done Jack Randolph, and the thought made the goal all the brighter. As for what Randolph had told him regarding a certain coincidence of relationship (having once recovered from the first undoubted shock), after all, it but lent a curious spice of piquancy to the situation.

"Ah, you miscalculated on that occasion!" he exclaimed, chuckling. "'When the cat's away, the mice will play.' When your back was turned, my solemn friend, I—picked up the cards again. I'm ready to bet you I hold some good trumps in my hand just now."

"You'll find I've got the joker, if you don't look out," said Randolph, at his grimmest and coolest.

"How am I to look out?" quoted Jewett, still smiling.

"You're to get out of this, just as soon as you can pack up and be off, and if ever I hear——"

"Pooh! So I'm to 'get out,' am I?" the other interrupted. "Well, I wonder at your cheek, Jack Randolph! What are you to the girl, anyhow—her keeper? I tell you what it is, I sort of admire the family. 'Like mother, like daughter'——"

"There's my joker then!"

Splash! Cawollop!

They had been walking in convenient proximity

to the ever ubiquitous swamp which was Moonsville's
pride and Moonsville's pestilence. With the toe of
his boot planted at a well-calculated angle, Randolph
had played his trump card, and it had proved—for
Silas Jewett—to be no other than the " deuce."

It was really a pity that the Wall Street broker
had not been thoughtful enough to wear his country
clothes. If a frock coat and a tall shiny hat had appeared unsuitable in the straggling streets of Moonsville, among the grey flannel shirts, the "butternut"
coats, and the flapping felt hats which turned to stare
after them, they looked doubly so, splashing about in
the thick black ooze of the bog.

To be sure, this was not the wild, mysterious
region of which Monica had thought with throbbing
heart a few hours previously. Had she carried out
the purpose which had loomed darkly in her mind,
she would have found her way into the fields, and so
on among the crowding trees which mourned over
the deeps of the swamp, and for all their sighing,
would have tried to keep her secret well.

Here, close to the road, none but a most determined
suicide could drown himself. But a man could have
as good and sufficient a mud-bath as any famous
German "bad" could afford him. He could be
coated with slime like coagulated ink from head to
foot; he could choke in it, be blinded by it, breathe
it in and swallow it—all of which Silas Jewett did,
though the author of his undoing did not wait to see
the result of his own handiwork.

Ready for all the actions for "assault and battery"
that any legal lights of Arkansas could set in motion
against him, he jauntily walked off with the air of a

man who has come out in view of a certain object,
and satisfactorily accomplished it. In reality, there
was no room for jauntiness in Randolph's heart,
which was hot within him, and would for the moment
have made the act of murder sweet to him. But then
there was no need to let the population of Moonsville
know with what ferocious earnestness he had revelled
in his deed.

Usually the streets of Moonsville (the inhabitants
were very particular about having them designated as
"streets") were desolate at this hour, which was the
witching one when even workmen eat—in Arkansas
villages. But "where the body is, there will the
eagles be gathered together," as everybody knows.
When anything happens out of doors, the observing
mind invariably has cause to marvel how, in such an
incredibly short space of time, a crowd can possibly
be collected on a spot innocent of all humanity. Yet,
the phenomenon always has taken place, and always
will take place; and the case of Jewett's accident was
not destined to be the exception that proves the rule.

Tall, thin, yellow men, with bare upper lips and
pointed beards on their chins, strolled upon the scene,
with their hands in pockets which otherwise would
have been empty. Women in calico sun-bonnets,
with bilious babies in their arms, dawdled out of
mysterious places of concealment. Young girls
stopped manipulating their omnipresent chewing-gum
in the interest of this providentially provided enter-
tainment. Grey-headed darkies scratched their matted
wool with ash-coloured fingers, and turned up their
whortle-berry-and-skim-milk eyes. Young darkies
frankly showed their ivories and coral-pink gums.

Little boys of the "poor white trash" order danced with glee at the ignominious fall of the elegant "city boss."

"Oh my, hi! ain't he a mud-pie? W'at 'ud yo' take to eat him?" yelled one.

"Reckon you'm had yo' peck o' dirt all to onct, mustah!" kertled another of larger growth, gingerly extending a stick to the dripping, inchoate object, as he might or might *not* have done to a drowning mongrel.

"Say, boss, how much'll yo' gib us ef we fish fo' yo' nice high hat?" chirped an adventurous third, and a chorus of irrepressible juvenile yells arose, as at length a huge, muddy scarecrow emerged, swearing such oaths as delighted Moonsville had seldom been treated to before, from the hospitable bosom of the swamp.

Jewett had had enough. He was not equal to playing future games of cards with Randolph. The joker had taken all his tricks.

CHAPTER XXVIII.

"Stay till I read the letter."

"I JUST wanted to tell you, Miss Nairne," said Randolph, "that that scoundrel isn't likely to bother you again. He got himself rather muddy this morning when he and I were out walking together, and it seemed to make him kind of sick of Moonsville. He just put on some clean clothes, and skedaddled, bag and baggage, leaving your poor old brother, so to speak, in possession of the field."

It was again in the Jefferson Davis House parlour, and the baby in the chromo "Awake" smiled affably, if inanely, on the meeting.

"But—he has papers that I signed, promising to pay money for the company's expenses," Monica faltered, half fearful, half rejoicing in her unexpected deliverance.

"Papers, has he? Well, I'll eat my head if he ever tries to use 'em, without so much as asking for tomato sauce to go with it. Besides, he'll be paid before he gets the chance. I'll see to all that, as a brother should. There's bound to be profit in this company, and, if you're agreeable, it's going to be kept right on. We shall have the marriage on the stage that all the hotel folks are talking about, and then, when I've had a piece of the wedding-cake, and seen you started on your way, I'll be off about my business. You don't mind if I stay till then, do you, little sister, and sort of knock things into shape for your big tour?"

Monica looked at him, but not for long. She did not trust her own eyes.

"I wonder if you understand just how bad I felt when I found that blessed little shoe in New York, and knew it had been sent out to give me its message weeks ago?" he went on. "It just seems to me as though, if I had more happiness piled up in my future than I ever had, or possibly can get, it wouldn't make up to me for knowing what you went through in those days, and I not here to——"

"Oh, don't let us speak of that any more!" said Monica, with a haste not born of impatience. "Though sometimes I wondered a little, I think I always have been sure in the bottom of my heart that you would have come if you could,—for you see—you had been so kind."

"Kind!" Randolph echoed.

Then he walked away to the window, with his hands behind his back; and, as he looked out on the blue mist that overhung the not far-distant swamp, he smiled the three-cornered smile which Monica often saw when she pictured his absent face. But the smile did not linger. It had been as superficial as evanescent.

"I was gone a little longer than I meant to be— that's one thing," he said, turning to Monica again, and standing with a hand on the back of a chair near hers. "I had considerable business, and it took some time to finish, in just the way I wanted it done. Part of it—er—took me to Leeds."

The girl glanced up, with a quickly drawn breath,

and a dilation of the eyes. But he was looking down, greatly interested apparently in fitting a leg of the nicely balanced chair into a particular blob of pattern on the preposterous carpet.

"You know you didn't say I mustn't see your friends, if it came in my way to do so, little sister; and it *did* come in my way. I guess I may as well confess, now the murder's out, that I made a special point of seeing them. By Jove! you didn't say too much. *She* is a Tartar, and no mistake."

Monica laughed a little hysterical, giggling laugh, her hands clasped tightly together, while she waited for what was to come. It was not to be the intelligence that had been meant to overwhelm Jewett. That secret would be jealously guarded after this.

Randolph went on speaking in a somewhat changed voice: "But your cousin, Mr. Eric Stannard, he's very different. He's a fine-looking, pleasant-spoken young man. Oh, yes, I had quite a long chat with him about you on two or three occasions. You see, my business in Leeds kept me several days. Naturally, thinking so much of you as he does, he was glad to meet any one who could give him news of you. And even his mother—the ' blood relation '—kind of weakened, towards the last."

He paused, and cleared his throat, for he was troubled at the moment with a slight hoarseness of the voice.

Monica tried to break in with speech—to say something; it could scarcely matter what. But her lips were singularly dry, and by the time she had moistened them, Randolph had begun again.

" Even if I hadn't got the little shoe, which gave me

so much pleasure and pain to find, I should have searched you out, and come to you as soon as ever I could, because I had something for you, from the other side of the ocean, that I wouldn't have trusted anybody to bring except myself—not even the mail. It's—it's a letter. The whole way home I carried it in my breast-pocket, so nothing could happen to it that didn't happen to me too ; and now, after all this time, here it is. You just take it, and read it. I've got an engagement out."

Into her hand he thrust a letter, sealed with a large, gold-brown seal, and warm from the heart over which it had been lying.

Monica knew that seal well ; and well, also, did she know the dashing handwriting on the envelope, with its elaborate Greek "es," and the long tails to its letters.

The fingers which received it from him had suddenly grown cold as ice, and begun to tremble.

"Don't look so frightened, little sister," said Randolph, smiling; "there's nothing in it to worry you— only the best of news, I'll stake my life on that. Now, good-bye. I expect I shall be seeing you again before show time this evening."

"Don't go—please," breathed Monica. "I would rather you were here while I read it."

Randolph wandered again toward the window. His quick ears could hear the breaking of the seal, the rending of the thick, white envelope, though his back was turned. And this time, when he looked out upon the swamp, he did not smile.

CHAPTER XXIX.

*"Oh, the difference of man and man!
To thee a woman's services are due."*

"MY DARLING," she read through the light, glittering veil of sparks that danced before her eyes, "ah, how good it seems to be able to say that dear word to you again. I would come to speak it in person, instead of sending this letter to cool before it reaches your charmingly pretty little hands; but I am engaged on very important business just now, which may mean much for my future. You remember old Sir Henry Evelyn? Well, he has taken a great fancy to me of late, since I advised him to the best of my poor ability about a law case of his which was pending. He pronounced me a remarkable young man, asked me to go to Baden-Baden with him for some baths he was obliged to take, poor old beggar, and now that we've come home, and the baths have proved no good, he's going to die and leave me a cool ten thousand in his will. So you see, it wouldn't be policy to run away just at present.

"Your friend Mr. Randolph has kindly offered to be the bearer of an epistle, which must be my representative at your court for a few short weeks—I hope no longer.

"And now, after this tedious but necessary preamble, let me turn to that of which my heart is full.

"*Apropos* of Mr. Randolph, he is indeed a kind

friend of yours. But no wonder he has come to take a fatherly interest in so fascinating a creature as yourself. If he were a dozen years younger, I don't know that I shouldn't be afraid of him. But then, joking apart, though he is a capital chap, he is not *quite* a gentleman, according to our standards here, is he ?— and, therefore, not my fastidious Monica's style at all.

" I do not entirely understand from him whether he has already accurately informed you of his intentions regarding you or not; but, at all events, that was a lucky hour in which you confided our sweet, sad love story to his sympathetic ear. In short, he offers to settle fifty thousand pounds on you the day you and I become man and wife—a happy day for me, my darling, though I had so long given up all hope of ever seeing its bright dawn.

" Even mother is dazzled at the prospect of this heiress-ship, and has already promised both Mr. Randolph and me to welcome you in her best style—a ' poor thing, but her own.'

" As soon as you have answered this (which I pray may be without delay), giving me your address, she will herself write to you.

" Now, my fairest one, as Mr. Randolph must go— on the principle that time and tide will not wait even for a Yankee millionaire—I must say farewell. Take my heart with it, which has, indeed, always been yours. And my prayer is that you may be as happy in this solution of all our apparently hopeless difficulties as is,—Your devoted ERIC."

" P. S.—It has just occurred to me, whether it might not be possible for you to sail at once for Eng-

land, from which you have been far too long away for
my peace of mind. This would save delay, conse-
quent upon poor Sir Henry lasting longer than we
think.—E."

When Monica had read it all, the hand which held
the letter slowly fell at her side. For a long time she
sat, absolutely motionless—as motionless as the statue
of last night.

Randolph was still at the window. He had not
wished to stay, and he had not dared to turn, although
the moments were slow in passing. It seemed to him
that Monica was an unconscionable age in reading the
letter. But then one must expect that a girl would
wish to read such a letter two or three times through
at least. He wondered if she would speak to him
when she had finished, or whether, since she appeared
to be so absorbed, he might not quietly slip out of
the room.

Meanwhile, Monica's eyes were fixed staringly upon
the Greek " es " which even at some distance were
legible on the white pages of her lover's letter. Once,
she had thought that Eric wrote a beautiful hand.
What change was there in herself that now it looked
superficial and almost offensively affected? Was it
wicked to feel a sensation almost akin to repulsion
against the writer, who spoke so calmly of waiting for
a dead man's shoes, and who was so ready to accept
her, enriched with a dower bestowed by the splendid
generosity of a stranger—a stranger whom he dared
to say was not quite a gentleman!

She rejoiced now that she had neglected Eric's photograph for so many weeks. She was even viciously

glad of a crack which had somehow appeared, on the last occasion on which she had gazed upon it, across the faultless nose.

It was a strange gladness, however, for there was not the ghost of a smile on her lips, which curved downward in sarcasm or displeasure, and though there were no tears in her eyes, the lids burned and smarted as if with the shadow of coming events cast before.

She rose, by a sudden impulse crumpling the letter in her hand.

Randolph, albeit hesitatingly, took the sudden crackling and the pushing back of her chair, as a signal, and came toward her from his retreat behind the dusty curtains.

"Well, little sister," he questioned, with creditable cheeriness. "Is it all right? Are you happy at last?"

"It's not all right, and I'm not happy," said Monica. "I'm—simply—the most miserable girl in the world. Oh, how *could* you?" And the belated tears came with the rush of a summer thunder shower.

He was aghast. "What have I done wrong?" he faltered.

"Oh—everything! It was splendid of you. Did you think so meanly of me as to believe I would accept it? I can't forgive you that."

"I meant to *make* you accept it, that's all. And I'll bet, little sister, that I've got a stronger will even than yours."

"You havern't got a strong enough will to—to make me marry my cousin Eric."

"Then he shall come and make you do that himself."

"He won't. I wouldn't let him. I—I never want to see or think of him again. He—you must have seen it when you met him, and laughed at me for cherishing a ridiculous ideal—he's not *nice* at all, he's *horrid*. If I had to marry any one, I'd rather it would be his mother than he."

When a woman vows that a male person of her acquaintance is not nice but horrid—still more, an old lover, nothing further remains to be said on the subject. Randolph, though not learned in woman's ways, realised this, and did not attempt argument.

"I'm sorry, little girl, I didn't do any good," he ventured dolefully, feeling that whatever he said it would turn out to be the wrong thing. "But—I can't help it—I'm *not* sorry you don't love that fellow. I guess he's good enough in his way, but he isn't worthy of you."

"Yet you took a great deal of trouble to—give me to him."

"That was because I thought you wanted him. Do you remember I told you once that if you wanted the Kohinoor I'd make as big a bid as I could to get it for you? though, to my thinking, it would hardly be worth having when you got it?"

"Yes, I remember," said Monica, through the medium of her pocket-handkerchief. "But you said that a long time ago."

"I mean it just as much now, and everything else I said then. Only I know better than to bother you with it."

"Oh, *do* you? Then—I—wish you would!"

"Would what? You've only got to say."

"Would bother me with it."

"What—why—Lord bless my soul, you don't mean——"

"Yes, I do. I'm afraid I've meant it for a long time, only I wouldn't let myself know. I've been learning such a lesson these last two months—about the difference there can be in men. And the more I learned the more I—wanted you."

"Jove! I don't care if I die to-morrow. I've had more happiness in this minute than any other man in his whole life!" said Randolph. "Honest and true, do you really—*like* me, little one? You're sure it isn't any mistaken idea about gratitude, or some rubbish of that sort, you've got in your mind? I worship you too much to take you on such terms."

"It's only love," answered Monica, emboldened to the confession by his humility. "Love that has been growing and growing in my heart ever since the very day you left me, though I tried to send it away ; and now it is deeper, and higher, and wider, than I thought I knew how to feel. It is the sort of love that can come to a girl just once in her life, I believe, for the one who is to be the only *real* man in her world."

"Thank you, my darling, for telling me that," he said, in a voice that broke a little at the end. "It's everything to me."

Then happened a thing which a hundred times he had dreamed of, but never hoped to realise, because the shadow of Eric Stannard had stood always in the way—she was in his arms. There was no one else in earth but their two selves. And for her—beyond the joy and thrill of it—there was a wondrous sense of protection and rest after storm.

"Will you marry me to-morrow?" he asked, sud-

denly. "No—there's no excuse—no banns, no waiting for a license, in this blessed country. Say yes—
say yes!"

But after all he did not give her time to answer,
save only with her eyes. Their response was satisfactory, though her lips were otherwise engaged.

This time the door did not inopportunely open.
Every one was occupied, in distant corners, wondering
what would happen next, and whether the company
was to "go on." It did ; but Monica did not go with
it. She had departed to join Dinah, with the Marquis
of Carabas, in her own private car.

THE END.

www.ingramcontent.com/pod-product-compliance
Lightning Source LLC
Chambersburg PA
CBHW030245030726
47493CB00023B/599